The taste in his mouth did not encourage a mood of self-love. Taking care not to disturb her, he lay and regarded his companion with misgiving. She slept [illegible] now differ-ent from the exuberant ma[illegible] daylight, her hair latticing the pi[illegible] as if it had spent the n[illegible] Indeed, it had been pressed, h[illegible] effect

TROY SAVAGE

Hard-Up

GRAFTON BOOKS
A Division of the Collins Publishing Group

LONDON GLASGOW
TORONTO SYDNEY AUCKLAND

Grafton Books
A Division of the Collins Publishing Group
8 Grafton Street, London W1X 3LA

A Grafton Paperback Original 1987

ISBN 0-586-07101-6

Printed and bound in Great Britain by
Collins, Glasgow

Set in Times

'The disintegrative effect of modern sex activity is undeniable. It is only less fatal than the disintegrative effect of masturbation, which is more deadly still . . . Mankind has got to get back to the rhythms of the cosmos and the permanence of marriage . . .'

A PROPOS OF LADY CHATTERLEY'S LOVER
D. H. Lawrence

'The gods are just, and of our pleasant vices make instruments to plague us.'

KING LEAR
William Shakespeare

Hard-Up

1

Michael woke up a little earlier than the elf-locked young person he had taken to bed the night before.

There was a vague pain in his head coupled with sensations of weightlessness.

The taste in his mouth did not encourage a mood of self-love.

Taking care not to disturb her, he lay and regarded his companion with misgiving. She slept now, how different from the exuberant madcap of the previous night, her hair latticing the pillow, her body curiously flattened as if it had spent the night in a wild flower press.

Indeed, it had been pressed, he recalled, not once but often.

She had made love with a sort of tenacious frenzy as if she had been climbing a rope.

'Horrible, horrible,' she had exclaimed avidly.

She was not a wild flower, however, more raised under glass, but somehow mundane as well as exotic, like a dandelion in December. Where had she come from? What had he done?

Michael's mind, sluggish as a beam engine, slid heavily into playback.

He had met her when she appeared at a casting session, hopelessly unsuitable for the part of a wholesome country girl in a shampoo commercial he was meant to be directing.

Her hair, if not like mouldy hay, had a brillolike bounce that would have accorded indifferently with the rustically romantic tresses envisaged by the scriptwriter, a self-made Cockney.

On the other hand, she did have a sort of urchin insouciance which, coupled with a pair of large cirrus-blue eyes (he discovered later that she wore contact lenses when he kissed one of them out) beguiled him into the momentary delusion that she might be the one with whom he could forget the world and throw up job, friends, financial crisis and all the infinite, tedious, clogging problems of being Michael.

An absurd delusion, of course, and one that he did not really believe in even when he was spinning the first fine gossamers of self-deception, but he was especially susceptible to innocence at the moment, having just ended a brief but emotionally (as well as financially) ruinous affair with a ravishing would-be cosmopolite.

So when Treacle, this was her professional name, had come in and said 'Know what I mean?' several times, he really felt he did know what she meant, and had rarely heard it so well-expressed. Besides, she had chipper little breasts. And so, though denying her the job, he took down her telephone number, and rang her the same evening. And later that night, after two bottles of Cotes du Rhone, he took down her Brutus jeans, and gave her everything that had been bothering him.

It was while he was doing this that he made a note (not for the first time) never to confuse naïveté with innocence. Treacle might not be a jet-setter or an Arts Graduate but she was no stranger to the lexicon of love.

A slight movement beside him disturbed his train of thought, and indicated that Treacle was accepting consciousness. He glanced sideways again, narrowing gummy lids, pretending to be still asleep. It was a ridiculous relic of childhood, he knew, but he hated people to know he was awake before he was ready. He almost felt – as he had when he played his first game of hide and seek – that if he kept his eyes shut no one would be able to see him.

He shut his eyes very shut indeed. But it was no use. He had been found.

'Mike?' she said. 'Mike?'

He hated to be called Mike.

'Mike? Are you awake?'

One thing he hated even more than being called Mike was being asked whether he was awake.

'Mike? D'you mean what you said?'

Perdition. What had he said? Some lustful blurt of love, a promise of a weekend in Paris, an invitation to move in with him, dinner with his parents, an offer of marriage? Pray God he hadn't said he'd lend her his car?

His mind was an empty palimpsest. The Cotes du Rhone and the night's activities had erased every syllable of whatever conversation had passed between them. He had the feeling that, though urgent, it had not been deep.

When on the run-in, Michael generally preferred to switch to automatic pilot. A light laugh, a little anecdote, an infectiously boyish grin, a smile of sympathy, a frown of understanding, a moue of self-deprecation, these were the reactions which needed no intellectual bull-working, no flagellation of the frontal lobes, and had proved over the years to be generally successful.

Oh, of course he knew there were exceptions, but he had learned from the earliest days to avoid women who talked about Jane Austen as his hand slipped with poultry-farmer's deftness into the warm nests of their 34A's, and any girl who raised questions of a philosophical or quasi-religious nature as his fingers played an erotic cantata up and down the keyboard of her vertebrae was never asked up to examine his Coffee-Table Book of Astrology a second time.

Not that he neglected the mental approach. He had found it of infinite service at the Making Friends stage. Spinoza at the first lunch, certainly (if his potted history of Western Philosophy had provided him with enough information on the subject, and the girl knew less than he). Kant over the cucumber sandwiches, if necessary. Carlyle, Thomas Lovell Beddoes, Restoration Comedy, Donne's View of Women, Jacobean Tragedy, Jonson, Johnson, Doctor Dee, the Malleus Maleficorum, the Welsh clergyman who wrote those sensitive diaries and had a taste for little girls, Sir Philip Sidney, Plato, Marx, Freud, Von Masoch, Lewis Carroll, Black Holes. All the random gleanings of an expensive but not exhaustive education were grist to his amorous mill.

Where was he? Ah yes. Treacle. He would never have talked to Treacle about such matters. The whole thing had been too sudden, too much of a romp. Erudition had not reared its head. At least whatever was now on her mind would require a minimum of ruminative effort on his part.

Realizing this, he let out a faint sigh of relief, no, less than a sigh, a very quark of a noise – but it was enough to indicate to Treacle that he was conscious and fit for conversation.

'Mike?'

He felt a sharp pain in his left leg as she gently kicked, piercing the skin with an irregularly trimmed toe-nail. Pray God she wasn't going to become violent. Or, worse, roguish, he submitted, as a small hot hand punched through the tundra of his pubic hair and clawed playfully towards his penis. She was going to become roguish. He took refuge in pretending to wake up. Much business with yawning, stretching etcetera.

'Aaaaaaargh. Aaaa-aaaaargh. Woroworoworoworo-wooooof.'

Near hernia in his efforts to simulate the spontaneous return of awareness, Michael was gratefully conscious that Treacle's hand had left the restricted zone and was now tweaking playfully at his left nipple.

'How d'you feel s'morning?'

This was better too. This was something he could understand. He knew how he felt this morning. He felt terrible, but uncharacteristically, he found he had no desire to go over this uncongenial ground with another person. Never one usually to stifle a tale of misfortune, this morning he felt reticent. Pain, like his penis, was a private thing. Besides, he did not think that Treacle was really interested in how he felt. She was just using the subject as a stepping-stone back to her original 'did you really mean it?'

'How d'you feel, Mike, how d'you feel?'

He felt the next problem was going to be his expression. How was he going to seem? Given the fact that the vague sensations of discomfort in his head had crystallized into a first magnitude headache, he could of course stifle his qualms about confiding in Treacle and simply take refuge in indisposition. But there were flaws in this course of action. Treacle would feign sympathy, hover around making filthy cups of coffee, nurse him into fitness again so that she could corner him with her questions. Besides, he had to see an editor about recutting a toffee commercial he had just directed and he couldn't be late because his client was going to be there, a crapulous producer from one of the big advertising agencies who, through ancient loyalty or sheer sottish confusion, was one of the few people still to give him work.

Shelving the problem of his expression, and filling-in with elaborate stretchings and flailings, Michael allowed himself a not-uncommon moment of self-commiseration. Here he was, forty years old, rented flat, two divorces behind him, in the red at the bank, no security, habitually under-employed. All he had got was an ageing Aston Martin (relic of a time when for a six heady months, he had himself been the current darling of the agency groundlings) and a string of affairs which, emptied now of their meat, hung round his mind like coconut shells making hollow noises in the wind.

'Mike. C'mon. Mike.'

She was getting petulant now. He decided he must face things rather than dodge and weave. He could feel persistence radiating from her like a pulsar. There was no escape. To the guillotine, then.

Hastily stitching on a smile (the crooked front tooth capped), he rose like a gammy linnet from the pillow. Was that an infectious grin breaking out all over his face? It was. Was candour stealing across his eyes like a Turner sun-up. It must not be doubted.

'Morning, luv.'

He liked that luv. It gave a demotic touch, the patois of the producer. In spite of his age, his hair had not yet lost its colour – brown with glints of gold like an old picture frame. His frank blue eyes, his hair, his face lightly tanned from a 3-day shoot in Morocco for a fitted kitchen unit warehouse, his capped white teeth, all gave the impression of a far nicer person than he actually was.

Treacle, who had found herself waking up beside a considerable cross-section of contemporary virility, was in spite of herself impressed.

'You're not a bad-looking geezer.'

This was promising. She had deserted the subject upon which she appeared to need Michael's reassurance, and was now ranging freely over mundanities. What might she not touch on now? Her plans for the day, whom she was going to meet for lunch, where she was going this weekend, the latest shock-horror film on at the Cinecenta (The Abattoir Massacre 'Your stomach will churn'), the price of fish? Michael sensed no danger in any or all of these possibilities.

As it happened, however, Treacle simply yawned. At length, luxuriantly, the feline yawn of the young wife in Marriage a la Mode, making Michael realize not for the first time, that the world suits women much better than it does men.

He glanced at his watch, at the window. The shadow of a bird outside on the sill seemed imprinted on the curtains, motionless, like the face of Christ on St Veronica's scarf. He experienced that sensation of out-of-timeness, of life frozen solid as in a block of perspex which sometimes precedes moments of massive unimportance.

He knew then nothing she could say, nothing he could do, nothing Destiny could serve up, would make the slightest difference to the mildly squalid, endemically impecunious, infinitely boring quagmire that his life had wandered into and from which, however much he flailed or other people proffered ladders or wattle sheepcotes, he would never be extricated.

His life, his career, London stretched endlessly, motionlessly around him like a joke bad egg.

Michael shuddered (taking care not to move). How had he got into all this? he asked himself, as Treacle broke the spell, reaching across to turn on the radio.

'Tie your mother down, tie your mother down', a raucous belial voice suggested.

No, that had not been the way. Quite the reverse. His mother had tied *him* down, tied him down by marrying into New England stuffiness (his father had been an ultimately unsuccessful banker with a family house in Vermont) and reserving for him an Old England style of education which had left him elaborately ill-equipped to cope with the necessities of either nation.

On leaving Oxford, his tutor had told him, in a rare moment of practicality, 'You have been perfectly educated to be discontented'. 'How true' he had annotated helplessly in the margin of experience. But what was he to do about it?

'Tie your mother down' Treacle insisted, wagging her shoulders to the rhythm of the neanderthal beat.

Not that he could bring himself to blame his mother. She had doubtless in her turn been tied down by the petrified precepts of her nineteenth century parents, and had died when he was so young that he could hardly accuse her of anything more than giving him birth.

Treacle looked round the bedroom proprietorially, encouraged and fortified by the crude vigour of the ditty.

'No,' she said.

No? He panicked momentarily. No what? No leaving without trouble? No peace for the wicked? No quarter asked or given?

'Them curtains.'

Blast. She'd caught him out, trapped him into speaking too quickly, denoting attentiveness and possibly relationship. Curtains? What did he care about curtains? They were irrelevances: small-time, womanish, jejune. Besides, what was wrong with his curtains? A trifle tawdry, perhaps. Fly-stained, possibly. But nothing clinically wrong.

And what was she doing affecting a Cockney accent? She was a bank manager's daughter from Tarporley, wasn't she?

'Those', he said, sending her racing back to the baseline with a drop lob. 'Those curtains.'

After all, the language is all we've got left these days.

'Don't give me all that shit.'

Though it was said good-naturedly enough, Michael discerned with alarm the note of chummy triumph in her voice. If he didn't look out, she'd move in.

Why did he get involved with them? Why couldn't he devote himself to work and, if one must have excesses, to the pleasures of the table. The great advantage of food was that it couldn't lecture one. Spinach souffle with anchovy sauce would not attempt to redecorate one's quarters in one's absence. Sole Veronique would not quibble with everything one said. Coq au Vin would not have fits of jealousy and pique. Scallopine alla pizzaiola would not be ostentatiously unfaithful or cause scenes at parties.

After all, sex wasn't that marvellous.

Men, led by their own ignis fatuus, plunging and blundering about in the dark. And women, splayed like dissectable frogs, missionary batrachians, twitching to the spark of the electric probe. Didn't Donne have it 'The short scorn of a brief bridegroom's play'? Donne did have it. Not once but often. And had thirteen children to prove it.

What? Why couldn't he, Michael, exchange the pleasures of a well-turned thigh for a cuisse de grenouille provençale?

In this moment of sleepydusted self-analysis, he thought he knew. He saw that he devoted himself to women because he was successful with them and not particularly good at anything else. Sex was his art, his hobby, his pastime, his exercise, his caprice. He might not be a great film director, but he had become a major talent between the sheets. And as he thought about it, the great wide inexhaustible river of womanhood, the strict, the gentle, the bashful, the abandoned, he felt (torpid though he was) a familiar stirring in the regions that Astrology assigns to Scorpio and that, in the nursery bath he and his Nanny had always referred to as the Parson.

Treacle who, it seemed, had a carnal Asdic monitoring at full alert twenty-four hours a day, homed-in on it in a trice.

Ping, ping, ping. This was the last thing he wanted. Morning sex, Michael well knew, was far more emotionally binding than the blacked-out anonymous bundling of the night.

He tried to think of intensely serious things to quell this development. Proust, the Equal Opportunities Commission, the St Matthew Passion, The Metropolitan Water Board, Findhorn. But before he'd even had time to select a suitable candidate, he realized that luck this morning was with him. The night's exertions had left him somewhat tender, and Treacle's hands had suffered considerably from a washing-up liquid commercial she had recently starred in. Her touch, so inflaming the previous evening, was today like emery-paper.

'Yeeow.'

Lust, like the williwaws of the Magellan Straits, subsided as quickly as it had sprung up. There were no men overboard. No spars broken. No harm done. But it had been touch and go.

Treacle's hands pummelled his member for a while with a determined barbed wire tenderness, but to no purpose. It was as listless as a geriatric's pyjama cord.

'Whassamatter?'

'I'm getting old', Michael thought hopefully.

To be relieved at the diminution of desire, was this the beginning of wisdom? Was he going to be finally free of the tyranny of the testicles? Was a Tiresias-like prescience, fore-suffering all, going to save him from the seduction of the minute?

No, on the whole, he suddenly saw, it was not. Treacle, rising to the challenge of his flaccidity, had suddenly dived under the sheets and appeared to be reciting the Major-General's patter-song from the Pirates of Penzance with his member in her mouth.

A familiar sweet powerlessness began to steal once more over him. This is dreadful, he thought, she's going to want to stay; lovely, dear, a little further down. Oh ciel. Oh dieux. Oh, here we go.

Just as he was giving up all hopes of hustling her out into the dog-spangled Kensington morning, however, he was saved by the bell.

Something between a trill and a whimper, it was an acoustic impertinence that had been installed when the flat was young and had had its bass notes blown off in the Blitz.

Yes. No. Carry on, luv, it'll go away. And on she carried.

'I've mastered all the details of the differential calculus, I've learnt the scientific names for beings animalculus. In short in matters animal and vegetable and mineral, I am the very model of a modern Major-General', she gabbled to his parson.

Ohh. Yes, luv. Wonderful. Yum.

But the wretched excuse for a doorbell sounded again and Treacle surfaced red-faced and cross, like a baby that's had its teat taken away.

'Whatthehell's going on?'

'Someone at the door, luv.'

Clasping his head to stop the scalp blowing off, Michael swung his legs out of the bed, noting but not censuring their malt-loafish heaviness and sluggishness of response, clutched at his bedside copy of Other Men's Flowers to hide his subsiding manhood, and shambled across the room in a manner that Karloff would have regarded as over the top. Paused to huddle on his Robinson's Lemon Barley Special Offer dressing-gown. Stumbled across the hall, nearly tripping as usual on the ragged bit of carpet next to the kitchen. Wrenched open the front door with fibrillating heart, knowing that such persistence at this hour could only betoken a Writ or Tax Demand. And felt his misgivings justified as he peered, in the Lubjanka light of the landing, at the triumphant face of the postman.

He struggled to modulate his expression from apprehension to languid interest.

'Yes?'

'Registered delivery. Sign here.'

He scribbled with malarial fingers.

'Trouble, I wouldn't wonder,' said the postman. 'It's all right for some. I got up at 0600 hours.'

'I suppose you've been sitting on your arse for the last three hours drinking tea,' rallied Michael.

'The day will come,' said the postman darkly. 'The day will come.'

'Yes, and a lot bloody quicker than the post.'

Michael slammed the door and slumped. He simply could not afford another bill. His financial situation, always tenuous as a result of two divorces, and the entertaining that in spite of women's emancipation a man was still expected to unleash, had been eroded to the point where even the façade of impersonality had crumbled from his Bank Manager's communications.

'Mike? What is it, Mike? You haven't buggered off, have you?'

He ripped open the suave official-looking envelope and steeled himself to read.

'Dear Mr Lambert,

This company is acting for the executors of the late Mrs Gloria Kovacs whom we believe you knew . . .'

Michael stopped reading. Of course he remembered Gloria, an impulsive boyish-faced widow whose only fault as far as he could remember (it was some three years since they had parted) was an inordinate possessiveness that had finally put paid to an otherwise jaunty relationship – that and her name. Her name was a drawback. No one was called Gloria. Was she dead? How sad. Poor Gloria. *Sic transit gloria mundi.* But what was that? Executors? A sudden wild hope beat like a trapped crow in the undergrowth of his heart. He read on.

'If you would call into our office at your earliest convenience, you will learn something to your advantage. Yours truly, signed for Mr Tooth in his absence.'

So. He had not been deceived. His hopes took wing. It wasn't a bill at all. Against all the odds, it was good news. Was it good news? He read again. Tooth, Boothroyd & Dulcimer, Solicitors. An address in The Gray's Inn Road. There was no room for misinterpretation. The old girl had left him something. The only question that remained to be answered was how much.

He was so moved, he kicked the other envelope, the one with the embossed insignia of Foxy Lady Casinos, right under the doormat where it lay undiscovered all week.

2

Lucy Dulcimer, sitting at the heavy Victorian desk in the dark brown study of an office that had been her father's, watched the busy bossa nova of the dust in the few strips of sunlight that Becket, the Clerk, had permitted to enter, and sighed.

She had just had a vigorous difference of opinion with Becket, a crabbed creature who, thinking he was indispensable to the effective running of Tooth, Boothroyd and Dulcimer, which indeed he was, seemed hell-bent on imitating the fate of his illustrious archepiscopal namesake.

'Who will rid me of this turbulent clerk?' she brooded venomously snapping her carefully-sharpened HB Venus as if it were a priest's patellum.

The situation between them, never cordial (Becket did not approve of women in the office), was aggravated by the fact that both her partners were once again away, this time on a golfing walpurgisnacht in Frinton.

Lucy, who had earnestly applied herself to her studies at Law School, and had won a first-class degree after long and diligent lucubrations had already shown herself mistress of many situations. Let other students explore the new-found freedoms. Not for her the fumblings over crumpets. Did she succumb to the amorous hectorings of pimply-faced trainee architects from the polytechnic? No she did not. While others were having their tights torn and gussets racketed about with, Lucy had stood firm.

With the result that she had passed the final examination with alpha query plus on every paper.

So she did not feel inclined to be sympathetic with Becket's dyed-in-the-wool sexist disapproval of her presence. What had sex to do with it? She had trounced the men where it really mattered – Coke's reforms, Rex versus Puddephat, tort, canon law and fiduciary discretion.

'Let him resent me,' she pondered brusquely. 'Any more trouble from that shrivelled Janus and I'll walk all over him.'

But would she? She sighed. It was difficult to get snotty-nosed typists these days, let alone Clerks. And old Tooth and Boothroyd would sigh, say how different it all was in the days of her dear father, and dig their stegosaurus-size heels in if she threatened to sack him.

She made a mental note never to underestimate the strength of weak men.

Now nearly thirty, Lucy had lost the impreciseness of youth, the misty shyness that makes young men feel that girls may be angels but which is soon dissipated by the revealing sun of maturity.

She had by this time turned into a competent hardworking little taskmaster with incisive mind and trenchant tongue – the sort of young woman that suddenly, as it were, springing up in the night after two or three years' misty marriage, makes startled husbands reach for secretaries, alcohol, hobbies or blunt instruments.

She did still suffer, however, like many other young women of her age, from a sort of romantic disappointment that she'd turned out the way she had. The mist beguiles the mountain as well as the spectator. She wanted still to be wreathed in rose-coloured Possibility.

As a matter of fact, at this stage, Lucy was not in a

position to startle her husband. She was unmarried and likely to remain so. Not that she was unattractive. She had a good skin, pleasant hair, a gaze that could be described as fresh or, as a rejected suitor once remarked, like the horizon off Novaya Zembla on a good day in January, and a figure that had made more than one young barrister contemplate a serious malfeasance.

But Lucy's trouble was that she had a vision of Duty. It was a family matter, really. She was an only child, and all her life she had tried to make up to her parents for not being a boy. In consequence, she dressed about five years older than she was, wore tortoiseshell glasses and an expression of pruny gravity.

This morning, she was in a particularly grave mood. It was not just Becket. With the approach of her thirtieth birthday, she was getting to that stage in life when people take stock. She was wondering about Success.

'Where are you going, Lucy Dulcimer?' she said to herself.

Tooth, Boothroyd and Dulcimer was not a dynamic firm. Lucy did what she could. She was a good solicitor. Her grave expression and tortoiseshell views encouraged the few clients who came to their door, while her bottom encouraged the young barristers. But she alone could not hold the firm together. Tooth and Boothroyd were dead wood. Golf was their passion, claret their pastime. Or was it the other way round? At all events, if they were not to be found at the Wig & Pen, they could be spotted scratching up the bunkers at Huntercombe.

Was there much point in holding the fort for those two old codgers? Where was Honour? Which way went Glory? Certainly, she thought, neither of them were hovering near the precincts of 436 Gray's Inn Road this morning. Quite the reverse. They had lifted their skirts and scooted. And she for one did not blame them.

What had Honour and Glory to do with telling Mr Michael Lambert whoever he might be, about a Will whose contents were both irregular and regrettable?

Was it for this that, in the Kent University School of Jurisprudence, she had resisted offers of weekends in Herne Bay or fought to preserve her bra-hooks from the prying paws of Academe? Had it all been not avoided but stored up, to wait for her here, now, in reeking heaps on her tooled leather desk top?

'Gentleman to see. Didn't tell me you was expecting visitors.'

Becket had stolen in like a smell of drains.

Lucy hastily threw a mask of competence over her features. It would never do to let him guess at the true state of her emotions, giving him cause to descant once again on the theme of woman's weakness, or make jokes about finding Documents done up with knicker elastic instead of legal ribbon. (Becket's sense of humour although legendary, would scarcely have raised a chuckle in the Intensive Care Unit of a Laughing Gas Clinic.)

'I told you yesterday, Becket.'

'No, yer didn't.'

'Mr Lambert at eleven. Please show him in.'

'Can't expect me to keep the place running smooth if yer don't pass messages. Women. You'll be asking me for Babycham in the sherry cupboard next.'

Lucy liked sherry and detested Babycham, and Becket knew it. She stifled an oath as the evil old man doddered out to summon her visitor, and opened the file on her desk to refresh her memory with the minutiae of the case. She liked to have a ready command of dates,

Christian names, number of siblings. It impressed the clients and kept her mind limber.

Here it was. *Kovacs, Mrs G.C.* Gloria Caroline. (Evidently her parents were torn between Hollywood and the Home Counties in the naming of the infant.) Née Mudford. Widow. No issue. No near family. Address: 38 Phillimore Walk, Kensington.

The notes, written in her father's hand, revealed that Mrs Kovacs' husband Tomas had been a Hungarian electronics engineer of considerable genius and industry who had fled to Britain during the troubles of 1956. He had set up a factory in Britain and by the time of his death in 1969, his personal estate was valued at around £8,800,000 after Duty. His widow was thus a millionairess and an electronics manufacturer.

Below this entry, Tooth's handwriting took up the tale. Gloria had promoted a trusted colleague of her husband's to be Managing Director, and had herself remained as Chairman. The company had prospered, specializing in the manufacture of micro-instruments particularly in the field of medicine (pacemakers for heart patients) and also in the area rather loosely described as surveillance. It had recently been awarded a government contract.

This made the next part of the story, written in fresher ink with perceptibly more clarity, all the more disgraceful and bizarre. Why should she pick up the dirt for Tooth?

Before she could warm to her resentment, however the door burst open (Becket never knocked) and her visitor was propelled into the room by a servile blow from Becket in the small of the back.

'Mr Nigel Lampard,' he intoned disgustedly, slamming the door behind him to emphasize the gravity of the charge.

Lucy felt that she had met Mr Lambert somewhere

before. She recognized those spuriously candid eyes, that smiling mock-apologetic mouth. She looked at him more closely. Tallish, irritatingly sunburnt, resilient brown hair going grey at the edges, he gave an impression both younger than his years and yet at the same time of one who has gone to seed. His boyish features were sicklied o'er with – well not, Lucy guessed, with the pale cast of thought. Too much womanizing and Dom Perignon, more like. That was why she recognized him – not him but his type – a type she did not much care for.

'Good morning, Mr Lambert. Won't you sit down?'

Michael took a chair and returned her gaze with all the equanimity he could muster. Silly cow. What was she being so calm about? He knew her sort. All pseudo intellect, and tight arse. He smiled at her mock-apologetically.

'I'm afraid I'm a little late but.' No, he was not going to do her the politeness of a lie. He had slipped in for a quick drink to steady his nerves. 'But here I am.'

'So I see, Mr Lambert,' said Lucy prunily.

They bared their teeth at each other.

'Would you like some coffee?' she said, knowing full well there was not the faintest chance that Becket would oblige with anything more palatable than infusion of henbane.

Michael shot her a lethal smile. Paused. And then gave in.

'There was a matter of a Will,' he blurted.

'Ah yes, Mr Lambert. By all means. Quite so. Good of you to come along.'

You stupid bag, he thought. Wouldn't you come along if someone told you that by doing so your crooked was going to be made straight and your rough places were about to be returned to the horizontal?

'The Will indeed. You were on good terms, I believe, with the late Mrs Kovacs?'

Lucy compensated for her youth and femininity by speaking in the way she felt solicitors ought to speak. It was understandable enough, but it got on Michael's already gratinéd nerves.

'Good is hardly the word, Miss Dulcimer.'

'Quite. I . . .'

'I would say wicked, smutty, or even goatish. I was on carnal terms with the late Mrs Kovacs, Miss Dulcimer. We made the beast with two backs.'

'Really. I . . .'

'To put it more formally . . .'

'I think I catch your drift.' Why did men have to be so beastly? But she could see he was nervous. He crossed his legs too often, and fidgeted with the shattered ends of her HB Venus.

'The Will,' he began again.

Oh well, better get it over with, she thought.

'I'm happy to tell you that the late Mrs Kovacs had bequeathed to you her entire estate which, at the last valuation, some twelve months ago, was estimated at being £8,800,000 after Duty. It mainly consists of . . .'

'What? Say that again.'

Lambert was on his feet, eyes popping, mouth afrog.

'It mainly consists of.'

'No, no. The first bit.'

'Mrs Kovacs has left you a bequest valued at rather over £8 million.'

Now Michael had heard his impossible expectations far exceeded, he could not believe it.

'It's . . . it's incredible. There must be some mistake.'

'I can assure you of the Will's authenticity, Mr Lambert. Here you are. Read it for yourself.'

Michael glanced at the ribboned document she thrust at him.

'I . . . I still find it . . . That sort of thing doesn't happen to me. I'm sorry about being . . . a bit over the top just now. I was rather tense. I'm sure you understand.'

She understood. The man was rapturous now. Feverish with pleasure. It was worrying what money could do to a character like that. She delved into her box of cliches in an attempt to moderate his exuberance.

'That's quite all right, Mr Lambert. May I remind you, however, at the risk of pouring cold water on your euphoria, that money does not necessarily buy happiness. In this case . . .'

'Pshaw,' he said.

She had never heard anyone say pshaw before. She was momentarily impressed by the head of steam necessary to produce the sound.

'The late Mrs Kovacs' estate consists mainly of her shares in her late husband's electronics company, Omicron Engineering, which has premises in Slough,' she said, at length.

'That's fine,' he said. 'Fine. I've always wanted to own an electronics company.'

'Of course, Death Duty has already been taken into account, but the actual value of your inheritance may diminish slightly in the light of one or two other concomitant disbursements.'

'Just so's I'm a millionaire,' he said.

'There is also a codicil that would prevent you selling your shares for at least three years – in order to ensure the continuity and stability of Omicron Engineering.'

'I don't quarrel with that,' he said.

'But there is one further clause.'

'Ah.'

Lucy had held back on this point, not because she was malicious (which she was not) but because she was embarrassed.

'The bequest is yours on one condition.'

'I'll do anything.'

The man really was in a bad way. But not as bad a way as he was going to be. She took a deep breath.

'The late Mrs Kovacs stipulates that you abstain from carnal activity for six months from the day you accept these terms.'

'WHAT?'

'Believe me, Mr Lambert, it is as hard for me to say these things as it is for you to hear them. It is all most . . .'

'Do you mean to say . . . no sex . . . no no no girls . . . Is that what you're trying to say?'

'I'm afraid so, Mr Lambert. If it's any comfort, it's one of the most extraordinary wills I've ever come across. The concept of death, Mr Lambert, seems to bring out quirks and oddities in people that ordinarily lurk far below the surface. I don't mind telling you that I've seen some most capricious and bizarre bequests . . . incomes for budgerigars while younger son starves . . . yearly pilgrimage to Builth Wells . . . wear nothing but natural fibres . . . but this one, to drop into the vernacular for one moment, this one, Mr Lambert, beats all!'

'It isn't. Any comfort, I mean.'

She knew she ought to be disgusted by the abject way he was reacting, but she could not help feeling sorry for the man. She had dealt him a body blow.

'Of course, you could refuse.'

'I can't.'

The cry was rung from him as from a stoat at bay.

'On the other hand.' A thought had struck him.

'Yes, Mr Lambert?'

'I don't want you to think I'm trying to bend the law or anything.'

She knew what he was going to say, and all the head prefect in her stood up and wrestled with nascent sympathy inside her bosom.

'What if I said I agreed, and then went away and did it?'

'Did it?'

'Went to bed with someone. No one would know. Would they?'

'As a solicitor, Mr Lambert, I could not possibly condone such an infringement. As an individual, of course, I am not unsympathetic to your predicament. But as executor of this particular Will, I must tell you that such an aberration on your part would not be overlooked. It would be registered.'

'Registered? But how?'

After the nervousness, the elation, Michael felt a plumb of gathering avoirdupois taking soundings along the bottom of his belly.

Lucy now forced herself to talk of matters which (though second nature no doubt to the slackers of her year, who got Third Class Degrees and who now sat at the back of the Legal Departments of popular Sunday Newspapers) were never raised in the one-bedroom Tabitha Twitchety flat off Marylebone High Street where she entertained girlfriends, organized play readings, and dispensed decaffeinated coffee to a small time consort of viols on Thursday evenings.

'Mrs Kovacs was a woman who had a somewhat pronounced sense of humour?'

'She was what you might call impish.'

'But she also, it would appear, had a practical side. She apparently commissioned from her electronics company a small piece of equipment which, inserted in the appropriate part of the person – your person, Mr Lambert – would transmit evidence of activity to another instrument, a recorder placed in an entirely different location such as, say, this office.'

Lucy opened a drawer and brought out what looked like a miniature barometric device encased in perspex.

'This is the recorder, Mr Lambert. It is entirely proof against tampering, I'm afraid, even if such a thing were morally defensible.'

Michael's complexion had gone the colour of a dogfish's underbelly. His face assumed the expression of one of those deep-sea creatures which swim at unbelievable pressures, whose mouths pout and droop, and whose boggle eyes never see the light.

'But. But but but. But this is monstrous. Unspeakable. To have something fitted to my. What fitted? What thing? What is this thing?'

'It's here, Mr Lambert.'

Lucy produced from the same drawer a tiny bright button the size of a large pinhead.

'It will be completely unnoticeable. The operation to have it inserted will be performed at the Wimpole Clinic and will be paid for by the Trustees.'

Amidst his shock and indignation, Michael somehow managed to keep some hold on reason, and he now thought of something which, though embarrassing to mention to such a po-faced virago, had to be a key factor in the outcome of the venture.

'What if, you know, I sort of brush myself with my hand?'

'What?'

In spite of himself, he could feel a rare blush spreading across his face.

'You know,' he mumbled, hoping the silly cow had acquired at some stage some primary sexual gleanings.

'Brush yourself, Mr Lambert?' she enquired.

She had been dreading this kind of physical detail. Surely even Lambert would not mention self-abuse?

'You know. Sort of accidentally. Or in the performance of one's er natural functions.'

She averted her face and tried to think of Monteverdi, but the beastly man was warming to his theme.

'What if I have a wet dream?'

'Oh.'

He took her involuntary gasp as an expression of incomprehension.

'Well, er a wet dream's a sort of . . .'

'Enough. That is more than enough. The monitor, Mr Lambert, do not ask me for the electronic intricacies, will only register physical contact with the person of another. You may, if you must, touch yourself as often as you please. Though I think I should warn you that the effects can lead to myopia.'

But her caution fell on deaf ears. The man was clearly beyond health warnings.

'She had it all worked out, didn't she? The bitch.'

Michael cast his mind back to his parting from Gloria. She had discovered him in some trifling peccadillo and had become quite unreasonably incensed. Even then, there was something febrile, hectic about her, clearly foreshadowing her subsequent illness. How beautiful she had been, the short dark hair, the boyish face, the small perfectly-curved biteable mouth.

Now he thought about it, he remembered that last row clearly. He had been told she was off with her revolutionary Philosophy Group (she dabbled in fashionable revolt, finding no incongruity in the fact that she was at the same time as rich as a King's ransom) and he had invited a girl in to share his Saturday evening. Gloria had unexpectedly returned, sent the girl packing (or rather dressing, he remembered), and vented a quite amazing arsenal of rage on him.

He, on his dignity, announced his own departure. Suddenly she had changed her tune. She implored him to stay. He, rather wanting an excuse to extricate himself, insisted on departure. It was at that point she had hurled first a Teflon-coated saucepan, and then a curious threat at his retreating backside.

'I'll get you, you bastard. You won't get out of this one. I know what makes you tick. I'll make you bloody squirm.'

Gloria had a taste for melodrama as well as a sense of fun. He had written off the threat at the time simply as a case of hell hath no fury and it would be better in the morning. But he realized now he had made a terrible mistake.

She had got him. And he squirmed like a conger.

'I won't do it,' he said without conviction. 'She's dead. I'm not going to be a puppet for a bag of bones.'

Lucy sighed.

'In that case, Mr Lambert, the entire bequest goes to the Philosophers of the Revolution.'

'The . . . not *them*? They're the ones she used to go to. A sort of ghoulish philosophical Marxist Buddhist group. They practise meditation, vegetarianism and social conflict. They've got a headquarters in a manor house in Berkshire somewhere. Gloria used to go down for awareness therapy and come back with nettle rash.'

‘They are the ones who will inherit if you fail, Mr Lambert.’

‘But they’re dreadful. They’re like dry rot, elm disease, athlete’s foot. I won’t let them have it.’

‘Bravo, Mr Lambert.’

‘But it’s asking a terrible lot. I don’t know if . . . if you’ve any idea how much the act of . . . the challenge . . . the pursuit . . . mean to me . . .’

‘No, Mr Lambert.’

‘Perhaps it’s just as well. At least I feel I can talk to you about it, Miss Dulcimer. I feel I can confide in you. I do not say this to many women. Maybe it’s because I don’t think of you as a woman.’

Lucy’s heart warmed to the man.

‘The point is, Miss Dulcimer, I shall be a man without a mainspring.’

‘Think of the new challenge, Mr Lambert. Think of the prize you stand to gain.’

Lucy was going on to talk about the wider seas of life, but it apparently was not necessary. Michael had seen light amongst the gloom.

‘I shall be able to pay-off my wine merchant.’

‘Excellent. Shall I telephone the Clinic, and book you in?’

Michael nodded. Lucy picked up the telephone on her desk, and waited until such time as Becket or the water-wing-breasted cake-faced receptionist decided to award her a line. She felt better now she had got the embarrassing part of the conversation off her chest.

A thought struck Michael, already reeling from a surfeit of conjecture.

‘These Philosophers. I’d put nothing past them. What happens if they try and push me under a bus or something?’

'The eventuality, though far-fetched, is covered in Mrs Kovacs' Will. In the event of your decease before your trial term is up, the bequest will go to some distant and, I'm authorized to say, extremely prosperous septuagenarian cousins in New Zealand.'

'Just thought I'd ask.'

'Live in confidence, Mr Lambert. The world, if not your oyster, do not let us become swollen-headed, is your winkle.'

An unfortunate choice of bivalve, Michael thought.

'Take plenty of cold baths,' said Lucy, warming to her theme. She once had to read the riot act to a couple of incipient lesbians in the school lacrosse team. 'Avoid intemperate companions. Play squash. Skip goulash. Shun Vindaloo. Ah. Thank you, Tracey. Get me the Wimpole Clinic, would you?'

Michael's mind was a fritto misto of emotions. Life without sex? It was unthinkable. Life without money? It had become impossible. And then there were those appalling Philosophers to consider. Why should they get a fortune from a company whose Hungarian founder had fled from just the sort of grey bullies the Philosophers admired? And yet. And yet.

Six months' abstinence. He had not contemplated such a lay-off since his voice broke.

What would happen to an instrument upon which so many obligatos had been played, so suddenly abandoned? There might be permanent damage. Should it be laid up? Was there some kind of service procedure?

Shying away from these imponderables, his thoughts lurched on to another consideration which had to be taken into account.

There had appeared at the door of his flat last week two very large and ominous-looking men who had come, they said, on matters relating to his account at the Foxy Lady Casino. A polite letter had been sent, they explained, but it had remained unanswered.

The trouble was, they said, he had not only transgressed regulations by fraternizing with one of the croupiers (a delicious and wilful girl whom he had found infinitely feral in her Foxy Lady outfit) but he had run up a debt of some £2,500 which was now outstanding beyond the normal term of the management's tolerance.

They were reasonable people, they said, and valued his custom, but if he could not come up with some constructive suggestions regarding payment, they would smash everything of value in his flat and duff him up so even his little old grey-haired mother wouldn't recognize him.

It was only by a dint of a considerable effort of oratory and a £20 note he had been saving for the newsagent, that he had been able to persuade them that the best way to settle the matter would be for him to come and explain the position to the management in person.

They had pocketed the £20, scratched their heads, said they hoped he wasn't messing around and wouldn't he rather take what was coming to him now because it'd be worse if they found he was wasting their time? But he'd been adamant – the management, he said, would thank them for their creative handling of the issue when it heard this proposal – and they'd finally lumbered away. But he knew that if he failed to keep the appointment they would be back.

If his inclination to comply with the will's requirement were in any way wavering, their visit had to be regarded as a stiffener.

The telephone broke through his reverie. Lucy picked it up as if it had been heeled-out through the back row.

'Hullo hullo. Wimpole Clinic? Reservations please . . .

Hullo. Reservations? Thank you. I want to book a room next Monday for three days, for Mr Michael Lambert . . . That's right. We've spoken about it . . . No no. Not a shared bathroom. And we'd like the meals sent in from Odin's . . .'

As Lucy laid down the law, Michael twitched meditatively at his boxer shorts.

3

The hospital is deathly warm,
Even the germs walk small,
Matron's in her element:
'Vasectomy? or gall?'

Bright nurses fly about the room
All optimism and soap.
They actually like saying 'Bowels'.
Yes, where there's death there's hope.

Michael, a man not without finer feelings, bit his ballpoint and peered hopefully at the paper in front of him, wondering whether a third verse would come. It would not. He sighed, rose, and walked tentatively towards the window of his third-floor room at the Wimpole Street Clinic, taking care not to discommode the dressing which clung to his parson like a surgical dog-collar.

The operation had been performed two days previously – to the total satisfaction of the surgeon – and Michael was now convalescent and waiting to be discharged. Despair about the next six months coupled with the gauze-scented accidie peculiar to hospitals made him shuffle off thoughts of the present and future (which might demand action) and dwell instead on the events of the few days leading up to his arrival at the Clinic.

After leaving Tooth Boothroyd and Dulcimer, in a state of considerable mental turmoil, he had had the misfortune to hail a taxicab whose driver was of a garrulous persuasion. His non-stop fusillade of patter and badinage had left Michael feeling so exhausted that he had stopped him some distance from his real destination. He could go no further. Reeling into the nearest pub, he ordered a quadruple scotch and began to feel better.

'There is a great deal to be said for a Jewish taxi-driver,' he remarked to the man next to him at the bar, a mild creature with watery eyes. 'And he usually says it.' His companion edged away from him nervously, while Michael ordered another large scotch.

As he sucked this down, somewhat more restrainedly, he pondered on his immediate course of action. At first he had felt that he would launch himself immediately upon a massive course of pleasure the like of which London had not seen since the Restoration, cramming his about-to-be privated parts between as many concupiscent thighs as he could find; but the whisky induced a more contemplative mood, a spirit almost of resignation, and he returned later to his flat, very drunk, with a book on Self-Control and a vegetable hamburger.

He threw away the book when he opened it because it reminded him of the Philosophers; and the hamburger tasted of guznuz; but he stuck to the spirit of the thing when Treacle came back from a boozy lunch in Soho and attempted, while still clutching a carrier bag and what looked like a prayer-mat, to take off his trousers. Mercifully, his jeans were modishly tight so her first efforts were foiled, but when she dropped her purchases and resumed the attack, escape was harder to secure.

Michael careered about the flat like a bluebottle, but she finally laid him low in the guest bedroom among a heap of Old Sunday Timeses.

'Pax,' he panted as she yanked viciously at his zip-fastener, the teeth sticking as ever.

'Never,' she grunted as she undid her own jeans with a

view perhaps to eliciting a sympathetic response in his Fioruccis.

Suddenly he had known that at all costs he must resist this invasion. It was a pointer to the future. Clutching his parts, he had half-hopped half-waddled, Fioruccis round his knees, into the bathroom and turning like a deranged gazelle, had managed to close the door before Treacle could slip inside.

Treacle tripped, fell, revived, beat on the door, blistered the paintwork with oaths, and sank into her customary torpor in front of the television with a bar of Swix (the flavour you'll love, the 'tween-meal snack you'll go bananas for).

Michael had considered his position. It was not good. Supine, on a carpet clogged with old talc and Treacle's make-up detritus (spilt mini jars of mascara and special offer tubelets of blusher), inebriated, besieged, about to be faced with an unshareable future, he could not remember when he had felt lower.

As always, however, or at least as sometimes, when one is as low as one can be, the feeling of solid bottom beneath provides resilience. Michael tapped on the bathroom door.

'Yeah?' responded Treacle, Swixfully.

'I want to talk to you.'

Treacle was so surprised at the suggestion of an even quasi-intellectual relationship between them that she started to put her jeans back on.

'C'mon out.'

'Perhaps you could keep your hands to yourself?'

'Whadda ya think I am?'

He knew what he thought she was, but he felt this was not the time to frame it in syllables. He opened the door cautiously. Treacle was standing there, open-shirted, braless, mouth open (regulation register for listening to television, commercial radio and disco music), her breasts as white as baked alaskas with a glacé cherry on each top. He had to confess that she had a sort of delinquent appeal, and he felt himself weakening. He pulled himself together sharply. No, no, this would not do.

'Whaddisit, Mike? For chrissake what a fuck-up. Ya think I come on strong? Ya oughta meet Hoggie.'

He felt instinctively that this was an introduction he could do without, and with this awareness strength returned. Yes, he could do without Hoggie whoever he or she was, and he could do without Treacle too. Her appalling voice, her arsenal of make-up pencils, the litter of knickers and knotted tights that had recently seemed to be springing up like boletuses throughout his admittedly not fastidiously maintained but previously more or less hygienic quarters.

'I want you to go,' he said.

'Get stuffed,' said Treacle.

'No, seriously.'

'Well, of all the fucking cheek.'

The conversation seemed to be taking an ugly turn. Michael tried an 'I thought we could talk about it like adults' approach.

'I thought we could talk about it like adults.'

Treacle suddenly kicked him very hard in the groin. Thinking about it later, he had to confess that her action would have evoked in him a lively sense of surprise had it not induced such sensations of pain. He rolled about in an ecstasy of discomfort, his projected six months' abstinence now seeming not so much debatable as de rigueur.

'You little bitch,' he crooned through a balaclava of agony. 'What did you do that for?'

'I'm a Scorpio,' she said. 'You don't louse up Scorpios. I'm tenacious and resentful.'

Michael clawed his way up the wall as she tenaciously and resentfully came at him again, caught her arm as her leprous-puce fingernails scrabbled within an inch of his left eye and grabbed her leg as she kicked out again like a mustang on loco weed. Both losing their balance, they tumbled to the floor in a travesty of the missionary position which she would have been swift to take advantage of, in other circumstances, but the fall had temporarily winded her, allowing Michael to struggle up again. Back she sprang in a trice with an alacrity that would have done credit to Grendel's dam, and they rolled about the flat locked in murderous embrace while glass, china, records, ivory statuettes, lamp shades and bachelor's bricabrac strewed the floor like chestnut blossom.

At the height of the affray, Michael became aware of an insistent drumming sound issuing from the hall. He managed to pin Treacle temporarily under a large green Habitat sofa, and raced across to open the front door. Whoever it was, it would provide some respite from the struggle.

A face like a haggard Norse god, as if Errol Flynn had been sent to the laundry and come back tumble-dried, peered at him out of the gloom.

'Everything hunkydory?' it said. 'Thought I heard a bit of an up-and-downer.'

Treacle at this moment chose to open the living room door and hurl a small pot-plant at Michael. It caught the Norse god squarely in the face. It went down, covered in peat-moss and pale suckers.

'Bugger off,' said Treacle, meaning Michael.

'Oh dear,' said Michael.

'Aaagh,' said the Norse god.

'Oops,' said Treacle. 'But bugger off anyway.'

The Norse god was, in fact, Tom Cornelius, accident-prone anglophile. His parents had sent him out of Holland as a child just before the war (or so he said) and he had taken to the ways of his adopted country with a ferocious attachment, refusing to go back to the land of his birth.

Sometime wallpaper designer, physical fitness fanatic, amorous inept, garrulous confessor, he lived in the flat below Michael's and kept what he considered to be a fatherly eye on him. It had, over the years, while doing the subject of his monitorship very little concrete good, left him with a remarkably comprehensive picture of Michael's sexual peregrinations.

On this occasion, it was also going to leave him with a black eye.

Tom, however, though floored, was not easily kept down and, while Treacle cast about for further ammunition, he leapt at her with all the zeal of a tidal bore. (He was, Michael recalled, some kind of belt at judo, and could destroy all sorts of things with the palm of his hand.)

Treacle was overwhelmed. Like a pinnace off the Horn, she disappeared from view; but then, in her turn, miraculously bobbed up again, arms going like pistons. In spite of the havoc she had wreaked in his flat, Michael could not help feeling a surge of admiration for her.

'Please, Treacle,' he said, 'be a good girl.'

'Fucking bastard,' she said as Tom let her down, but she had stopped spitting and scratching. 'I was going anyway. Who'dya think ya are? I don't shack-up with geriatrics.'

Michael was pleased the argument had reached this

more ruminative stage. He did not like to part on violent terms with his girlfriends for reasons that were only too pressing.

With Tom, he watched her pick up the Marks and Spencer bag which housed all her impedimenta, fumble under the bed for boots and lip-gloss, stuff the tights and the mascara in among the tissues and the pop-out Pill packets, and make for the door with a toss of the head and an odour of freshly-sprayed Calumny (one of the new Hell's Smells she had done her last modelling job for).

Michael felt a pang as he noticed a small glistening dewdrop at the corner of her eye, but he made no comment. He was in enough trouble without Treacle. Besides, for all he knew, it might have been Max Factor. He turned to Tom.

'Stay a bit, Tom. I'm in a spot of bother.'

Tom responded like an old charger at the sound of the bugle.

'Bother?' he enthused. 'Girl bother? Money bother? Law bother?'

Michael sat him down and gave him a drink of orange juice ('Never touch alcohol, old boy, kills the bacilli in the small intestines') and told him everything that was on his mind. Tom was beside himself with excitement.

'I say,' he said. 'You've got into the odd scrape or two in your time, but this beats them all. One thing's for sure. This condition they've set you. You've got to keep it up.'

'Or down,' said Michael mournfully, thinking of his pleasant vices.

'Or down,' agreed Tom. 'Down, that's the ticket.'

Tom had a habit of agreeing with almost everything you said.

'You've got to keep it down,' said Tom again, warming

to his theme. 'You've got to keep it down, and I'm going to help you.'

'How?' queried Michael.

'I'll move into your flat.'

Michael supressed a too-immediate refusal. Fond though he was of Tom, he did not wish to see his quarters turned into a cross between a Juice Bar and an assault course. Besides there was a sort of high-frequency vibrating quality about Tom that could, if over-exposed, crack a man's mind.

'No,' he said, 'I've got . . . I've got to face this on my own.'

At this moment his bleeper went. It indicated that there might be a job for him at the film-company which organized his directorial destinies, and that he was to telephone the office with all speed. It gave Michael an idea.

'That's it,' he said. 'Bleeper. Why not play them at their own game?'

'Don't quite follow you, old boy.'

'Electronics. I'll carry a homing-in device wherever I go, and you'll have a bleeper. So if things seem to be . . . getting out of hand . . . I can switch it on and you can come to the rescue in the Porsche.'

Tom normally responded to a challenge, and was glad of any opportunity of showing-off his car, but even he scented drawbacks in Michael's plan.

'They don't make that sort of bleeper for the man in the street.'

Michael's work in films brought him into contact with all manner of recondite technicians.

'I'll get that recording engineer, what's his name, Wally, to run one up. He can do amazing things with little bits of wire.'

'Sounds a bit hare-brained, old boy.'

Michael had argued, and Tom had finally agreed (as he usually did), on the tenuous strength of the bleeper proposal, to abandon his plan to stay in the flat, and instead to maintain a watching brief from his apartment below, and Michael had made a mental note to look up Wally and find out if such a device were feasible. It occurred to him that it might, after all, be more than just a ruse to get Tom to withdraw from his quarters. It could actually work.

And so next day he had driven to Battersea where, in a basement workshop, Wally, friendly engineer, electronics buff and whey-faced gnome, listened attentively as Michael outlined his requirement.

'I want a tailing device, Wally. Something I can carry and switch on in a crisis so someone can follow me. James Bond usually has one.'

Wally had thought for a while, massively. It was as if Michael had asked him to take the plug out of the Atlantic Ocean. You could sense his brains screaming for mercy as he racked them.

'Yes, it could be done,' he finally said. Wally talked in a curiously clipped way, like an army message. He had been a Corporal in the Signals once, and had had an illicit affair with a NAAFI girl. It had been the high-spot of his married life. Even today, the smell of chips gave him sweaty palms. His wife, who had discovered the liaison, never served them.

'It could be done,' Wally repeated. 'It's all a matter of parts. Come back next week.'

Michael, who had been expecting a contemptuous rejection, was considerably elated at the prospect of electronic assistance, and offered to pay him in any currency he chose, including pommes frites . . .

Fortified by these reminiscences, Michael returned to the present. The sun had come out. Fleecy clouds gambolled over Oxford Street. He assayed the future. All in all, he reflected, whether it was thoughts of electronic assistance or simply post-operative lift, the next six months – no, what was he saying – the next five months and twenty seven days did not look quite as hopeless as he had feared. True, he was going to have to abstain from spicy foods and inflaming thoughts, but a diet of Proust and bean shoots might work wonders with a system poisoned with Prawns Pil-Pil and the Story of O.

It was while he was thus philosophically consoling himself that the door opened and Staff Nurse Lundquist entered, advancing upon him with brisk pumps. He was glad it was Staff Nurse Lundquist. Neutered as he was by the circumstances of his arrival in Wimpole Street, he had registered from the first that here was something altogether different.

Staff Nurse Lundquist was a glorious creature from Uppsala, soft yet brisk, fresh, flaxen-haired, breasts like bofors under the subduing camouflage of her uniform, and legs that seemed made only for two things – hiking across mountains or thrashing uncontrollably in a hayloft.

She smelt of hay as she bent down to stick the thermometer in his mouth.

Even this routine duty, she contrived to make wonderfully intimate and suggestive.

He tried to say something, but she poked the little glass cylinder back into his soft palate.

'Aieee,' he murmured in pleasurable protest.

'Sorry. Did I hurt you?'

'Yes, Staff Nurse, you certainly did. You hurt me very much indeed. You made me realize exactly what I'm going to be missing, just when I was getting philosophical.

Unleash your Oerlikons. Shoot me down in flames with your nipples. Let me bale out into the forest of your hair and find sanctuary in the nape of your neck. Let me hole-up in the farmhouse of your thighs. Oh sweet nurse, let me be your staff,' Michael thought.

But all he said was 'Uhuh', shaking his head and smiling dashingly (a difficult feat with a thermometer in your mouth).

Smiling back, she held his wrist and took his pulse, while he drank in the glorious cloveriness of her. It was only after several minutes of absorption that he suddenly realized that she had been holding his wrist far longer than was necessary. And that she was stroking, very softly, the inside of his palm – that area which chiromancers call the Mount of Venus.

He looked at Staff Nurse Lundquist and she looked back at him, the blue eyes searingly bright, the lips pinker than a cat's tongue, half-parted.

'You know,' she said. 'You're rader sveet.' And she crossed her legs lingeringly, revealing (oh horrors) a tender glimmer of white thigh above the stocking-top. His brain allowed a half-formed moment of query. Were stockings regulation wear in the Wimpole Street Clinic? Were lacy suspenders on issue?

Then suddenly, he didn't know how, her starched pinafore fell forwards. All that lay between him and those titanic bosoms was a thin striped frock whose fabric was being subjected to pressures far greater than those for which it had been designed. You could hear the cotton screaming.

'Undo der buttons, undo der buttons,' the excitement had made her lapse into a thicker accent.

With crazed fingers, not stopping to think, on automatic pilot now, Michael plunged at the warm tumuli. She sighed and swirled her head. It was like the South Wind soughing in an Ingmar Bergman cornfield.

Nibbling lavishly at her mouth, her ears, her neck, Michael noticed one of his hands sliding down her striped uniform towards the dark glossy mushrooms of her knees which were sliding against each other with sly little silky sounds.

Then up, up . . . his hand caressed the wicked welt of the stocking-top, and reverently started its journey over the swansdown reaches of the upper thigh.

All thought of the legacy had now left him. A nebula blazed between his pyjama legs.

Ye gods . . . she was wearing briefs of such vestigial flimsiness they made a travesty of the name of knickers. (Another quirk of the Wimpole Street Clinic?)

Dimly he heard her moaning and calling to him.

'Let me . . . dulling . . . look at . . . your drezzing.'

And then she was on him, tearing away the bedclothes, pulling at the pyjama cord, and finally laying bare his parson which, in contrast to the clean white bandage, wagged and fulminated pucely like an Old Testament prophet on the verge of a crise cardiac.

At this moment, the door opened and a carrier bag surmounted by a hyacinth walked in. Staff Nurse Lundquist, with commendable speed, whipped the bedclothes over the offending member, contriving at the same instant to button-up her apron. So that when the carrier bag had been set down, revealing Tom, nothing remained of the episode apart from a sensation in Michael's loins that an atom bomb had been suppressed within the confines of a ginger-pop bottle.

Murmuring an excuse, Nurse Lundquist slipped from the room, never to return.

'Dammit, Tom. Why'd you have to come barging in?'

‘Well. I like that.’ The hyacinth nodded aggrievedly.

Michael felt contrite.

‘Sorry. It was just that . . .’

As lust slowly ebbed, Michael began to realize what an incredibly lucky escape he had had. He decided not to tell Tom. Tom would only panic.

‘It was just that they were changing my dressing. Bit private.’

A wave of tristis post interruptum swept over him. If he was going to win his legacy, he would have to pull his heel-reinforced Morley stretchables up. At the same time, a little minnow of concern darted about behind his frontal lobes. Nurses in suspenders? A schoolboy’s dream. But, even for the Wimpole Street Clinic, wasn’t it pushing patient welfare beyond the frontiers of medicine?

‘Cheer up, old lad. I’ve brought you some of my very own muesli.’

4

Three days later, Michael was discharged from the Clinic. His dressing had been removed, revealing only the faintest tracery of tiny stitches just above the member where a sort of tonsure had been effected in his pubic hair.

Arriving back at the flat, he half expected to see Treacle and her flotsam strewn around the place as usual, but it was deserted and almost ominously orderly.

He poured himself a large whisky (brandy was too rousing), and thought about his options. His first instincts were for evasion. He would hole up somewhere; go into a retreat; find himself a rainforest; sail around the world. But the more he mused, the less attractive the notion became. He had heard of monkish quirks; rainforests were notoriously ticklish; as for sailing, a sheet was something you put on a bed . . .

He had another drink and decided that what he had to do was to rule out the element of the unexpected. It is the surprising, the bizarre, the alien that lower one's defences. He had to maintain normality . . .

Besides, he could not simply walk away from his debts. He did not have much in the world, but what he had he valued. It would be sequestered if he simply disappeared. No, what he had to do was bury himself in his work. It was the classic recourse . . .

Next morning, nursing a small hang-over, as well as his stitches, he formed up at the offices of The Box – the television commercials company with whom he was loosely affiliated – in Wardour Street.

Karen, dark-haired houri, receptionist, chain-smoking production-assistant and rumoured lesbian, was at the switchboard and gave him a curious look when he arrived. She could not know about his predicament, but all the same, he felt suddenly bashful.

'Scratcher around?' he asked quasi-masterfully.

Scratcher was the resident producer and managing director of the company.

'Anything wrong?' she asked, crushing a light buzzing waspishly on the board with ruthless fingertips.

Michael started, a shiver running across his dominican pubis. Did the girl have X-ray eyes?

'Wrong? What d'you mean, wrong?'

'Come on. You never come in looking for jobs, lazy sod. Or did we bleep you?'

'Yes, as a matter of fact, you did.'

'I can't imagine what for.'

This was a reference to Michael's unimpressive position in the director's league table.

'Anyway,' he said, 'I've decided to devote myself to my work.'

Karen fell about.

'Good grief,' she said. 'What's happened? You got a hernia or something?'

Michael drew on his reserves of dignity.

'Certainly not,' he replied quietly. 'There are times in a man's life when hard work takes his mind off the vapid and the trivial, and helps him sort out his direction, his philosophy, his very ethos.'

'I'd take it to the doctor if I were you.'

Michael felt the conversation was not progressing along constructive lines.

'The trouble with you, Karen,' he said, 'is that you're utterly circumscribed by the tinsel world of advertising.

You are blinded by the sights that dazzle. The tempting sounds roar in your ears like enraged bull mastodons. You do not simply ignore the finer things in life. You are impervious to them. Wit, beauty, truth, art, skip across the street and walk on the opposite pavement with averted head when you come blundering by. I discard you. And now I am going upstairs to see Scratcher. Good morning. I advise you to apply for a lobotomy.'

'Get stuffed,' he heard Karen rejoin crisply to his retreating backside, and he pondered once again on the decline in young ladies' language since the advent of sexual ecumenicalism.

Upstairs, the fashionable green furniture which lent an impression of dynamic contemporaneity to the reception area of the converted 18th Century cabinet-maker's quarters that housed The Box, had turned to a richer more fin de siècle subfusc.

Victorian trinkets and knick-knacks festooned a knocked-through saloon which a young designer-turned-film director who had recently joined the company (putting Michael's already wobbly nose still further out of joint) had created for Scratcher, sparing neither expense nor taste.

Burgundy-coloured flock wallpaper, commodes, chaises longues of hideous discomfort, aspidistras, candelabras, an early gramophone with a horn larger than a triceratops, stuffed birds, and wax fruit overflowed in appalling plethora across a vast stained carpet that had once graced a knocking-shop behind the Alhambra believed to have been visited by the Prince of Wales.

The particular pride of the neophyte film-director was a series of Edwardian nudes which hung around the walls in attitudes reminiscent of a pork butcher's with generous views of hams, collops, belly and trotters.

At the end of the room, by the window overlooking the multi-storey garage which, though daily yielding its tribute of grinding gears, tearing bumpers, madly revving engines and impenetrable yells as the Nigerian custodians called to each other down the well of the ever-sticking lift, was quieter than the hubbub of Wardour Street – sat, behind a Victorian tea broker's mahogany desk – Arthur Barrington Sitch: small, rotund, touchy, machiavellian.

Arthur's father had been a mortician in Bristol called Sitch. His mother had had very little sense of the absurd. She had given him a Christian name which, abbreviated and coupled with his patronym, suggested a condition Arthur's schoolfellows were not too slow to appreciate. He had become known as Arsitch and had laboured under this cruel handicap for many years. It had pursued him into adult life. Even his friends, he did not have many, called him Scratcher.

Coming to London, away from the humiliations of childhood, prepared to turn over a new leaf and make a great deal of money just to show the provincial hobbledehoys who was the witty one now, he had added a Barrington to his Sitch. For no particular reason. He did not have any connections of that name. It simply suggested respectability and liniment-like smoothness. But Fate was against him. He had embarked upon a career in celluloid which he saw as providing a speedy avenue to wealth and the beautiful life, and had taken a job as editor's assistant in the cutting-room of an industrial documentary company making films about latex, sugar beet and the private life of the boll-weevil.

All had gone well at first. Before very long, he had risen by creeps and bounds to be producer for the company before it went broke.

He had thereupon set up his own documentary outfit;

but, a slump coming on, he had astutely switched to commercials (sensing that, in hard times, manufacturers are keener on selling their products than explaining their service to the community). At this point he had engaged as director a tiresome young copywriter from Pratt Bouncer and Vipan, an advertising agency which promptly gave him three road-safety commercials to do, to make quite sure the writer didn't return to them. These, Scratcher (drawing on his father's experiences as police surgeon) helped to make so unspeakably shocking that they won first prize at the London Television Advertising Awards; and the company's and the tiresome young copywriter's and Scratcher's names were made.

The only tsetse in the Germolene was that an old fellow-pupil of his from Bristol turned up as someone's client on the next table at the Award Dinner, and the secret of Scratcher's original soubriquet was out.

He was now 'Scratcher' to the entire advertising and film industry, a cross which he bore with secret rage and spleen but all the appearances of stoicism.

'Morning, Scratcher,' said Michael.

Scratcher grinned back with unrevealing hatred.

'Ah, Michael, just the man I want to see.'

Michael, who had been expecting a rather more low-key welcome, was pleasantly surprised. He had thought there might be a certain amount of leafing through files and 'Let's see what we've got coming up'ing. He tried not to look gratified and flared his nostrils slightly. He had found this contributed to an air of virile insouciance though if you didn't look out it sometimes made incipient bogies stick the insides of your nose together.

'Yes,' continued Scratcher, apparently satisfied with the virile insouciance, 'Bunnage McGee have a cigar commercial they want you to do. Looks like a foreign location job.'

'Oh really,' said Michael, wrinkling his nose disadhesively, and trying not to look pleased. Bunnage McGee was a fashionable advertising agency who normally only used established star-directors, especially for foreign locations. 'Bit of a bore. Not the West Indies again.'

'Idiot. It's a £90,000 shoot. That means at least two grand for you. When did you last earn that much? You're bloody lucky. I was thinking of giving you the elbow.'

'Oh.'

A quirk of dismay gripped Michael by the tonsils. He mustn't overplay this insouciance thing. He needed money desperately and he knew he'd have difficulty finding another production company at short notice.

'Oh well. Needs must, I suppose.'

'You're goddam right needs must. But you won't say that when you see the script. It's a nubile half-caste rolling about in a palm-fringed lagoon with tobacco where her fig-leaf should be. Can't think why they asked for you, but there it is. Walter would've done it so much better.'

Walter was the incompetent art-director who had decorated the room. Anger flared momentarily.

'Walter couldn't direct his way off a traffic policeman's podium.'

'That's quite enough, Michael. Casting here at half-past two if that's all right by you, and indeed even if it isn't. This one's a rush job.'

Michael's mind raced. He had suddenly seen a major snag. Warning bells were sounding in his brain like carillons (or was it a police car racing down Wardour Street to seize the latest sado masochist epic at the Compton Sinema?) A frollicking quasi-nude half-caste was the last thing he needed. Why could they not have given him a nice quiet commercial featuring smokeless briquettes or Captain Birdseye?

'Well?' said Scratcher, tapping his gold-plate teeth with his Pentel and smiling like a piranha.

Michael pulled himself together. Really, he wasn't a child. Of course he was going to do it. He would meet it head-on, grasping the nettle till the verjuice gushed.

'Yes,' he said. 'Yes, Scratcher, I daresay I can fit this one in. Just going to meet Jeremy at the Fontana, and I'll be back here on the dot.'

The Fontana was a fashionable film-company restaurant and Jeremy was creative head of one of London's biggest agencies. He knew this would impress Scratcher, and it did. Scratcher became oppressively cordial.

'Stay for a quick noggin. It's ages since we had a proper chat.'

'Sorry, Scratcher. Another time. Must dash. See you at 2.30ish.'

'Two thirty.'

'Ish. Goodbye.'

Leaving the building, Michael turned and waved enigmatically to Karen who tossed contemptuous curls in the window and then made his way down Wardour Street, branching off before he came to the Fontana. He had lied to Scratcher. The agency chief he had spoken of was no doubt even now tucking into noisettes of Lamb Shrewsbury with a dyspeptic Brigadier (Recruiting) at Boodle's.

As he passed through the pullulating lunchtime streets, it seemed that the whole of Soho was privy to his problem. Carnality whooped and hooted at him from a myriad photographic windows where vealy young ladies pressed their bosoms and arched their bums for the delectation of pimply greenhorns up for the day from West Hartlepool.

'Hot Acts of Love', 'Office Drawers', 'Whip-hand', 'Gland', 'Leather Forecast', 'Obeisance', 'Lickety-Split', the very titles of the magazines seemed to run along beside him like small Arab boys, clutching at his attention.

He looked down and there *was* a small Arab boy clutching at his attention. He shook him off gently, stumbling into a fruit stall. Oranges, aubergines, peppers and pomegranates splayed in every direction. The place was getting more like Port Said every day.

Overhead, the sun did what it could to confirm this impression, though even at full blaze, its light was still ineradicably English, like a typist from Staines doing nameless things at a Black Sabbath and saying 'pardon?'

The lunch-hour passed, hot and strong, as Michael reeled through the familiar streets trying not to weaken. Finally, he had to stop and stiffen his resolve with a glass or two at the French Pub, and then with a chaser at the Intrepid Fox.

It was well after half-past two, in fact it was nearly half-past three when in a more limpid state of mind, he passed through the fashionable smoked-glass door of The Box for the second time that day.

Karen gave him a smile that would have been more at home in an inmates' performance of Titus Andronicus at Colney Hatch.

'Good of you to drop in. I do hope you're not troubling yourself too much. They've only been waiting for you three-quarters of an hour.'

It was then that he saw them. No wonder Karen was so keyed up. The whole reception area was alive with beautiful houris. There were mulattoes from the rain-forests of Wandsworth, Indian girls from Africa, African girls from Paris, Israeli girls, Peruvian girls, totties from Tijuana, silken Samarkanders, anyone who was dark and beautiful from Clapham to the Cocos had heard the call and congregated at Number 345, Wardour Street. The whole place glowed with the lustre of their pearly teeth and their merciless marmite-brown eyes.

And the noise. The susurration of saris, the slitherings of satin, the sweet swish of legs being crossed and uncrossed. It was too much. Michael's good intentions, softened by the lunchtime liquids, fell from their ordered course like tipsy tightrope walkers.

Even as he was mentally consigning his inheritance to the four winds, he was brought back to the job in hand by an evil laugh from the switchboard.

'When you're quite ready,' Karen cried roguishly, eyeing the girls with gentlemanly relish, 'perhaps you'd sort of wander upstairs. The client's there already. But I wouldn't hurry. I expect he enjoys wasting his time. The only thing is, Coucou here's got to be somewhere in five minutes.'

Michael turned, smiled a general benevolence (especially at Coucou whom he had met once before and found derangingly beautiful), and mounted the stairs three at a time, confronting Scratcher at the top, red and dangerously swollen, like a sun at the end of its life-cycle.

'Not late, am I? Thought we said three thirtyish.'

Scratcher stood there, red-gianting.

'Ah,' said Scratcher.

'Hullo, Peter,' said Michael to the other man who sat there, a dapper venal bird-like creature of indeterminate age called Whapshott whom Michael dimly remembered having seen climbing up the frocks of coltish production assistants at Christmas parties.

'Steve,' said Scratcher.

'Hullo, Steve,' said Michael.

'Wotcher, Mike,' said Whapshott, odious popinjay.

'Shall we commence?' said Scratcher, indulging his taste for latin roots.

And what a vile Latin root it is, thought Michael. Like 'toilet'. Designed only for local government officials and market research questionnaires.

'Shall we commence toilet?'

'I beg your pardon?'

'I said, it'd be a pity to spoil it. By waiting, I mean. All those girls down there.'

Scratcher gave him a holocaustic look, but light springy steps sounded on the stairs, and in bounded the dusky Coucou.

'Hullo, love,' Michael drawled as coolly as he could. 'How are you keeping?'

As a matter of fact he could see that she was keeping very well indeed for under her silk blouse the breasts were as buoyant as young Brie; but chatting-up the models was expected of the director.

Scratcher looked at him with surprise and annoyance. He had not thought Michael would be on familiar terms with such a star.

'Not so bad, Michael.'

Excellent, thought Michael, she knew his name, she remembered him. He was scoring all round; even Whapshott seemed impressed. Scratcher butted in with unctuous tone.

'This is Steve Whapshott from Bunnage McGee. I gather you've met our director.'

'Sure have.'

Coucou flashed a look of unmistakable turpitude at Michael and contrived to seat herself so that he could see all the way up her divided skirt when she crossed her legs. As in a dream he heard the litany of question and answer. Yes, she came from Martinique via Paris. No, she had not done a television commercial in this country, just a cinema film for L'Oreale. What had she been doing recently? She had been working in New York, California and Germany. Did she mind taking her clothes off in front of the camera? She would take them off now if they liked. She had nothing to be ashamed of.

'Yes, if you would, please,' said Scratcher, moistening his lips.

'We would like to be reassured on certain points,' Whapshott said.

Michael's attention suddenly snapped to full alert. Could it be true? There was no doubt about it, Coucou was already unbuttoning her blouse. Merciful heavens, was there to be no relief? He sprang up.

'Er, I've just got to make a quick call,' he mumbled, knocking over his chair in his alarm.

'I think you ought to see this, Michael,' said Scratcher reprovingly. 'You're the one who's got to be happy with it.'

With a superb and careless grace, Coucou stepped out of her clothes and stood before them like a Hyrcanian dryad. The light appeared suddenly dim and shadowy. The room seemed full of foresty sighs and whispers.

Coucou, mercifully, had retained a tiny bra and brief ensemble and her skin glowed, shiny as conkers, against the pale polyester. When she breathed her breasts threatened to clamber out and press themselves into waiting hands. Her nipples bulged like Cape gooseberries.

The nectarine and curious peach, into my hands themselves do reach, thought Michael, giving a sort of moan.

'Happy, Michael?' said Scratcher, thickly. 'Perhaps we should have the bra off?'

No, no, no, no, no. What was he thinking of? This would not do. He must be mad. He was going to be a millionaire, he was going to be free from financial panic for the rest of his life. Was he really going to sacrifice all this for a week's rutting in the West Indies (or wherever they went on location) with an octaroon? He braced himself.

'Thank you, Coucou,' he said, non-committally. 'That will be all.'

He felt he had never done anything nobler.

Coucou pouted, slid into her clothes, and retreated, her buttocks waggling with displeasure like cross stop-cocks.

'Well?' said Scratcher.

'Too . . . not . . . virginal enough. She comes on too strong,' said Michael, floundering.

'I'd like her to sit on my face,' said the egregious Whapshott.

'That would be an excellent criterion,' said Michael, rallying strongly, 'if the product were bicycle saddles. What it has to do with Senorita cigars escapes me.'

'No, no, you're right, I suppose,' retracted Whapshott. 'You're the director. Let's see the whole shooting-match.'

And so they did. One dusky beauty after another sprang up the stairs, answered her questions, and took her clothes off. Michael was at his wits' end. He knew that if he were to go on location with any of these creatures, he might as well kiss goodbye to his inheritance here and now, give the job to Coucou, and call her round to his flat for a quick rehearsal. Of course, it was true he didn't have to take the job on, but he needed the money. There was a solicitor's letter on his doormat even now. Senorita cigars would tide him over nicely.

Then, hallelujah. Salvation came in the form of a young

lady from Lavender Hill who had arrived around lunch-time hoping to be taken on as office runner. Being of a shy disposition, she had entered Reception unnoticed, and taken up her position at the back, dubious of her success among so many sophisticated ladies, and taking the assemblage of beauty as being quite natural for a job in films in the West End.

When the last model had come down from the casting-room upstairs, she had modestly, (clutching her bag and hat) assayed the stairway before Karen, who was fluttering her eyelashes at a coconut-chested chum from Tobago, could stop her.

The girl from Lavender Hill was not merely dusky. She was coal-black. This, in itself, was somewhat contrary to the script which had suggested mulatto; but this was not the real problem. It was true she was thin. It was also true that she had Brobdingnagian bosoms. But she had no style. She moved badly. The insolent pertness of the model was not to be found in any part of her features. She giggled. Her face, though pleasant, was so open you wanted to put enclosures on it. One of her front teeth was missing.

She answered all the questions with either a rolling of the eye or a cautious negative. She was firmly of the opinion that they were deranged. Her puzzlement, however, changed to mortification when at the end of the interview, they ritually asked her to take her clothes off, at which point, she burst into tears, but (because she wanted the job very badly) at the same time she complied with their request (thinking that perhaps this was a prerequisite for all labour appointments in Soho), revealing a brassiere built on the lines of a Brunel suspension bridge.

She was so upset by this time that she could not explain

the reason for her visit, and was led below by Scratcher while Michael poured Whapshott a drink. He could not think of anything else to do with him.

'Well?' said Scratcher again, on his return, meaning to have a little chat about the general standard of the candidates and his views on whom should be chosen.

Michael seized his chance. He had realized he could spend a year on a desert island with the last girl without doing anything more physical than dig for clams together.

'Amazing, fantastic,' he said.

'What?' Scratcher was baffled. 'Who?'

'The last one, of course. Such innocence. But what sensuality. Did you see how she walked?'

'Yes,' said Scratcher. 'Like a ruptured plesiosaur.'

'You're joking,' chimed in Whapshott, his little cushiony face covered in a fine film of anticipation. You could see now that his features would look their best framed between buttocks.

'Really, you two,' chided Michael, warming to his theme, 'where have you been? What are you doing? We are in the communications industry. We are meant to be, if you'll pardon the expression after such a heavy afternoon, abreast of the times. That girl is an original. She is not a cliché. She is this year's face. Warm, brutal, friendly, ravening.'

And so, by playing on their reluctance to appear out of touch, he worked them round to his choice, and there it was. Lavender Hill, as she was to be known, was launched upon her modelling career, Scratcher and Whapshott withdrew to an actors' drinking club (because they were not actors) to drink, and Michael returned to his flat feeling that, though the day had been threatening, Shepherd's Delight had come in the evening.

It was only when he was seated in front of his window

reading the second chapter of The Old Curiosity Shop (the most unarousing book he could think of) over a whisky and water that the blackness overtook him again.

What was he going to do with himself? Lust flickered round his cortex like summer lightning. Even the thought of Little Nell made him cross his legs.

It was then that there was an abrupt whimper from the bell, throwing Michael into a paroxysm of anxious speculation. Who could it be? Not Treacle, pray God. Whoever it was now decided to eschew the bell, and turned instead to the more personal touch of the knocker. What would this mean? He put down The Old Curiosity, and moved towards the door with crab-like caution.

Rap, rap, it came again. It could never be Tom who had his own fortissimo way of announcing his presence. Michael put the door on the chain and shot a finny glance through the aperture.

'Yes?' he called.

'It's only me,' said a voice. It was not Treacle, but Michael was far from reassured. It's only me is always the prelude to trouble. He squinted out again. It had sounded like, and now he saw it was, Coucou.

'What are you doing here?' he said, dismay and delight vying for supremacy.

'Thank God it's you,' she said. 'I didn't know I had the right apartment.'

Michael just stood there.

'I've got to talk to you,' she said.

Michael stood there some more. A myriad of emotions played like grylle around the spongy wreck of his determination.

'Oh well,' he said weakly, 'I suppose you'd better come in.'

As he poured her a Kümmel on the rocks, he speculated

on the sheer navigational difficulty of piloting a body like hers around any large conurbation.

There would be so many contenders wanting to do naughty things to it. He had once seen a Rolls Royce in a stock car race. It was that kind of thing.

Away from the quasi-professional atmosphere of the casting-session, her attractions appeared to have been given full rein. She was wearing a simple cream-coloured dress which came down just below knee length, and it suited her colouring as much as it did her corporation. Her body was like a single superb Spanish quote. The inverted comma of her breasts opening the remark at one level, the callipygous curve of her rump closing it at another.

'I say, Coucou,' Michael stammered. 'Agua passada no molino molare.'

It was the only superb Spanish quote he could think of.

'Peeg,' she replied in her charming evening English.

'Oh come,' he remonstrated. 'Surely not.'

Suddenly she stepped out of her frock and stood before him completely naked apart from a body-stocking spun out of 33% polyester and 77% moonshine. If the King had happened to come by, he would have wanted it immediately for his new clothes. Michael gulped.

'Zere,' she said. 'Aren't I better zan zat liquorice all-zort you chose for ze part?'

'Oh yes,' he said, his wits flying out of his head like the Venerable Bede's bird in the beer-hall. 'Oh yes, Coucou, you certainly are.'

'I'm sorry,' she said unrepentantly, 'I know is not done to call on director like zis. But I see you like me zis afternoon. You like me, yes?'

All at once they were lying on the sofa, and his hands

were skateboarding over the elastomeric integument of her torso.

He had never had a conquest quite like this. Beautiful girls normally needed a great deal more application and sycophancy, he had found. It was almost too good to be good.

He could feel her breasts blossoming under his touch, and a moist warmness where his hands ran thigh-high in lycra. Her legs moved luxuriously. She sighed like the South Wind. As he kissed her left nipple, the fine denier tickled his tongue, inflaming him to the point of no return.

Coucou's costume, though, however enticing, was absolutely impenetrable, and he now started to remove it with the utmost despatch.

The body stocking is not a garment designed to be taken off, couchant. One careless wave of the arm or wiggle of the leg will not suffice. It was while Michael was bending all his powers to this problem that the malignant doorbell once again set up its wheezy ululation.

This was followed by a fusillade of peremptory thumps.

There are many harmless fears that lurk in the heart of the Anglo-Saxon, and one of them is called forth by a particular kind of knock on the door. It was true that Michael had not been born in England, but he had sucked English guilt in at his mother's breast and, in the course of his long sojourn in the country, this early foretaste had become confirmed.

The rat-tat-tat at the door was the knock of authority, presaging the bailiff, the beadle, the constabulary, or the Pest Officer. It penetrated, perhaps as nothing else could have, the hiss and crackle of lust which filled Michael's ears and diverted his glissading digits from the matter in hand.

'Cheri, cheri,' moaned Coucou.

'Hang on,' panted Michael. The start he had given at the first rap had caused his watch to become inextricably entangled in the fibre. It was a particularly expensive gold watch and he had no intention of wrenching it.

As the knocks redoubled in authority, indicating that if no answer were forthcoming, force would have to be used, Michael had no recourse but to hoist Coucou off the sofa and hobble, almost kneeling as she walked sideways, protesting and gasping the while, into the hall and up to the front-door.

He was just about to reach for the latch, purposing to open the door no more than a chink, when the treacherous portal flew open, knocking Coucou and himself to the ground where they sprawled like sinners on Judgement Day as interpreted by some minor artist of the settecento possessed of more enthusiasm than talent, and admitting two large officers of Her Majesty's Customs and Excise, attended by a smirking hall-porter with a large bunch of keys.

They were all surprised to see each other. The porter rolled his eyes, and the two officers went to considerable lengths to adjust their expressions.

Remarkably, Michael was the first to recover. The ominous sight of the excisemen reminded him of his financial position and the vast sum of money that had nearly slipped through his irrepressible fingers.

'Am I glad to see you,' he said, nursing his funny-bone. In the fall, his watch had miraculously become detached from Coucou's second skin.

'That's very kind of you, sir. Indoor sports, is it? I like a spot of dumb-crambo myself. And now, sir, if you please, there's a little matter of £1,500 owing on the Value Added Tax . . .'

5

The offices of Foxy Lady Casinos & Leisure Enterprises were in a discreet mews off Half Moon Street.

Michael rang the front door bell and after a longish wait, was greeted or, to be honest, grunted at, by one of the heavies he remembered from his own hall-way. The man did not actually put a hand on him, but Michael had the sensation of being propelled as he indicated a deep leather-upholstered sofa in front of a low table which crouched beside the reception desk.

It was one of those sofas which give you an option either of lolling in its depths or perching on its edge, both of which alternatives struck Michael as being unsuitable for the mission in hand. The one denoting an excess of insouciance, the other suggestive of stark terror. His compromise between the two, however, was equally unsatisfactory, and necessitated a strenuous exertion of rarely-used back muscles. It was as nothing, though, compared with the turmoil going on in his mind. He had given his repayment proposal considerable thought, night and day, and he had still not come up with a solution.

The large man sucked his teeth. Michael adjusted his position. The minutes ticked by on an ornate French clock whose face was held aloft by an epicene Mercury, god of gambling, commerce, communication and sharp practice.

Finally, a buzzer sounded, and the massive attendant, with a crook of his leg-size little finger, indicated that Michael should follow him.

A door opened into a study decorated in the style of an up-market hotel. Michael received an impression of yet more leather, deep beige carpet, marble fireplace, and twinkling brass. The whole effect was of someone's idea of someone's idea of what a rich person would feel at home in. It made Michael feel considerably alien. Behind a capacious mock-Victorian desk sat a woman in a grey business suit. Michael guessed her age as around thirty five. She had the most flamboyantly red hair he had ever seen. He judged that it was natural – the original Foxy Lady. Indeed, there was something of the vixen in her manner – alert, twinkly eyed and cold as a night in the fields. This was how the Virgin Queen must have been, he reflected.

She gazed at him frostily for some moments without rising to shake hands. Michael comforted himself with the thought that at least he didn't wish to sleep with her. Quite clearly the feeling was mutual.

'Come in, Mr Lambert,' she said finally. 'Sit down.'

Michael did as he was told. There seemed no point in doing anything else.

The large man waited by the door.

There was another pause while they all looked at each other.

Michael thought that perhaps the onus was on him.

'Er, I've come about the . . .' he started, but the Foxy Lady cut him short with a gesture, as though she were snapping off a pullet's head.

'We have done a little research on your financial status, Mr Lambert,' she observed, 'and we do not like what we have unearthed. You appear to have no security whatsoever. You are also, it seems a noted lecher.'

This kindled a flicker of revolt. He was not here to receive a moral thwacking.

'I don't see that this is any of your business,' he countered.

The burly stirred, but Foxy motioned him back.

'Everything is our business when you owe us money. Besides, Bryony's tiresome infatuation for you cost us considerably more than you may have realized. It took her eye off the ball. It is lucky for both of you that the money we lost through her carelessness did not find its way into your pocket. Even so, can you think of any reason why I should not let Beamish here give you the drubbing of your life?'

'Yes, I can, actually.'

'Have a care. I have heard of your glib ways. You could talk the hind leg off a donkey, but not, I am glad to say, off Foxy Lady Enterprises. I am inured against charm. I advise you to make a clean breast of your guilt, and then we may at least have the thing out in the open.'

'I am sorry. I fully accept responsibility towards Foxy Lady.'

'That is better. I see there is some moral sense left in you.'

'I am also sorry about Bryony's lapses, but I cannot totally shoulder the responsibility for the affair. The blind god also has something to answer for.'

Her lapidary manner of speech was infectious.

'Pray continue, Mr Lambert. You say you can discern some reason why Beamish should not tear you limb from limb, but I must confess that at present it is lost on me.'

'Well, you see, it's er sort of hard to explain . . .'

'Come, come, Mr Lambert. Do not shilly-shally. Neither my patience nor my time is infinitely extensible.'

Suddenly Michael was inspired. He hadn't planned it this way, but he saw now with the glaring clarity of the desperate that the only thing to do was to tell her the truth. For once in his life, it was his trump card.

'It's like this . . .'

She listened intently, giving nothing away, as he plunged on with the story; but when he reached the bit about the Will, and its basic stipulation of enforced celibacy, he began to get worried. The woman started moaning to herself and swaying slightly as if suppressing some intolerable inward passion.

Had he gone too far? Did the whole tale seem to her a grotesque tapestry of mendacity from beginning to end? Her fists started to drum a tattoo on the leather-covered desktop. He sensed the man Beamish breathing down his neck; but he could not stop now, he was committed to an explanation and it had to be completed.

Finally, as he reached the delicate issue of the electronic monitor and the operation to insert it, she exploded with a wild volley of sound. He half rose to his feet, only to be gripped by the attentive Beamish.

'I'm sorry,' he muttered, 'I . . .'

'Ha,' she cried, writhing in her swivel chair and kicking her legs, 'ha ha ha hahahahahahahahHAAAAAAA.'

Bloody hell, he thought with mingled relief and indignation, the bitch is laughing at me.

When she had finally calmed down, she addressed him again, dabbing at her streaming eyes.

'Very well, Mr Lambert,' she said, 'I've heard many stories from bad debtors in my time but this one caps the lot. You have won a reprieve. I do not often laugh. But don't think, Mr Lambert,' here she pulled herself together and summoned a measure of the old menace, 'don't think that just because we have shown you a modicum of leniency that Foxy Lady is soft. We are not in the business of charity – except, of course, for social purposes. We shall expect to see you here in six months' time with a cheque for £3,500 in your by then, no doubt, palsied hands. Or else . . .'

'But I only owe £2,500.'

'Come, come, Mr Lambert. Have you never heard of interest?'

'Oh well. All right.'

'And don't let us down, Mr Lambert. Or you may have a more permanent and painful celibacy enforced upon you by Beamish here. Tell him, Beamish.'

'I was place-kicker for Widnes.'

'I think I catch your drift,' said Michael.

'I advise you to most strongly. We shall be watching you,' said the Foxy Lady.

And Michael found himself out in the mews again. He half hailed a cab that was turning round, then remembered he had used his last pound note in getting there. He started to walk, sweating slightly, the sound of the Foxy Lady's laughter still mocking him from the gently billowing net curtains, mingling with the admonitions of the taxi-driver, baulked of his fare.

6

Michael was not an outstandingly attractive man. He stood five feet and eleven inches in his socks, and still had most of his hair. His complexion was fresh. His eyes, by no means dazzlingly cerulean, or seemingly fixed forever on distant fields of pack-ice, were of a regulation water-colour blue. His figure, though not as willowy as he might have wished, was not exactly portly. His breath, while inoffensive, was too tinged with the flavour of cigarettes to be reminiscent of the choicest ottos.

His whole turn-out, in fact, was beta-plus, marginally better than average but by no means knee-trembling.

As a child, at his English-style private school in Maine, he had always been better as a scholar than a sportsman. He had been good at irregular verbs and remembering poetry but indifferent at football, and the chilly humiliations on the pitch had left him with the firm impression that he was not at his best in purely physical arenas. It was only later when he came to England and discovered cricket (a game which seemed to contain within its slow observances all the meaning and pent-up drama of a copulating turtle, but to which, because it was so unlike American football, he became perversely attached) that he formulated the Lambert Law of Batsmen and Bowlers.

It appeared that, in cricket, for some reason of eye and muscle which he could not fathom, good bowlers were very seldom good batsmen (and vice versa), though very often they keenly wished to be so, and would get more satisfaction out of a modest score with the willow than from taking all ten wickets before lunch.

Michael, with a sort of haymaker sweep of lateral thinking, had related this manifestation to Life.

He observed that most of the great bloodbaths of the last four hundred (and quite possibly the last four thousand) years had been started by weedy eggheads. He noticed that thugs would often get more pleasure from writing a thick-pencilled birthday rhyme to Mother than from coshing a whole convoy of Securicor guards. He registered that beautiful girls wished to be loved for their minds. Whereas he, with all his intellectual and educational equipment, simply wanted communion with their bodies.

They were all bowlers wishing to be batsmen.

He did not, he knew it, have the greatest natural genius for women, but that was the point. It explained why he was so captivated by them. To be a gambler and always win would be stultifying, and so it would be for the irresistible man: no excitement in the chase, no hair-breadth encounter, no agony of suspense, no desperate retrieval, no intricate ruse; no fun, in short, at all; just boring conquest after conquest. That's why irresistible men are often so strangely sexless, he had observed. It all explained to his own satisfaction why he had adopted and pursued his chosen calling.

And yet, next morning, as he padded round his flat, still shaken by the Coucou encounter, drinking coffee and dipping into a soothing collection of Black Hole stories (astro-physics fiction was one of his few remaining areas of cerebral interest, to the point where he even worked occasionally on a film-script he had devised on the subject) his mind kept coming back uneasily to the less astro and more physical aspect of his life. The batsman in him was troubled.

In spite of having to work at being successful with women, he was normally prepared to admit, even on the most conservative reckoning, that he had become quite adept in his chosen sphere. But, even so, beautiful girls still didn't just drop into his lap. Windfalls, of course, were nice, and he didn't want to seem ungrateful, but it still struck him as odd that he should have had two such absolute pushovers in rapid succession. No, they weren't even pushovers. They had pushed him over. It was flattering, of course, but it was undeniably rum.

Did it mean that his embargo had in some psychological way added to his attractiveness? Was the gizmo on his parson somehow hoisting a secret semaphore? He sincerely trusted not. It would make a precarious situation even more ticklish.

A flopping from the direction of the front door distracted his attention, indicating the arrival of the mail, and he put down Event Horizon and trailed unwillingly towards the mat, wondering why it was that business letters always made a duller noise than tidings of joy.

He knew from the flop that morning that there would be trouble, and he was right. A bill from his Wine Merchants, third time round, an immediate remittance is requested, and a solicitor's letter from his garage.

He needed that legacy desperately. Meanwhile, he had to work.

Stifling his finer feelings, he presented himself that afternoon at the The Box's office, both to try and drum up more work, and to make quite sure that the administration for the cigar-commercial was progressing smoothly.

Karen was bubbling over with spite like a cauldron of Borgia minestrone.

'It's a wrap,' she said, before he'd even had a chance to explain what he'd called about.

'What?'

'Senorita Cigars. It's been called-off. Caput. Finito. You got up their nose if you ask me.'

Michael stifled a sensation of being swallowed by a triffid, and tried not to think about the VAT Collectors and the other creditors whose images hissed and chattered in his brainbox like seventeenth century playwrights at a rival's first night.

'Sometimes,' mumbled Michael austerely, 'I feel you need reminding which company you work for. I mean, we do all labour for the same great enterprise, do we not? My loss is the company's loss, wouldn't you say?'

'Go mumble yourself,' said Karen.

'Look here . . .'

But further conversation was rendered impossible by the chatter of the telex machine as it spelt out urgent details of someone else's South African brisling commercial. Michael bounded upstairs.

Scratcher was being measured for a suit by his tailor, but it might have been for a halo, so smug was his demeanour.

'I'm sorry, Michael, but I'm not at all happy about the way you handled that yesterday. Whapshott wasn't happy either. I could see he was dismayed when he left. And now I've had a call saying the whole thing's on ice. Indefinitely. Well, it may be on ice indefinitely. Or it may be you. And if it's you . . .'

He paused, meaningfully.

'And if it's me . . . what?' said Michael, beginning to get angry.

But this was too frontal for Scratcher.

'Let's leave it at that.'

'No, dammit, I won't leave it at that. He wanted Coucou to sit on his face. I'm not here to set-up Arabian nights for blur-lensed admen. I'm not here to . . .'

'Let's leave it at that, Michael, old boy.'

Michael left it at that.

'What about other jobs, Scratcher. Anything doing?'

'Nothing at the moment.'

Michael's heart sank. He had known what the answer would be, but he had nursed a quarter-hope that something would have come up.

'Except . . . oh yes . . . MultiCo want you to go down to some hotel in Sussex where they're having a Conference on communication. They'd like you to talk about making commercials. On Thursday week.'

'They want me?'

Hope surged and flapped like a chained dirigible.

'They asked for you specially.'

Whatever the reason for the predilection, Michael imagined that this must be the reason why Scratcher had not already told him to find another production company. MultiCo, as well as being one of the country's biggest food-groups, was also the fourth biggest commissioner of television commercials in London.

'But I don't know anyone there.'

'More people know Tom Fool than Tom Fool knows,' said Scratcher sententiously. 'Take your reel with you – it's a good excuse for showing your work. And a magnum bottle of alka-seltzer. The big-company seminars are hard on the liver.'

'What are they paying?'

'Five hundred. Payable Thursday week.'

'That's good.'

It would settle the garage and placate the Wine Merchant.

'It's bloody good.'

'But I don't really know much about making commercials.'

'True. But they're not going to notice. As long as they've got a speaker, that's all they care about. Until the bar opens.'

It sounded very much like Michael's sort of gathering, and he descended the stairs with limber feet. Pausing only to exchange a malediction with Karen, he strode authoritatively into the street and took a cab to Battersea.

Wally was waiting for him with a small plastic thimble-like object.

'You put this,' said Wally, 'in your pocket. And you switch it on.'

He then produced another plastic piece, mounted in rubber, which he squeezed. It started to emit a piercing pinging noise.

'If this is switched on by your friend, it'll start to bleep. If your friend goes in the right direction, it'll get stronger. Otherwise, it'll get weaker. Takes a bit of time to tell which is which. That's the only nigger in the woodpile.'

'Thank you, Wally,' said Michael, slightly dismayed, knowing Tom's tendency to get everything wrong.

'That'll be fifty quid,' said Wally.

Hell, thought Michael, as he wrote a cheque post-dating it to Thursday, there goes the Wine Merchant. But he managed to convince himself that the purchase was a vital one, and took a bus back to Kensington in a mood of reasonable optimism.

Ringing Tom's doorbell on his return, he was momentarily disconcerted when it burst open almost on the instant, revealing Tom in an oriental posture and a Japanese wrestler's jockstrap, breathing hard.

'Just practising my aikido, old boy. Got to keep in shape. Went out with this female last night and had half a bottle of wine. Only eighteen. D'you think she fancied me? I think she did. You can tell. They like older men. You know? Finesse. I could tell by the way she looked at me when I ordered the Valpolicella. You'd have liked her, my eighteen year old.'

Michael told him of the latest developments, over a glass of carrot-juice, Tom becoming almost uncontrollably excited as he described the casting session and the body-stocking.

'No? Really? I say. Body stocking? I've always been somewhat intrigued by them. Do they wear them non-stop? I mean, how do they cope in the loo? Do they have to take everything off, frocks and all?'

Michael had more pressing things on his mind than the putative contortions dictated by an item of underwear that had already caused him quite enough trouble in the last twenty-four hours, and wondered why Tom could never find out these things for himself. The truth was that Tom was a nervous wreck when he went out with girls. Anything more physical than blowing his nose was unthinkable, and even that caused him grave moments of self-doubt.

Michael showed him the bleeper.

'Just keep it switched on when I go out, I'll give you the word when I do, and if it starts bleeping, drop everything and come after me. Matter of life and death, Tom. Don't let anything stop you. Barge in anywhere. Private house, company office, women's changing room . . .' Tom brightened. '. . . Bank, blue movie complex, seance, vestry, green-room.' Michael paused, hoping Tom was following him. 'Just follow, like a bull at a gate.'

'Follow you. That's the ticket. Bull at gate.'

'The only thing is, Wally says, you've got to know whether I'm getting stronger or weaker.'

'Weaker, I should say, with all those Delilahs after you.'

'I'll tell you the general direction I'm going in before I leave. So you should have some idea. It's only got a range of about five miles, though. It won't be much good on Thursday week.'

'Thursday week?'

'I've got a job in Sussex.'

He told Tom about his lecture for MultiCo, stifled a general feeling that he was clutching at straws, and they went out to test the bleeper, putting the receiver in Tom's Porsche.

After one or two false starts, Tom, to Michael's great surprise, seemed to get the hang of it, and successively tracked him down to a wine bar in Fulham, an editor's cutting-rooms in Soho Square, and a public library in Cricklewood (much to the annoyance of the Librarian, a spinster of uncertain years and liberal persuasion, who was only partly mollified by Michael's explanation that his activities had something to do with Amnesty International).

'But I don't see why you have to buzz so,' she complained.

'It's for the Third World,' Michael assured her, mysteriously putting his finger to his lips, and when Tom came rushing in, he introduced him as a Peace Corps commando.

7

Ten days later, heartened by Tom's apparent mastery of the homing-device, and refreshed by successive nights sleep untroubled by Treacle, Coucou or even dreams of Nurse Lundquist, he set off for Sussex in a mood robust enough to take stock of the situation.

He knew, of course, that he should not be so absurdly, so humiliatingly positioned by a Will. Here he was, being led by the horn, as it were, by a dead woman who had known that he would do anything, give up his pastime and dear self-proof, in pursuit of the golden dream.

The masters of antiquity, the most profound of philosophers, and (more importantly) his childhood Nanny had universally condemned the stuff, but somehow Michael could not be of their kidney. He believed that the slogan 'Money doesn't buy happiness' was invented by the rich to placate the poor, and that there was a public relations fund, paid into by the wealthy every year, to propagate this monstrous piece of bromide.

Money did buy happiness. It bought him, when he had it, theatre tickets, places at expensive restaurants, tables at night-clubs, weekends in charming hotels, holidays in dapper resorts, all the essential trappings of seduction without which he would have been reduced to crass fumblings in ricks, lofts, spam-flavoured back rooms of small-time cafes, back seats of dusty jalopies, and scented bedrooms in New Town housing estates.

No, no, give him Money. Give him Love too, of course.

Money without Love was as meaningless as Love without Money.

'Love and Money, Love and Money, Go together like a spoon and honey,' he carolled as Streatham succeeded Clapham, and Croydon prolapsed into Purley.

True, he knew how petty, in terms of Ultimate Things, his twin gods were. He had been to university. Indeed, his perverse love-affair with England, though starting with his English mother, and fostered by an English stepmother, had been confirmed at Oxford, and there he had reiterated corroborations that there were spiritual and artistic values to be striven for. He had friends who talked about the Inner Life. But somehow, at the end of the day, and it usually was the end of the day, there was nothing quite so satisfying as a good meal followed by a fuck. He couldn't help it. That was the way he was made. And that, of course, was at the root of his trouble at the moment. Didn't King Lear have it somewhere? 'The gods are just, and of our pleasant vices make instruments to plague us.'

Still, as the may-scented hedgerows slipped by, and London wallowed further and further in the background, Michael found it difficult to be censorious with himself. He had not realized the trees were out.

He waved to passing villagers, he beeped at a pretty girl in a summer dress showing a ravishing flicker of knicker as she pedalled her Raleigh towards a pillar-box.

'I sometimes think that I would like to be a saddle on a bike,' he chanted, thinking of Whapshott.

The sun shone, the wind was soft, it was the springtime of the world again, and the electronic bug on his penis seemed as far away as a space-probe.

The MultiCo conference on Communications and Marketing was being held at a large neo-gothic grange near

Lewes, erstwhile seat of an ironmaster's son who had built it to make his German bride feel at home. She, however, showed her appreciation by dying as soon as she moved in. The sprig of the ironmaster, deranged with neo-gothic grief, could neither bear to sell it nor to live in it, and it had stayed empty for many years, mouldering away in a tennysonian fashion, until the sprig, walking through Portman Square one day, had stepped on one of his own cast-iron manhole covers which had snapped in two, depositing him into a vault full of empty wine bottles, and neatly breaking his neck.

There had been much talk at the time about the curious fittingness of his end (even the preacher at his funeral had used the word 'ironic' more than once). The 'Money doesn't buy Happiness' brigade had played the story up for all it was worth. And potential buyers, deterred by the general publicity and the frankly repulsive aspect of the house, were given the kibosh when it turned out that the place was haunted. (The unhappy fraulein was said to stalk about, eternally wringing her hands, and wanting to go back to Bremen.)

And so it had mouldered on until someone had the idea of turning it into a preparatory school, which lasted for ten years; after that it became in quick succession a health farm, a lunatic asylum, a maternity home, and finally a luxury hotel and conference centre. The people who had done the last conversion had spared no effort in making the place civilized and comfortable, but the sensitive could still discern in it the traces of all its pasts – melancholy, austere, dotty and cathartic.

As Michael turned into its main gates, however, and saw the turrets and pinnacles outlined against the Downs, the red-brick mellow in the early-summer sunlight, he could not help thinking that there were worse places in the world to waste a day in. Windows winked, frumpish castellations glowered almost prettily, deer dotted a park still equipped with immemorial trees, and, on the great sweep of front lawn, two cedars supported a greenness that dropped rich as butter-icing.

All was as it should be, right down to the panoply of expensive cars drawn up outside the portico. The very gravel as he drew up crunched like Fru-Grains.

Inside, he was welcomed by a grey man in a grey suit with a grey shirt and a grey tie. He could not tell whether this was the grey man's preference, MultiCo's company colours, or the general motif of this particular seminar, and he did not pursue the matter as the grey man led him first on a brief tour of the main areas of the hotel, and then showed him his room, a baronial affair with a four-poster bed facing a view over the valley of the Glynde.

Finally, he led him down again to deposit his reel in the projection-room, and ushered him into the bar for pre-prandial gin-and-tonic.

'This is our speaker for the afternoon,' he announced to no one in particular.

Michael was pleased to note that the MultiCo crowd were about as sexually arousing as the Plotters of Cabbage Patch Corner.

There were middle-aged executives in suits; there were younger executives in sports jackets; there were, it was true, one or two she-executives, but they wore that frightful air of seriousness that women sometimes adopt when they feel they're competing with men. All femininity had left them. They'd have grown moustaches if they could, and one of them could.

It was all most gratifying. A gong sounded, and the flower of MultiCo management took its nose out of its glass and trooped into the neo-gothic dining-hall.

Michael feared for a moment that they might be served boar's head marinated in mead so authentically medieval was the setting, but first a freshly-made vichyssoise was presented to him, which was excellent, and then a glass of Poilly Fumé which was even better. He relaxed.

'Tell me,' said a low voice soupily in his ear, 'something I've always wanted to know. How many feet of film are there per second?'

He turned, and there, right beside him, was one of the most beautiful women he had ever seen in his life.

'Oh no,' he was so shocked, he actually groaned aloud, causing several MultiCo executives to pause in their spoon cycle, a thing they had never been known to do before. The woman was not disconcerted.

'I expect you get a lot of stupid questions about your, if I may say so, rather glamorous profession.'

'It's not that,' he babbled. 'It's just . . . well . . . you're so astonishingly beautiful.'

'Thank you. But you appeared to be in some way anguished?'

'I rather hoped there wouldn't be anything . . . distracting . . . down here. My . . . my my talk, you see. It means a lot to me.'

'Evidently, if I may say so, women do too, Mr Lambert.'

Michael's heart went out to her. Yes, here was a woman who understood. She must have been in her late thirties, possibly older, but she was superbly preserved. No, that was the wrong word. She simply had not grown old. A girl might have envied her figure; slim legs, svelte waist, canteloupe bosom. Her hair was soft and dark with that patina upon it that betokens health as well as hairdresser. Her skin was blushing apricot. Her lips as plump and smooth as lychees. Her clothes were unmistakably French: a cream-coloured suit, a floral blouse, worn with an easy carelessness that made the effect all the more upsetting.

Michael had always had more of a penchant for the younger rather than the older woman, the maid rather than the matron, but now he took it all back.

Courses came and went. Southdown lamb roasted with rosemary, strawberries with kirsch and chantilly cream, Stilton and celery. Michael left them virtually untasted. The woman's presence made him reel. Her voice blandished his ears and inveigled his senses like a Mozart Wind Serenade, though afterwards he could scarcely remember a word she had said.

'Tell me,' he implored, as the meal drew to a close, 'your room? What do you do? Why are you here?'

'Ah,' she said. 'Allow me my mystery. Tonight, after your talk, I'll tell you everything. But you'll have to find me first.'

She got up. Coffee was being served, Michael knew, in the drawing room. He rose to walk through with her, but a blundering ape of an executive momentarily got in his way. When he recovered, she was gone.

'Come back. I don't even know your name,' he called.

The baboon-face turned.

'Talking to me, laddie?'

Michael rushed back to where he had been sitting. There was no one left but an elderly marketing manager tucking into a last wedge of Stilton.

'Who was she?' Michael was so excited, he clutched the man's shoulder.

Droplets of Stilton fell from the grizzled moustache. He reminded Michael of the White Knight as he turned a pale blue watery eye upon him, sighed deeply, and took a swig of claret as if to fortify his memory.

'She?' the old man said. 'She?'

Michael shook him like a rag doll.

'She. The beautiful woman sitting at the end here.'

'Beautiful woman? End there?'

'That's right. You must remember her.'

'Pass me that bottle of claret, would you? I fancy there's a drop at the bottom.'

Michael slid it along to him. The old man poured himself a sedimenty bumper and sucked his teeth ruminatively.

'Beautiful woman, d'you say?'

'That's it.'

'Good skin?'

'Right.'

'Good hair?'

'Absolutely.'

'Nice figure?'

'You've got it.'

The old man drew liberally on the lees of St Emilion.

'Sorry, old boy. Don't remember anyone like that.'

Michael was about to do something violent when the grey man appeared like a ghost.

'We'll be ready for you in about ten minutes. Perhaps you'd like to liaise with the projectionist.'

Frantically he looked in the hall, the conservatory, the library, but with no success. And when he finally turned up, late in the conference room, she was not there.

How he got through the afternoon, he never knew. The MultiCo executives, addled after their lunch, were in no mood for the finer flights of fancy, which was just as well, for Michael, had he even wanted to do so, was in no condition to remove his chocks.

Playing for time, he showed them a bunch of bra and corset commercials he had made some five years previously, which seemed to please them, talked about scripts and casting sessions, editing and processing, lighting and opticals, dubbing and sync-sound, and quite surprised himself with his apparently firm grasp on a subject which he normally thought little about and cared for even less. However, his impromptu approach seemed to go down with the executives a great deal better than the swotted-up meticulousness he might have delivered had he been feeling less unhinged, and when he showed them the out-takes he had not been able to use in the corset commercials because of their somewhat too revealing nature, he had them eating out of his hand.

Afterwards, they crowded round, wringing it.

'Best talk we ever had.'

Somebody even asked him if he could get his out-takes made up into post-cards as a seminar souvenir; but all the while his mind was in a fever of conjecture. What did she mean 'mystery'? Had he lost her for good, or would she show up again? What did she mean 'you'll have to find me'?

He shouldered his way through the plaudits and steered for the Reception Desk.

'I'm looking for a woman,' he began, addressing himself to the rinsed-haired custodian of the keys.

She looked up so sharply that the glasses tobogganed down the thickly-powdered slope of her nose, and pressed what was clearly an Emergency buzzer. The Manager, suave as an otter, appeared as if by magic from a room within. She whispered a few hundred words in his ear. He spoke regretfully to Michael.

'I'm sorry, sir. Royalty comes here, you understand. We can't afford a whiff of scandal.'

'May I rephrase my question?'

'Alas, sir, I regret, but it is not a matter of verbal legerdemain or linguistic gymnastics. This hotel is not a knocking-shop in anybody's language.'

'I'm looking for a lady who sat next to me at lunch. She is a guest here, I believe.'

'Ohhhh. That puts a different complexion on the matter.'

'I was hoping it might.'

'You do not know her name? Could you describe her?'

'I would say she was about forty. Dark-haired. Very beautiful.'

'Well, sir. MultiCo do not have many ladies at senior executive level. I know of only four staying at the hotel. Miss Hatchard, the Managing Director's secretary, a lady of some fifty summers. Miss Spigott and Miss Buntrock, two bespectacled young ladies – mild myopia, I understand, nothing recondite – Women's Products Marketing Managers. And then there is the projectionist's wife, a person of a proprietary disposition who insists on accompanying her husband wherever he goes. She is resting in the staff wing at the moment and being given tranquillisers by the Housekeeper. Thank you very much, sir. Your key, sir? Certainly.'

Michael climbed the baronial stairs with a heavy heart, and having gained his room, lay disconsolately on the four-poster while the executives circled and clucked like Wyandottes on the lawn below. He could not remember ever having been so aroused and intrigued. He pushed aside all other speculations. One question remained. Would she be at dinner?

And at the cocktail hour, when the sun slipped behind the great whale-hump of down beyond the house, and the shadows played grandmother's footsteps on the topiary lawn, the question remained unanswered. The birds in the garden were calling, 'Maud, Maud, Maud,' in a way that would have gratified the poet but that brought no relief to Michael's feverish imaginings.

At last, the gong sounded for dinner. Michael stood by the door peering hopefully at each delegate as they came bounding forward, nosebags at the ready, but as the last one surged through, he was forced to admit defeat. She was not there.

She was not there to enjoy mousseline de saumon fume aux crevettes, washed down with Corton Charlemagne, filet de boeuf en croute sluiced with Hospices de Beaune '78, or the Boodle's Orange Fool assisted on its way by Beaune de Venise. And that was a pity, Michael thought, because apart from anything else, she was the sort of woman who would have enjoyed it.

For himself, though, long training at private school in New England had taught him to eat what he could when it was presented – because you never knew when the next even quasi-comestible repast was going to grace the scrubbed pine – he merely toyed with the delicacies, not even minding when his neighbour, the White Knight, again asked him if he'd object to his snitching a crevette or two from his plate. He was in an ecstasy of suspense and desire.

After dinner, the delegates became bibulous. It was the last night of the conference, and MultiCo was letting its hair down. The grey man appeared at Michael's elbow, and murmured at him mothily.

'We're going to have the treasure hunt now.'

Michael's interest, in spite of himself, was stirred.

'You mean . . . treasure hunt?'

'We have it every year on the last night.'

'What's the treasure?'

'Ah,' the grey man looked positively puckish. 'That's for the winner to find out.'

Michael's interest quickened. Could it be? . . . No, the idea was ridiculous. But there was something about the man's manner, a faint twinkle in the greyness of his eyes, like a buoy in a sea-fog, that suggested naughtiness. He joined the delegates as they staggered back into the Conference Room.

To qualify for the hunt, you had first to fail a breathalyser test. The rest of the contestants – including, Michael noted, the dragon-wifed projectionist – had no difficulty with this initial condition, but Michael, who had kept himself on a tight rein, had to go back and down a large Armagnac before the crystals responded to his puff.

The grey man distributed folded clues, fired a toy pistol, and they were off.

The first clue set the delegates back considerably.

> 'Where the ewe, the lamb, the tup,
> Cannot enter, find my cup.'

There was much unrest over this. They considered it bad form of the doggerel to use an unfamiliar word, and wasted a great deal of time grumbling about it. Michael, recalling Iago's 'An old black ram is tupping thy white ewe,' dashed outside on to the now crepuscular lawn, and headed straight for one of the ornamental urns standing beside the ha-ha that stopped the sheep in the park grazing the garden.

In the fading light, he saw the white clue folded on the lip of the cup. Taking it down, he found it was composed in a similar style to the last. It despatched him to a goldfish pond which, in turn, transmitted him to a large greenhouse which sent him to a satyr holding a reedy pipe which ordered him to the kitchens where he had to sniff from five secret bottles, deduce the odours, take the first letter of each, and make them into a word.

There was aniseed, nutmeg, lemon, egg (hard-boiled) and peppermint, which he finally made into PLANE, as the rest of the field cantered crapulously after him.

Plane? Plane-tree? While the executives jostled and snuffled at the bottles, Michael raced out into the billiard-room where a huge painting of a Sopwith Pup waiting eternally for its prop to be swung, straddled the wall. Sure enough, stuck in its corner, was the next clue. Taking it out, Michael observed that the author had forsaken rhyme for a finely compressed prose: 'My young man is up.'

Simple as it seemed, however, this message did not blurt its secrets at first glance. Was it a reference to some lapidary tumescence in the park? Michael mentally traversed the grounds for a priapic statue, but could remember nothing outstanding. Then, suddenly, the words of the old music-hall song came back to him. Up? Of course. Up in the gallery.

He leapt up the oak baronial like a goblin, leaving the delegates baying and burping around the billiard table. At the top of the house, a replica of a Tudor exercise gallery had been added to the original structure. It was a room of enormous length, nearly fifty yards, commanding a stupendous view across the wooded valley, but it was now almost completely dark, save for a few electric candles burning yellow as tiger's eyes in the arching gloom. Outside, the crest of the downs rose like a tsunami, blacker than the blackness.

The room seemed light-years from any human connection. There may have been the lights of villages somewhere out there, but they twinkled like distant galaxies. He was aware there was someone else in the room.

He advanced cautiously from one candle to the next, touching the wall with tendril-like hands for guidance. His fingers felt miniatures, a tapestry, and then teeth. He dashed his hand away with (he had seen it written in books but never experienced it before) a cry of revulsion, and then replaced it, realizing that the teeth belonged to something stuffed. He had just had time to register that there was a twist of paper lodged inside the mouth. Extracting it from an upper incisor, he took it back to the nearest pool of light and read: 'Follow a shadow, it still flies you.'

This was poetic stuff. In fact, he rather fancied someone had written it before. But before he had time to rifle through the lumber of quotes and phrases that spilled uselessly about the truckle furniture of his upper storeys, he sensed a movement halfway up the room. Was that a draught? Was there a flutter of white in the abysmal, the ultimate, the Shwarzkild darkness?

He advanced towards the bear's head again, replaced the clue, and set off into the shadows. Yes, there was definitely a rustle, a susurration of silk. His pace quickened, and he fell over a small stool. Crazed with excitement, he sprang forward on his knees. He had caught the faintest whiff of the scent that She had worn. Another flicker of white. Was it an avatar, an incarnation of his desire, or was it the real woman? He neither knew nor cared. He had to get closer.

He was now nearly at the end of the gallery. He could just discern the wall ahead. The scent (a sort of hyacinth out of Paco Rabanne) eddied in the darkness, troubling the sense. There was a stirring in the air. Yes, a door was open. He fumbled forwards and found himself at the head of circular stairs, dimly lit by a skylight above. Racing frenziedly down, he tumbled into a long corridor off which sprouted a multiplicity of passages.

'Where are you? Wait,' he called softly in the catacomby gloom.

Did he imagine a ghost of a laugh?

He started foward again, trying one passage after another, like a laboratory rat. At one corner, he saw it. A glimpse, a very nano-second of long skirt. But on investigation it turned out to be a curtain blowing softly in the night air.

Finally, lost as well as exhausted, he slumped against a cupboard at the end of yet another corridor, and caught his breath. The delegates had been left far behind. They were even now, no doubt, desecrating a tapestry, but here a muffling silence ruled, as if darkness had fallen from the air, covering the corridors with black snow.

And then, just as he was deciding to give up the chase, and return to bedroom or bar, he heard the sound of a door being closed, somewhere over to his right. He whipped round. The sound had seemed to come from a short passage, a veritable blind alley, in which there was only one door. Creeping up like a cougar, he suddenly wrenched this open. A chair fell over, exploding against a tallboy.

'Come in,' a voice said. It was hers. 'I think you've won.'

He took a jelly-kneed step or two forward.

'Shut the door,' she said. 'Would you like your prize?'

The curtains were not drawn, and he could see by the light of the Milky Way, that she was lying on a four-poster bed. He suddenly realized that this was his room. He sat down rather quickly.

'Who?' he said. 'Where? What? How? And why?'

'Shhhhhhhh.'

She had taken off her gown, and was wearing the most deliciously shimmery silken slip. She crossed her legs, the sound of silk making him almost faint with desire, and patted the bed. He advanced like a pilgrim, and suddenly was embracing his saint with a fervour that surprised them both. His mouth sucked kisses from her as if it had had a longish spell in the Kalahari, and then it turned its attention to more corporeal matters: her neck, her ears, her breasts, while his hands slipped autonomously over the undulations of silk beneath.

'Darling,' he gasped, as a grape-size nipple sprang up into his soft palate.

'My sweet,' he murmured, as his hand quick as a shoplifter slid under one of her buttocks.

She was making little noises now, and his other hand, envious of its fellow, reached down and spreadeagled itself across a bank light and springy as camomile suffused with cinquefoil. He realized that he was now completely naked. She had removed his clothes without his even noticing it, and now she reached over and made little passes and veronicas with her tongue towards his parson.

All thought of securing his legacy had now left him. This was the very apex, the apogee of his experiences with women; she was his Cleopatra – let the world burn.

Thirsty again, his lips hovered over the long arum lilies of her thighs and sank towards the nectar, bee-mouth at the ready.

Just at this moment (he on the verge of soixante, she on the very brink of neuf) the door burst open, and an irate female voice was discernible, loudly upraised and shouting raucous abuse.

'Got you, filthy bastard,' appeared to be the burden of her message.

The light was switched on.

As Michael cursed himself for not having locked the door, they struggled to recover from an entanglement of sheets and limbs that would have given Houdini serious cause to wonder whether it wasn't time to consider a career in banking. But before they could do more than re-orientate themselves in the four-poster, so their heads at least poked out of the right end, the ogress at the door started to advance on them, throwing things as she came.

'Dirty, rotten, lousy, stinking.'

'Do something,' urged Michael's lovely companion.

'Whore, scum, hussy, no better than you should be.'

'Um,' said Michael, remonstrating with the hag who appeared to be ten feet tall, and had a face made of red plasticine. 'Look here.'

'Oh my gawd,' said the gorgon, 'I thought you was me 'usband.'

It was, it turned out, the projectionist's wife, of whom Michael had heard tell earlier, a woman who seemed to embody all the jealous matrons of mythology. Clytaemnestra, Medea, Mrs Hercules; they may have given their menfolk a hard time, but it was as nothing compared with the severity of Mrs Benamore. When her dander was up, her approach was not dissimilar from the Giant Polytheme's: 'the forest shakes, the mountain nods, the giant roars'.

Just now, however, her rage had vanished like a mighty wind, leaving only wreckage in its wake, and this she now addressed herself to tidying up, ludicrously clucking round them as they lay there, re-arranging the sheets and patting the pillows like a sort of Peggotty turned procuress.

'Oh dear, oh dear,' she kept repeating, 'I'll never live this down.'

'That's quite all right. Please go.'

'It's that Mr Benamore. He's led me a merry dance, I can tell you I always suspect the worst when he's got a pint or two inside him, regular valentino, wouldn't think so to look at him. Just keeping my eye on him, I was, when I come all over drowsy. Think they're slipping me something? I don't trust that housekeeper. Next thing I know there's this door here creaking down the passage, so I come on over and bingo! Hot drink? Biscuits?'

'Thank you. No.'

'There's your eiderdown. Slipped right off, it had. Just like Mr Benamore, if you get my meaning.'

At this point, just as she was enjoying her little joke, and preparing to tell them about her corns, the delegates arrived. They had formed a sort of conga and came hopping unsteadily in, whooping and falling about.

'I say, I say, I say, what have we here,' they called, congregating round the bed.

Michael had for some time felt the passion ebbing away from him. Loss of dignity, he had always found, was a great eraser of lust. Mustering all the sangfroid that remained, he pulled the curtains of the four-poster together, slipped on his trousers, thankful that he kept his keys and wallet in them since they were the only part of his wardrobe he could find, planted a valedictory kiss on the cheek of the mysterious lady, a merci as it were for the belle dame, and hared out of the room and down the stairs before the executives had a chance to collar him and throw him in the rose-pond.

He reached his Aston Martin as they rushed out of the house, still whooping and cat-calling, and with a fine spurt of gravel, he accelerated away and out into the Sussex night, leaving them capering goatishly among the company cars.

As he traversed Purley, the dawn trembled and danced across the municipal playing fields as merry as a secondary-schoolgirl on the Pill, but, for Michael, the morrow loomed with the malignity of a poison gas cloud, pendulous with menace.

He was finally convinced that someone was after him.

8

From time to time, as her duties at Tooth Boothroyd and Dulcimer permitted, Lucy had allowed her mind to wander in the direction of Michael and his bizarre predicament.

For herself, of course, the interdict on fornication would have mattered little. It was something she usually preferred not to think about, let alone activate.

True, she was not a virgin. To celebrate her twenty-eighth birthday, she had slept, twice, with a hairy sociologist: once to see what all the fuss was about, and the second time to show she had not just been seeing what all the fuss was about.

The whole experience had been tasteless and embarrassing. The sociologist may have been primus inter pares when it came to analyses on the effect of a monetarist economic policy on infantile delinquency in high-rise blocks, or reviewing the gotterdammerung of capitalism, but he had about as much idea of The Sexual Woman as St Simon Stylites. His idea of foreplay was a beard in the bosom.

Given all this, she was surprised at the way the little recording box in old Tooth's office kept tugging at her attention. It became quite a ritual for her to go and examine it every morning before Becket got in. (Becket, to whom nothing was sacred – particularly enforced celibacy – would have made regrettable jokes about it. Although recently she had begun to wonder whether Becket had some kind of inkling of its presence if not its purpose. Nothing escaped his goblin intelligence network for long, and she thought he had recently been looking at her particularly intently with those rheumy X-ray eyes of his.)

At all events, it was with distinct sensations of pleasure, mingled with qualms that she should have such sensations, that she heard the cake-cheeked receptionist announcing:

'Mr Michael Limpet on the line.'

'Thank you. I'll take it in my office.'

Becket, who was shredding dead mice with a pencil sharpener in one of the top drawers of his desk, paused and gave her another look. Lucy walked through to her office, taking care not to hurry. It would never do to show interest.

'Mr Lambert? Everything all right, I trust,' her voice quivered strangely, and her thoughts kept reverting to the box. Come, come she thought, I must be brisk and business-like.

'Still keeping your end up, I see.'

Damn. Why had she had to use that phrase? Even she realized it was ill-chosen under the circumstances. And she had virtually told him of her morning pilgrimage to Tooth's office. And why was there this wretched wobble in her throat?

His voice came back, strangely haggard.

'I think we've got a problem.'

Wonderful. He was involving her. But why did he sound so neurotic? His unhealthy London life, no doubt. What he needed was a good long hike.

'What's the matter, Mr Lambert?'

'Someone's trying to nobble me.'

'Nobble?' she wobbled.

'They're deliberately trying to seduce me.'

She reeled.

'These are strong words, Mr Lambert.'

'I feel strongly about it. I doubt whether anyone has ever felt so strongly about anything; Napoleon about his piles, Samson about his hair; even on a good day with a following wind, their feelings were playful and kittenish compared with mine. I don't think I can hold out if this goes on.'

'Perhaps you had better come round.'

And later, when Becket had shown him in with his usual mixture of contempt and distaste, as though he had caught a snake with its tail in the till, Lucy was shocked to see what a toll the ordeal was exacting. The man twitched. His face was pale, his manner highly labile.

'Please tell me everything about it, Mr Lambert. I am a woman of the world. That will be all, Becket.'

Why wouldn't the odious creature go?

Nothing loth, Michael launched into his story, omitting little. Lucy listened rapt, shocked and fascinated. So this was what went on; so that was foreplay (he was telling her of the Coucou episode); suddenly a whole new world of experience opened before her. She crossed her legs ardently. She wanted to reach out and take him in her arms, but she was her father's daughter still. As a solicitor, she could not possibly countenance foreplay with a client, above all not with one in Michael's circumstances. It would be tantamount to tampering with evidence. She pulled herself together.

'What you have told me is indeed disturbing, Mr Lambert. But I can discern no evidence of malfeasance. I mean, who could possibly wish to do such a thing? You have no enemies?'

'None that I can think of.'

'I'm afraid it's just the luck of the draw, then. You're an attractive man, in your way, Mr Lambert.' There. She had said it. 'This is the cross you have to bear. No doubt Mrs Kovacs had it in mind when she drew up her bequest.'

'Beautiful women suddenly appearing in my bedroom in silk underwear? Surely, Miss Dulcimer, this is more than being attractive in my way?'

'I'll have to get some.'

'I'm sorry?'

'I'll have to get some . . . of my files. One moment.'

Lucy busied herself at the cupboard, back turned to hide her blushes. What was happening to her? She had never wanted silk underwear in her life.

'I'm afraid, at this stage, I must regard your allegations as pure hypotheses.'

He wished she would drop the lawyer's cant. She was really rather attractive in her way herself. He wondered idly what kind of underwear she wore. With anyone else, he might have impertinently enquired, but he didn't want to risk her displeasure. He needed help. So all he said was, weakly:

'There's something funny going on.' And he didn't mean oolala brassieres.

There was a pause. She wanted to help him, and she wanted to see him again. A Racine-like struggle between Duty and Love racked her demure and legal frame. Had she not been warned, practically on her father's knee 'Remember, my dear, just as doctors must not have affairs with their patients, so we must avoid entanglements with our legatees.'

'I tell you what, Mr Lambert. If you can get any evidence, the merest whiff of something tangible that might support your thesis, I'll bend over backwards . . .' another ill-chosen phrase . . . 'to bring the perpetrators to law. But I have to say I think it's most unlikely. There's only one party that would stand to benefit if you ah failed to maintain your position, and that's the Philosophers of the Revolution, but I really can't think that . . .'

Michael bounded from his chair and embraced her.

'Mr Lambert . . . I must ask you to . . .' Do it again, she wanted to say.

'Sorry. It's just that it suddenly makes sense. You're right. It's those appalling Philosophers. They're capable of anything.'

'Nonsense, Mr Lambert. You're too dramatic. My advice to you is: cultivate the Horatian virtues, Reflection, Tranquillity; lay off the whisky; get London out of your system. "O quiet have I found thee here, and Innocence thy sister dear." Try a health farm. Walk the Ridgeway. Follow the Fosse . . . And if you do stumble across anything . . . not on the Fosse, naturally, but on your return . . . well, I'll be the first to rally round. Good day, Mr Lambert, and good luck.'

And with a bright smile, she extended her hand and a man-size portion of her heart, and opened the door, neatly pitching Becket forward across the carpet. Lucy only just managed to restrain herself from grinding him into the shagpile, but kept her grin on until Michael had left the premises.

He did so with a titanic sense of foreboding. The Philosophers. Ah yes. It all made sense now. The Philosophers had laid it all on. The nurse. The model. The mysterious lady. What else had they got in store? Who could he trust now?

On reaching home, he once more addressed himself to Tom's doorbell, and, though this time he had a longish wait, he was gratified to find his crazed neighbour in residence. Tom answered the summons with a towel round his waist and what appeared to be a pair of enuretic drawers round his head.

'Taking a sea-weed bath, old boy. Ah. I see you're looking at my invention.' Tom patted his strange mantilla. 'Anti-steam. Rots the follicles. Over-stimulates the sebum. Stumble in.'

He snatched off the headpiece, however, and shepherded Michael into his living room. Here, amid every kind of gadget and appliance designed for the improvement if not the comfort of the corporation, Michael took his seat on an exercise bicycle while Tom rowed manfully beside him.

'Something up, old boy? Got to keep exercising after a sauna or the muscles form what we call a crust.'

'I think I'm going to need your help.'

'Just say the word. I'm a Black Belt now. A walking textbook of controlled violence.'

'I don't think it'll come to that. I just need tailing. We need to activate the bleeper routine.'

'No problem. I get the idea. Can't trust yourself, eh? Want to borrow my Iron Will course? Be a Bismarck in Three Weeks.'

Michael gently declined, and told Tom about the Philosophers and their grey insidious ways.

'They're after the money, Tom, and they know my weaknesses, God knows how. And that's not all. They know my movements too. There's nothing they won't do to sabotage me.'

'We'll have to keep tabs on you, then. Better have another practice.'

Michael went up to his flat for the apparatus. Tom changed, quite unnecessarily, into a track-suit. And once more they essayed the streets. It soon appeared that their previous success with the device had been a case of beginner's luck.

Michael drove round and round the Albert Hall, bleeping vigorously, but this time Tom did not seem to be receiving him (or else the steam had got to his frontal lobes).

After an hour, Michael was just about to give up and retire to the flat when Tom shot round the corner in his clapped-out Porsche, hurtled past Michael's car, screeched to a halt, reversed into a stationary limousine full of startled Arabs, and finally, with half the Diplomatic Corps of the United Emirates clinging vociferously to his trouser elastic, doubled over to the Aston Martin's window.

'Sorry, old lad. Ran out of petrol.'

'That's all right,' said Michael wanly. 'It's just that if this were for real the Philosophers would be millionaires by now.'

'Early days, old boy,' Tom breezed. 'We've got to keep practising our scales. Tell these chaps to tool off, laddie, would you. I hate a baggy track suit.'

Michael, without too much difficulty, was able to convince the Arabs that Tom was possessed by devils, and they retreated, warding off the evil eye.

He and Tom spent the rest of the day polishing their technique.

Michael would sneak out, drive in any direction, and switch on the transmitter. Tom, ears finely tuned to the bleep, would dash out after him, sometimes in no more than a bathrobe, and drive like Jehu in pursuit.

It was a somewhat crude device, Michael reflected, as he waited at dusk outside Westminster Cathedral while Tom drove frenziedly up and down Pimlico trying to assess whether the bleep was getting louder or softer, and at the same time to negotiate the Minoan one-way system. It was crude, but it was something to clutch at.

And in the weeks that followed, as no further assaults were made upon his person, his spirits slowly rose again.

9

At the very toe of South East Buckinghamshire, a suburban sprawl with no particular name ends in a series of low brick streets, known locally as Babylon, which had once housed artisans working in a (now long-disused) railway repair depot, but which now straggles purposelessly across a featureless landscape, petering out in an industrial estate built beside an abandoned aggregate site.

Desolation is the keynote of the place. Stagnant mires (giving the locality its nickname) lick at ferro-concrete mini-hangars, and chilly little signposts indicate the location of profit-centres such as Genuflex Venetian Blinds, Nutrino Hair Products, and the Desjean Douche Company.

Apart from the daily coming and going of small work-forces, nothing normally disturbs the whistle of the wind through the coarse grass and sparse reed-beds, and the plaintive chirk of the moorhen.

Suddenly, however, this unlikely venue was the scene of exceptional activity.

Yesterday, it was true, there had been some small burst of unaccustomed to-ing and fro-ing. A florid man in a white coat was to be seen standing importantly and gesticulating towards the gates of one of the larger and newer factory sites, arguing with another man, of slighter build and sallower complexion, in a managerial suit.

Also the workforce, mostly female and of Asian origin, had left the factory a good couple of hours before the normally appointed hour. All this pointed to a mild departure from the norm.

But today something was definitely up; the workforce had not appeared at all. Instead, little groups of strangers – jean-clad – twos and threes with haversacks and pale faces, like fluff attracted to the electricity of trouble, started to congregate outside the factory entrance.

They didn't have to wait long. Soon, the genuine activists started to roll in, the shock-troops carefully trained in remote farmhouses in Derbyshire, the graduates from flying-picket school in Glasgow, delegations of miners from Doncaster, hospital porters from Welwyn Garden City, and all the other stock characters in the often-repeated mise en scene – puzzled rank and file, joyriders, thugs, hobbledehoys, sight seers, and even the genuinely committed.

They variously took up position outside the gates, and waited for developments.

The florid shop steward was still in evidence, this time backed up by a whey-faced individual with watery eyes and a cloth tie, something to do with the Union at local level. They both stood at the security bar, arguing ritually with the Security Officer who was equally ritually refusing to let them in.

Soon the police arrived, and started urging everyone to clear the roadway. You could see they didn't really expect anyone to take much notice, and they were right. They were hopelessly outnumbered.

The whole thing, at this stage, was like an under-rehearsed Greek tragedy; everyone had some notion of his part, but no one quite knew where to go.

Then Bert Scrannell appeared.

Everyone knew Bert Scrannell.

Christened Herbert, but clipped of his first syllable in

early manhood, he was the son of Sir Hereward Scrannell, the famous conductor, and some of his father's feeling for orchestration had undeniably been passed on to him. He had the gift of order. Wherever he appeared, people instantly seemed to know their place. So it was in Babylon. A ripple of purpose went through the crowd, and the police called up extra reinforcements.

Herbert was a tall man in his early forties. He had lacklustre hair and a glittering eye. He spoke endlessly about the workers, and rarely smiled.

He and his mother Lavinia, the noted portrait painter, had made activism their life's work. They were not prepared to rest, it was said, till they had turned the country upside down and shaken it until the tears ran down its face and its sweeties had gone spinning into the wainscoting; but what they were going to do with it then had not yet been disclosed.

Lavinia would be along later with a stop press issue of their paper, Mayhem, but Bert had come early to grip the situation by the lapels. He went over to the two men at the security-bar and greeted them unsmilingly.

'What's the issue, brothers?'

'Slave Labour.'

'Excellent.'

Another of Bert's characteristics was a strangely protean quality. He had the ability, having come to the front, to merge into the crowd and wait at the back. He turned on his heel, the mob opened, and he was gone.

For a few days, nothing changed very much. The crowd had swollen to several hundred, but it ebbed and flowed as it grew hungry or the pubs closed or it went to have a pee.

A now-substantial police contingent kept a path open to the gates with forced good humour, and was more or less successful in keeping the peace.

A Mister Whipsee van had appeared and was doing a roaring trade in frankfurters and soft drinks, and various touts were similarly employed in cashing in on the assembled company. The whole thing was like a rather depressing day at the races.

Then, suddenly, the entire tone of the proceedings changed. It was precipitated by a bus turning up, and obdurately forcing its way to the barrier. It was patently not full of activists or even rubbernecks. The passengers seemed to be mainly Asian girls, and puzzled. They were in fact employees of the factory.

Mr Lee, the Managing Director, had asked them to stay away until the trouble was over, but they had grown tired of being at home and getting ordered around by their fathers, so they had asked if they could now go back to work, and Mr Lee, being naturally anxious to keep production going, had agreed.

As soon as it was established that they were indeed employees, the cry went up.

'Scabs.'

The girls were puzzled. They had mostly been working at the place for several years, they were reasonably well paid, the conditions if not exactly de luxe were considerably better than a hundred other factories in the vicinity, and not to be compared with Bengal. Many of them were more than aware that it was something to be in work at all these days.

They were harangued for some minutes by the pickets while a posse of hard-line white collar workers menaced the driver. Another group started to rock the bus. The girls started to scream. The driver panicked. Reversing too sharply, he ran over a white collar worker's umbrella.

This was the signal for a well-orchestrated moment

of violence. Brickbats flew. The bus's windscreen was shattered. And the police finally had to move in.

Cordons were formed; baton charges were launched; a particularly vehement social-studies student from Loughborough was dragged along the pavement and bundled into a waiting Black Maria; an elderly Fabian made an impassioned speech from the top of a hastily commandeered patisserie truckette which nobody paid the slightest attention to.

A semblance of order was restored, but the bus was still not able to leave.

To loud jeers, Mr Lee, an Anglo-Chinese from Singapore, emerged once more from the administrative block and made his way across the forecourt to speak to the police at the barrier, apparently with a view to gaining admittance for the bus in order to take the girls out of harm's way.

The police Chief Inspector looked at his watch, peered at the sky as if in the hope of some divine intervention or, at least, guidance; finding none, re-addressed himself to his walkie-talkie, shook his head at Mr Lee, murmured official sympathy, made a gesture at the crowd resembling a circus seal-master's 'off your stools and I'll feed you' motion, and inwardly wished all wogs and lefties would go away and duff each other up outside his manor.

Mr Lee retired under a barrage of epithets and a selection of Grade Four eggs gleaned from a passing milk float.

The Whipsee van, temporarily commandeered by a contingent of dustmen from Galashiels, set up a derisory rendition of the Bluebells of Scotland on its carillon.

And a television news-team arrived with a couple of van loads of stores and supplies. It was clear that they were anticipating a lengthy sojourn.

The Chief Inspector, when things had quietened down a

little, and he had finally managed to extricate the busful of girls without further violence (only through a piece of overt sycophancy to the strikers, but arse-licking was part of the job these days) walked over to a quiet spot behind one of the hangars with his driver, and listlessly started throwing pebbles into the slime-grey depths.

'By the waters of Babylon,' he said to his driver, 'I sat down and wept.'

But his driver was not a God-fearing or even literary officer.

'I wouldn't sit here, Chief,' he said, 'you'll catch your death of piles. Hang on a mo and I'll fetch you the rug from the Black Maria.'

10

Michael's first two months were nearly up.

He spent much of his time now pacing his flat, debating how to prove to Lucy that the Philosophers were really after him, and reading. He had laid in a stock of science-fiction novels and quasi-scientific treatises on Black and White Holes, quasars and Naked Singularities, but many of these appeared to have been appropriated by Mrs Fitches, his cleaner, as had indeed one or two other items around the flat recently, and the only other book he hadn't read in his shelves (apart from The Old Curiosity Shop) was Barchester Towers. This, with no great sense of expectation, he started to peruse; but whether it was Trollope's leisurely style or ecclesiastical content, he found it strangely relaxing and congenial, in no way exacerbating his problems or inflaming his imagination, a sort of literary Benger's or Slippery Elm, nourishing and soothing, to be sipped at leisure.

It was a great novelty for his mind to dwell on any topic for long other than the roads to carnality. The comings and goings of Barchester exercised a murmurous fascination. Why had he neglected them so long? Had he been blinkered all his adult life? Was there something he had in some way overlooked?

It was June; tennis weather. Prior to his later interest in cricket, tennis was the one game Michael had been good at as a boy. It had, of course, been frowned on by his school where it was regarded as all right for girls but scarcely inculcatory of team spirit, besides it was played with a soft ball and didn't hurt. He still pricked up his ears, however, like an old charger at the bugle, when he heard the plung of ball on racket; and every year he played in a tennis circus on Monday evenings at the Rockingham Club, an elite piece of parkland and garden miraculously preserved among the savannahs of Fulham.

An acquaintance of his organized the circus – eight mixed doubles of a reasonably high standard – notable for the fact that the men all seemed to be merchant bankers and the girls were all pretty and appeared to have been to the same high-pitched school.

It was Jenny, one of these creatures, who suddenly rang him up and suggested a game. Glad of an opportunity to get out of the flat without putting himself at risk, he agreed readily enough, and she arranged that they should meet at the house of a prosperous uncle of hers, which had a private grass-court in its garden, somewhere off Kensington High Street. She said she would organize the other couple.

Next day, Michael turned up at the address she had given him with a lively sense of anticipation.

His almost religious feeling for tennis had completely overwhelmed any thought of his predicament, and he left his flat swinging his racket and practising his follow-through with a rare abandon, almost decapitating the old biddy who lived on the other side of the landing, and completely forgetting to tell Tom where he was going.

Jenny answered the door looking very fetching in a short white dress. She gave him a radiant smile.

'Michael,' she said, pitching low for a change. 'How nice to see you.'

He had thought the previous year that she and the other girls had been a trifle stand-offish, possibly because he wasn't a merchant banker (though decently hard-up themselves they always seemed to have an ear cocked for money), talking only to their friends and politely treating Michael as a rough boy who had as it were been brought in from the farm, all right to play with but not for serious things like dinner parties and weekends. Now, however, he revised his opinion. It must've been his insecurity coming out before. What a nice friendly girl she was.

'Come in,' she said, 'and meet the others. Prosperous Uncle's away in California and we've got the place to ourselves. There's a swimming pool we can use afterwards.'

She took him into the drawing-room which gave on to a wide and gracious garden containing a pool, a tennis court, a lawn, rose-bushes, honeysuckles, statues, and al fresco furniture. The uncle must be exceedingly rich, thought Michael, and cheered himself with the thought of what sort of quarters he would be able to afford when he was similarly placed.

The room itself was beautifully furnished, as one would have expected. He noticed a Chippendale mirror, a Queen Anne chest that must have been worth £15,000, a couple of Stubbses on the wall, and two girls dressed in white on the sofa.

'I'm sorry,' said Jenny, 'I couldn't seem to get hold of any more men. This is Trisha and this is Jo. They both played at Junior Wimbledon. I think we should have quite a good game.'

The girls smiled hello and looked, Michael thought, both friendly and unworryingly attractive, with the special cleanness which comes from a lifetime of Mummy putting the right soap in the bathroom, and keeping the vowels open.

After a few pleasantries, they all trooped out into the garden, down a rose-lined path, and on to the tennis court. It was decided that Michael should play with Jenny against the Junior Wimbledon duo, and they all started to knock up. The girls on the other side of the net were as good as Jenny had cracked them up to be, and Michael was hard put to it, being (what with one thing and another) considerably out of training, to appear even vaguely competent. And his abilities were further impaired when, stopping after five minutes or so's play to retrieve a ball, he could not help noticing that Jenny was wearing pants of a taut sheerness that would have been better suited to the boudoir than the baseline.

Silly girl, he thought, we can all make mistakes. He supposed, in a moment of abstraction, she had climbed into the first articles to hand, but it was a bit of a bloomer on her part. That sort of thing could put a chap off his stroke. Besides, it was just the sort of thing he didn't need at the moment. It was true that she did have two glorious moons down there, but the combination of the simple healthiness of the tennis dress and the lascivious twinkling of the buttocks aroused in him sensations he had hoped to have put aside for the evening.

He fluffed a simple smash, and served a double fault.

Damn. She was a high-powered secretary for some property company, wasn't she? She had obviously mislaid the regulation bee's-bottom frillies she would normally have worn on court. But a girl with such responsibilities shouldn't make mistakes like that. One day it's knickers and the next it could be a vital, multi-million-pound contract-note. He felt like writing to her employers.

'Love forty,' sang out Jenny cheerfully.

Should he tell her? She clearly had no idea of her faux pas. But in the end he decided it would be undiplomatic. What would one say? 'Excuse me, but your knickers are out of court.' No, he must try and concentrate on the ball and keep his eyes off those bobbing beacons. In spite of himself, he was somewhat intrigued that a nice girl like Jenny should wear things like that at any time.

It was now their opponents' turn to serve, Trisha to Jenny. She had a beautiful serving action, swinging her whole body into the ball. Michael opened his mouth to compliment her as the ball went whizzing into the very corner of the court out of reach of Jenny's outstretched racket – but the little twitch of the body she gave as she served had revealed something else. She was wearing briefs that, if anything, were more indecorous than Jenny's, and as she addressed herself to serve and thrashed down another winner, he was still in a state of shock. What did this mean? Surely they couldn't both have made the same mistake? What delectable creatures they were, though.

Half in joy, half in dread, he dished up a long high lob over Jo's head so he could catch a glimpse of her withers when she smashed. Up, up, the ball soared, and he could feel a certain sympathetic response from his own person as it elevated.

Jo ran back a little, steadied herself, and hit the ball as if it had personally impugned the honour of her high-pitched family, belting it straight at Michael who stood rooted with mingled delight and horror as he drank in the picayune postage stamp of translucent frivolousness that adorned her perspicuous loins.

The ball caught him like a high-velocity armour-piercing piat-shell smack on the forehead, spun him round, and dropped him to the floor. He passed out for a second.

The girls all clustered round, murmuring solicitously, and he looked up their frocks as they stood over him, his eyes watering with pain and lust.

'It's nothing. Really.'

He recovered himself after a few moments, and the match progressed. Somehow he struggled through three sets, but he had to admit his game was not at its best. He seemed, the girls agreed afterwards, to spend an awful lot of time crouching low at the net and rolling his eyes.

When it was all over, they made their way across to the swimming pool. It had been an inordinately hot evening, and the walled garden soaked up the heat like a tandoori chicken.

'Oh super,' cried Trisha. 'Golly, just what I need.'

'Yes,' agreed Jo, 'pools in England never seem to be around when one needs them. Like policemen. They come out on cold days covered with leaves and smelling of chlorine.'

Michael made a weak joke about never having met a policeman attired like that but the girls' minds were elsewhere.

'That's why I thought it'd be nice to play here,' Jenny observed.

'But we haven't brought our swimming things.'

'That doesn't matter. Bra and things will do. That is, if Michael doesn't mind.'

Did he mind? What a dreadful punishment. Why hadn't these things happened when he was just an ordinary unattached bachelor? No. He must be strong.

'No. Not at all. I think I'll go up to the house, though, if you don't mind. Bit of a headache.'

'Nonsense. You're being shy. He's being shy.'

'A swim's just what he needs.'

And Jo slipped out of her dress without further ado and plunged into the water. Oh my god, what creatures, thought Michael, as the other two followed suit, filling the air with flying bosoms; but he turned – he had never felt prouder of himself in his life, he knew where duty lay, and money too – and started padding resolutely up towards the house while the girls splashed and chirruped as if they were entertaining Hylas himself.

Suddenly he felt a wet hand on his shoulder. It was Trisha.

'Don't go,' she said. 'We'd really like you to swim with us.'

He mumbled an excuse, not daring to look at the wild roses blooming underneath the dripping traveller's joy of her bra, when all at once he felt hands seize him – soft, irresistible, bower-of-bliss type hands – and he was propelled back towards the water.

'No. Look. Hang on,' he muttered, and only just had time to switch on his bleeper (a last-ditch gesture) when his shirt and blazer were removed and he was hurled roguishly into the cerulean waters.

Halfway across Kensington, Tom, spoonful of nut burger arching towards his mouth as he wrestled with a propped-up volume of 'Body Language and Macrobiotics', heard the blip-blip-blip of the machine with a mixture of concern and exultation. This was the moment he had been waiting for. Cramming on his track-suit, the nuts of nine nations dribbling down his chin, he darted ferociously out of the building, sprang into his Porsche and set off like a maniac down the King's Road in the opposite direction, as it happened, from the emergency, spreading ruin and scattering tourists. He had scarcely time to notice that the blips were getting weaker when a policewoman sprang out of a traffic island, and demanded to see his driving licence.

Back in the pool, things were not going too well. The water, simmering all day in the expensive Kensington sun, was now nearly at blood temperature, and served merely to exacerbate rather than subdue the oriflamme in Michael's lower portions.

The girls, having ducked him, had taken off their bras and were, like wanton Renaissance princesses, splashing and giggling and tweaking each other's nipples. They now set about removing Michael's shorts, and what they found underneath set them crowing and giggling even more.

'He's only got two,' cried Trisha, with a Junior Champion's wit. 'But I think we can get a game together.'

Tom, meanwhile, attempting to explain things to the policewoman, had only made matters worse. Thinking that she was dealing with some kind of addict or deviant, she instructed him to take her to Chelsea Police Station, but no sooner had she got in the car than Tom sped off into Sloane Street and hared up towards Kensington with the policewoman churning about in the seat beside him and alerting half the panda cars in London with her walkie-talkie.

Tom cared little. The blips were getting stronger again. He shot three sets of traffic lights and careered into the Park.

Michael, hitherto torn between delight and duty, now recognized that there was no way out. He had given up hope of Tom. He realized that he had never had any real hope of him in the first place. He knew when he was beaten. So when the girls finally threw him a towel and suggested they go into the gazebo for a drink, he complied with ready concupiscence.

The gazebo was a grand affair. It had been built as a pleasure pavilion in a style and on a scale that would have done credit to Haroun al Raschid. It was mainly furnished with cushions, and it was fitted out with every conceivable aid to civilized luxury. Drinks, ice, music, air-conditioning, audio-visual devices abounded. And subtly-shaded blinds admitted a half-light that was madeira-coloured, cedar-scented, at once soothing and suggestive.

The girls had momentarily disappeared, as Michael was taking all this in, so he swathed himself in a sheik-like bathrobe and poured himself a drink, while music which he recognized as a selection from Gilbert and Sullivan, not the most erotic choice one would have thought but strangely congenial, filtered from cunningly-placed loud speakers.

At Lancaster Gate, the policewoman, fainting with fright as Tom took the one-way system at eighty mph against the stream, offered him leniency and a fair trial, but the blips were getting stronger and stronger, and Tom was in no mood to dawdle. At Notting Hill, she proffered her body and tickets for the Police Ball, but his sole never left the accelerator.

A movement from the far end of the room made Michael look round. There was no one to be seen but he got the feeling that something was up and it wasn't just his parson. (Although he had had a little time to consider his position, his mood of carnality had not been replaced by one of caution. Indeed his whole frame now seemed to be consumed with fire, popping and crackling like Pudding Lane timber.)

He got up and padded silently towards the far end of the room where, through a chink in the drapery, a sight that he had often dreamed about first as a pimply pubescent and recently as a dirty old man, but had never set eyes on in either role, now met his gaze, to the strains of 'Three Little Girls from School'.

At the very same instant, before he could register so much as an extra infinitesimal flicker on the Richter Scale of tumescence, the flaps at the other end were torn apart with a force that compared very favourably with the blow-out at Thira, and Tom appeared with an electronic monitor in one hand and an hysterical policewoman in the other.

The policewoman flung herself on Trisha.

'Save me,' she cried, unbuttoning her tunic.

Tom flung himself on Michael.

'Down boy,' he said. 'Out of bounds. Cut along now.'

Then suddenly the room was full of Alsatians and policemen flinging themselves at everyone.

'Fuck off,' said Jenny, which was true.

'A fine kettle of fish,' said a Chief Inspector.

'Woof,' said the Alsatians sniffing eagerly hither and thither.

Later, down at the police station, Michael tried to explain, but he couldn't dissuade them from charging Tom with dangerous driving and failing to stop when instructed by a police officer. And it was only by the skin of their teeth that they convinced the Chief Inspector that they were not trying to abduct Policewoman Fowler for a group sex corroboree.

'Really,' said Michael to Tom as they drove home, 'I think we got off amazingly lightly. I like that policewoman you picked up. I've always had a bit of a thing about policewomen. I think it's those black tights and the thought of what they might be wearing underneath. Did you see the bra she was wearing? Strictly non-regulation issue.'

'If you finally get this legacy of yours, old horse,' said Tom, 'it's going to be a bloody miracle.'

He was cut up about his driving offence.

'Cheer up,' said Michael, 'I'll buy you a new Porsche when I get my money.'

Later that evening, Policewoman Fowler rang Trisha up.

'Come up to my place,' she demanded brusquely, 'and I'll thrash you within an inch of your life.'

'It's the Philosophers,' said Michael, 'that's the only explanation. They've somehow got at those girls. They were just nice ordinary high-pitchers before, and now they're raving lesbians. You see how insidiously evil they are, like dry rot, they stop at nothing. Junior Wimbledon too. Is nothing sacred?'

11

Few among the encamped host knew how the strike had started and, if you had told them, even fewer would have cared. The fact that it was there was enough. Its origins, however, had been remarkably simple.

Somebody, not one of the older staff, and certainly not one of the Asians, had been given his notice by Mr Lee for failing to follow simple safety instructions in the matter of waste disposal – the management had experience of vital parts being thrown away by mistake, and the disposal squad had subsequently been issued with a precautionary routine that, with repeated instances in this particular case, had not been followed. The man, it was generally agreed, must have been almost deliberately stupid.

Stan Brewfitt, however, their Shop Steward, had called them all out in sympathy. They did not feel sympathy, and said so.

'We are not feeling sympathy, not in the very very least, my eye, no,' they clamoured.

Nor did they, for they had nice clothes to buy, as well as video equipment, and who wanted to stay at home all day in a sari being bossed around by your parents from arsehole to breakfast time.

But Sid Brewfitt knew better.

'One for all and all for one,' he lectured them. 'Turn a blind eye today, and somebody may not like the colour of your skin tomorrow. Look at Hitler's Germany. You know what Mick's fault was?'

'No.'

'He was a good union man. The management couldn't forgive him.'

'We are all union men,' said the girls.

'Not quite the same,' said Sid. 'Mick really felt for the workers.'

'That is true,' said pretty Miss A. Bismullah who had been brushed against by the youth more than once in the Canteen and Leisure Complex corridor.

'There you are, you see,' said Sid, noting the lass, and running his mind lightly over her tender little coffee-coloured titties, 'we were grooming him for promotion. He would have gone far.'

'That is true,' agreed Miss A. Bismullah.

Dirty little monkey, thought Sid, I'll kick him in the proper channels when I catch up with him.

'A lifetime of potential service,' he continued declamatorily, 'now callously cast aside. Who knows what harm that may do to a sensitive lad? He has been thrown on the human scrapheap, sisters, tossed aside like a used tissue. Just like what the Raj did to your native land.'

This was a mistake. The girls did not like to be called native, and started to mutter rebelliously. Sid called them to order.

'Anyway,' he lectured them, 'you do what I tell you and we stick together, or you'll be back in Calcutta, washing pots in the Ganges at the first whim of the Tories. You see? Who knows what the future may hold? And your Union will be able to do nothing for you because you did not stand shoulder to shoulder over a little local issue when a show of hands was called for. Savvy?'

The Asians were none too happy, but when Sid promised them emoluments from Union funds, they reluctantly went along with him.

'What is emolument?' said Miss A. Bismullah afterwards to her friend Narriman.

'I do not know exactly but I think it is very good for the skin.'

Many of the girls had complexion problems. It was something to do with their mixed diet.

It was only later that rumours started to circulate. The real reason for the strike, it was said, was that the company was making parts for a defence project, and certain vested interests wanted a disruption. Meanwhile, it was widely agreed by liberal opinion – as Bert Scrannell had so reliably forecast and indeed engineered – that the dispute was rooted in discrimination and cheap labour.

As usual, no one allowed the facts to distract them from their natural prejudices. There were all the ingredients for a first rate set of loggerheads.

12

As a result of his new-found involvement with Trollope, abetted by the more serious frame of mind induced by his current predicament, Michael had taken up the habit of jotting his thoughts down in an old address book. In between the erased telephone numbers of erased girl-friends, the rough tendrils of his reflections were sprouting like weeds among concrete.

Sitting in his flat, unmolested now for several weeks after the tennis debacle, but by no means off tenterhooks, he strove to find some reason beyond the mere exercising of an acquired talent that would explain his extraordinary passion for the other sex. An understanding of the cause, he thought, could possibly lead to a cure.

Clumsy from desuetude, his fingers guided the ballpoint through the concrete jungle of Oakley Gardens, Sloane Square, Earl's Court and Prince of Wales Mansions where Annie and Jane and Belinda and Yvonne and Pamela and Rosie had, in days gone by, welcomed him with open legs.

'Women,' he wrote, 'are sailing ships; men are motor vessels.'

He didn't quite know what it meant, but it sounded good. Encouraged, he tried again. 'Women are the Law,' he wrote, 'Men are merely the Executive.'

He rested from his labours. Is that why I want to make love to them? he wondered. To try and topple their inviolable grown-upness?

And then, catching sight of an old photograph that had

slipped from one of the drawers of his desk, he thought of an early love in his life which had nothing to do with women at all, the boy de Blaye at school. Their common bond of being half-American (de Blaye's American mother had married, and divorced, a Frenchman) had first drawn them together, and then a passion which only de Blaye's sudden departure from the school to live with his mother in Greece could quench. True, de Blaye had looked like a girl, the apricot skin, the soft brown eyes, but perhaps after all, Michael thought, it's nothing to do with the sexes at all, it's simply to do with sex, that burning bag, that mischievous martinet, that quartain fever that can only be doused for a pitifully brief spell before it breaks out again. Yes, that's what it is, a crass physical necessity one tries to dress up with words, but it keeps pulling its clothes off like a dog in a dinner jacket.

Why should I try to find human reasons for animal sensations? I've seen apes masturbating in the zoo. I recognize myself. Those terrible red parts. That's me. Take me to your Keeper.

That was one of the things that depressed him about the idea of an after-life. All those spirits, and God for that matter too, clustering round the bars looking in on the living as they picked their noses and sat on the loo and lay with their faces in some lady's lap. Spirits who could, when you were dead, come up and say 'Ho ho ho, we saw you.'

As he scribbled away, he wrote himself into a lower and lower mood without hitting the heart of the matter (proving that a willingness to face unpleasant fact is not necessarily a short-cut to the truth). The truth in his case was that he enjoyed both women and sex, and made the mistake of confusing them for one and the same thing.

At this moment of his painful inner pilgrimage, the

doorbell groaned as if in sympathy, and Michael, answering it, found Tom outside leaning against the lintel in a considerable state of shock.

'It's gone,' he ululated. 'Gone. Gone. Gone. Gone. Gone.'

His tones would have done credit to King Lear.

'What's gone, Tom?' said Michael, trying not to sound like Reading Without Tears. The reply, if he recollected rightly, was 'Someone has taken my gun, Sam.'

But it was not Tom's gun, it was his car. And not just his car. Tom had left the bleep receiver in the Porsche and it had vanished with it.

'I detect the hand of the Philosophers again, I'm afraid. I've been expecting something like this. It's been too quiet. I'm sorry. It's my fault.'

Tom slumped despondently on the sofa in the living room, too dispirited even to drink the macrobiotic tomato juice that Michael had laid in for him.

'If only,' Michael continued, 'if only I could find some proof. Without the bleeper we've nothing to fall back on. I don't have the funds to get another one. And even if I did, they'd steal it again. One feels so naked.'

'But my Porsche, old lad. That's what hurts. No girl's going to take me seriously without my Throbbing Monster. It was only insured Third Party.'

'Your body's in good shape.' In spite of his concern at the Philosophers' renewal of activities, Michael could still feel very sorry for Tom, and he knew references to his physique usually cheered him, but this time it didn't work.

'That's all very well,' Tom riposted. 'True. But a body will take you only so far. You can't piggyback a girl to a Hunt Ball. You can't tootle off to jolly old Paree on a sixteen inch bicep. You can't bomb down the Motorway for a few days at Mummy and Daddy's on an exceptionally well-developed pectoral muscle. To be honest, I feel like chucking it all in and getting blotto.'

The fact that Tom had never been to any of these places when he had possessed his Throbbing Monster was beside the point. Michael knew that Tom's physical honing was a preparation for a perfect relationship that would never happen, but he had not realized to what an extent Tom depended on his Porsche to keep him living in hope. His heart bled for the poor wimp. Just because he couldn't generate a relationship like everybody else, it was no part of the Philosophers' brief to lop his main support. He was an innocent, though crazed, bystander in all this. Michael suddenly felt very positive.

'Look, Tom, you'll probably get it back, and when I inherit the money, I'll buy you the most expensive Porsche they make. Meanwhile, I'm going down.'

'Down?'

'To talk to them. To tell them to lay-off. I'm going down. Now.'

'But you can't. They'll eat you alive. They'll come at you with ticklers and fallen women.'

'I'll leave a note with you to give the solicitors saying I'm going to see the Philosophers, and if I come to harm or lose my celibate status, it'll mean I've been tampered with, and they'll forfeit the legacy.'

'I don't like it. I'll come with you. Safety in numbers.'

'You've done enough already. I wouldn't hear of it. Go and see that Chief Inspector and tell him about your car.'

Michael scribbled his note, addressed it to Lucy, thrust it into Tom's hands, and took off westwards down the motorway.

A week or so previously, he had done a little research

on the Philosophers. He had been anxious to locate their place in the country, their headquarters, their nerve-centre as it were (no doubt of substantial size considering the reserves of nerve they seemed to be able to draw upon), where they went for special projects and socio-politico-philosophico lavage.

The address had not been easy to find, (he had not liked to ask Lucy for it), and he had devilled away assiduously but without success until a chance remark by a Council for the Preservation of Historic Buildings library assistant had led him to them. He had known, via Gloria, that the place was Jacobean and somewhere in Berkshire, and he had simply asked the librarian for details of all such houses. She in her turn had gone through endless gazetteers before she gave a little cry of triumph, a sort of archivist's view-halloo.

'There's a Sambrook Manor here, near Newbury, sold to the Neo-Buddhist Society twelve years ago. I think that must be the one.'

Michael, at the bottom of the ladder, staring up at her jeans-clad posterior and thinking wistfully of the days of skirts and stocking-tops, responded with a jerk that nearly landed the little librarian in his arms.

Gloria had been thoroughly steeped and sluiced in Buddha in the early days of her association with the Philosophers, and would make the night hideous with her 'OM'.

So that was where they hung out. A thirty-bedroomed mansion built by Sir Thomas Johnson, wool-merchant's heir and sometime courtier, in 1616: superb carving, Italian plasterwork, a couple of Van Dykes, and a yew-maze.

Now, turning off the motorway at Newbury, he branched left a mile or so before the town, following the signs to the village of Sambrook, which lay slumbrously astride the River Kennet, and then on towards the house which could now be seen at a distance, its gables and chimney stacks jutting up like cardboard cut-outs, its pixie-size formal gardens giving way to a handkerchief of park which sloped down to a puddle where a walnut-shell boat was moored.

He could even see on the right, the dense rectangle of what he supposed was the maze, about the same size as the house itself.

As he drew nearer, he saw that all around the estate, which comprised some three hundred acres, was a lofty glass-crusted wall and when he arrived at the main gates, he saw that their spikes were as sharp as halberds.

There appeared also to be some kind of electronic eye in operation for as he braked on the gravel, a bell rang, and he could hear the baying of dogs.

A nice place for a spot of meditation, he thought, and he remembered how he had chaffed Gloria about how hungry she always was when she returned from her sessions.

'Don't they serve bread with their Buddha?' he would quip, ever mindful of her missiles.

A large lobster-like man emerged from the porter's lodge and looked at Michael balefully. He appeared to be wearing dungarees made out of rush matting.

'What d'you want?'

'I want to see your Head. I don't mean your head. I mean your Head.' Michael always liked to get this sort of thing absolutely straight.

'The Master is out.'

'I want to see your Next Best Thing.'

'He's out too. Who are you anyway?'

'I'm from . . .' Michael's mind darted minnowishly,

'The Kennet and Avon Water Authority. We've had complaints,' he added darkly, 'I demand to see someone in charge.'

'Wait here.'

And the man turned and went back into the lodge. Five minutes later he was back.

'You're to go up to the house. Do not talk to anyone unless you are addressed. Do not smoke. Do not take photographs.'

'Do not collect £8 million,' said Michael.

'What was that?'

'Oh. Nothing.'

The gates creaked open in traditional Castle Perilous fashion, and Michael eased the Aston Martin up the gravel drive. Two or three figures dressed in similar dungarees, busy about the grounds, looked up incuriously as he passed, but when he parked the car at the foot of the great steps leading up to the front door, there was no reception committee.

He got out, mounted the flight and walked into the hall. There was a large oak table, an elephant's foot umbrella stand, and an odour of polished wood, museumy and cheerless.

'Anyone at home?' he called.

He was beginning, in spite of his earlier determination, to find the whole place decidedly worrying.

'"Is there anybody there? said the Traveller."'

Michael whipped round. The woman appeared to have sprung out of the woodwork.

'Do not be alarmed, Mr . . . er.'

'Matthews. Fred Matthews. Water Authority.'

'Do not be alarmed, Mr Matthews Water Authority. The manor is riddled with secret passages. I happened to use one as a short cut. There are many even we do not know about. It is rumoured that more than one cavalier still lies walled up within the house. It was a great centre of resistance. Personally, my sympathies have always been with the Roundheads. But I digress. You wished to talk to us?'

The woman was offensively bland. Of no noticeable age, dungareed like the others, she was slightly built, with close-shaven blackish hair, and a complexion that steered a wretched course between grey and sallow. Her eyes, however, burned Bessemer bright, with a noxious and implacable mockery, like chimneys in the Black Country or Hell on Saturday night.

Michael pulled himself together.

'Talk. Yes. Indeed. Perhaps we could go somewhere . . . a little more private.'

He wanted to get as much of a look at the house as he could.

'There are no secrets here, Mr Matthews Water Authority. However, if you wish, please come with me.'

And she led Michael down an unrevealing corridor and into a small study.

'Well, Mr Lambert?'

'You knew who I was?'

'Of course. We've been watching you since you left your flat.'

'For all I know you've been watching me since before I left my flat.'

'For all you know.'

'But this is monstrous.'

'Yes.'

'You'll never get away with it.' Michael felt himself weakening as he took refuge in clichés.

'Try us.'

'I suppose you know that your organization stands for everything I despise and loathe?' Stout words.

'Yes, we do. But it does not worry us unduly.'

'And that I shall do everything in my power to see you don't get the money. Not so much that I want it for myself, but because I don't want you to have it. Everything that's jolly you make drab. Everything that's light, you turn to lead. Because you can't have a good time yourself, you want to stop everyone else from having one. I saw it happening with poor Gloria, using words she didn't understand to express concerns she couldn't feel. Karmic Awareness! Third World! Elitism! Even the language you use has had the stuffing taken out of it – presumably to be put into rush-matted dungarees.' Michael paused for breath.

'Sticks and stones, Mr Lambert, sticks and stones. You can rant and rave as much as you like but it won't delay for one second the ultimate triumph of the Philosophers whose original activities, whose outward and visible signs, the vegetarianism, the self-negation, are simply passing disciplines for something infinitely bigger. You are just a very little man, Mr Lambert, an oblivious tick sucking happily on the back of a beast which goes you know not whither. Fool that you are. The day is coming, Mr Lambert, and quicker than you think, when you and your sort will be smoked out. We simply need the money to make one or two short-term financial arrangements, a bribe to this Union, a disgrace for that Minister, a catastrophic explosion, a shortage of fuel, and the whole country will drop into our hands like an over-ripe medlar. So we're going to activate that absurd little monitor you carry around down there, and you won't be able to lift a finger to help yourself.'

'If you touch me, Tooth Boothroyd and Dulcimer,

especially Dulcimer, will know of it. I have deposited a letter with them telling of my visit. If you force me to do anything against my will, if you tamper with my person, you forfeit any claim you may have to the inheritance. Codicil 4A paragraph 3. So yah if not boo.'

'Do not be so naif, Mr Lambert. We are Philosophers. That is the cornerstone of our power. We have power over ourselves. You will succumb to our temptations because you are weak. You are not a Philosopher. You have no inner granite. You are shale, Mr Lambert, mere oolitic limestone. There will be no evidence of our complicity. It will be all you. Do what you will, you cannot escape.'

'Over my dead body.'

'If that's the way you want to go, Mr Lambert. We certainly shall not lay a finger on you either to dissuade or encourage. And now, if you will excuse me, I have much to attend to. Plans for the eradication of crass individualism in this country are necessarily complicated. It all has to start (I concur with the Roundhead view) with the abolition of levity, a censorship on humour, that nervous tic of humanity, Mr Lambert, so highly personal, so alien to the common weal. I have been doing much research into Cromwellian times. They throw the most interesting light on how to put into general practice what has previously been a philosophy. Not just, for instance, preaching against theatres but actually closing them. I would not myself contemplate following exactly that route since some of our best and most humourless disciples are of that profession, but I am sure you follow my drift. What we shall do, by controlling the media, is to ensure that people will have entertainment but no, how does the poet put it, "no love, no liking, no delight". No spontaneity. No Joy, Mr Lambert. Things are already, thanks to our efforts, going our way. Hence Vain deluding Joy, Mr Lambert. Good day to you.'

She opened the door and ushered Michael out, and down the steps.

Michael, as he churned up the gravel and headed back towards the gates, was consumed by mingled alarm and exultation. The Philosopher had exceeded his worst fears, but at least she had made him see that his problems were not his alone, a purely personal affair; they were now the country's. But was she serious? She was certainly mad. Somehow he had to tell the world. How ironic that his opponent should be a woman. What luck he had had the foresight to bring his pocket recorder, and had now got her poisonous tones on tape.

The gates loomed ahead of him, and he pulled up sharply, tooting for the lodge-keeper.

'Get out.'

The man did not appear to have been schooled in the Chesterfieldian niceties of address. His manner was, if anything, even more surly than it had been when he arrived.

'If you have the manners of a whore, I suppose it would be too much to assume that you have the morals of a dancing master,' Michael observed, rather wittily, he thought.

The allusion was lost on the lobster who appeared to be looking for something inside the car. Michael tried again.

'If manners makyth man, you make Procrustes seem like Little Lord Fauntleroy.'

The lodge-keeper now started looking for something on Michael.

'Hold on. I say. What's going on?' he demanded feebly.

'Oh you would, would you,' said the lobster, taking the

recorder from Michael's pocket and extracting the tape before handing the machine back.

Michael opened his mouth but could think of nothing to say.

'Drive on.'

The gates swung open and Berkshire gaped to receive him.

As he drove back to London, Michael sought for some cause for optimism but could find none. He was alone, facing an empire of dirty work, and the whole balance between Good and Evil rested on the flimsy fulcrum of his erectile tissue.

Immediately upon reaching Town, he drove straight round to the Gray's Inn Road where the gateau-faced girl and Becket did their best to make him feel unwelcome, and Lucy flew at him in a rage, when he finally saw her, a rage (though he was not to know it) begotten of anxiety tinged with frustration.

'How dare you?' she ranted. 'How dare you go and disturb and make allegations to The Other Party? It's frightfully bad form verging on a tort. The Other Party has done nothing wrong. It's all in your mind. You're weak, that's the trouble. Any normal man would just shrug the situation off and get celibately on with it. But you, you let it prey on your mind, creating chimeras which . . . The fact is, Mr Lambert, all you think about is . . .'

And then she thought it was all she had been thinking about recently, and how she had had that peculiar dream, and how worried he looked and how she would do anything to help him.

'I'm sorry if it wasn't good form,' he said, placatingly, 'but they're after my parts, and that isn't good form either. And what they're planning to do when they've got the money is beyond form altogether. We have to think of something.'

'We need proof, Mr Lambert. I must have proof. Without proof my hands are tied.'

But later, sleepless in the fastidiously clean flat in Marylebone High Street where she had entertained so many decent string players and now played host to how many riggish fantasies, she did conceive a notion which, though fraught with many perilous possibilities as far as she herself was concerned, did have the advantage of being a positive step in the quest for testimony. There was something she could do for him, and she was going to do it.

As for Michael, he felt not so much that she had failed him in his hour of need, but that he should never have tried to enlist her sympathy. She was a po-faced solicitress with a trimly-turned ankle and a salient bust and that was all there was to it. He could rely on no one.

He went round his flat searching for hidden microphones, and found nothing. Were they making a fool of him? One way or another, they had him on the run.

13

A month had passed, and there was still deadlock. The crowd remained constant, replenished by ordered contingents. The weather continued fair.

Today, however, a sportive wind had wheeled in from the direction of the gravel pits, whirling aside the disused cartons and the empty crisp packets, and chasing tiny flecks of conversation around the drab arena as if they were sea-mousse near an effluent.

'Heard the one about the.'

'Wanker.'

'Like I mean.'

'Caring person.'

'Give us your views?'

'Harassment.'

'At this stage.'

'Sarnie.'

'Consult my.'

'Pierced nipple situation.'

'Life-style.'

'Onions?'

Every now and then the foam would be whipped into a crest of excitement.

'He's coming out . . . He's coming out . . . HE'S COMING OUT . . .'

Only to be broken off.

'No . . . No . . . he's going back in again . . .'

And licked once more into the murmurous flat swirl of the crowd.

14

Things went unexpectedly quiet again after his visit to Sambrook. Days turned into weeks, but the respite brought Michael no peace. He could not lift up his eyes to the end of his term (which was now getting almost copably close) because he knew the Philosophers were not going to leave it at that. It was simply a question of when they would make their next move.

Finally, the telephone rang, disturbing his dire meditations: it was Scratcher with a project. One of the other directors had a cinema commercial lined-up for the South of Spain, but had suddenly fallen ill. Would Michael take it on for him?

Michael, who was desperately short of cash again, roused himself from his lethargy, found inspiration in the idea of putting as many miles as he could between himself and his tormentors, and accepted the offer.

It would mean leaving in the morning and taking a plane to Almeria from whence he would be conducted to the location, a ghost town left over from the days of the spaghetti westerns.

The product, he was told, was called Badlands, a spurious-smelling unisex under-arm deodorant for teenagers.

This was a world Michael knew. He did not like it, but he knew it. It made a change, at least, from the uncharted marismas of subversion and intrigue that were threatening to engulf him

'Oh, and one other thing,' said Scratcher sinuously,

'I'll be coming too. Just to keep an eye on things and see you don't balls things up.'

'Good to have you on board, Scratcher.' Even better to have him over the side.

The flight took off at 11.30 next morning, and soon Michael and Scratcher were wrapping themselves round cardboardy chicken and ham washed down with bubble-bath size bottles of Mumm. The vibration of the aircraft, the champagne, his long abstinence, were all combining to give Michael increasing occasion to cross and re-cross his legs.

'The models are coming on tomorrow,' gurked Scratcher.

'Models?' Of course. He had hardly read the script yet.

'Eight teenagers. Four boys. Four girls. Really nice kids. You'll love 'em.'

Michael refrained from commenting that if he had his way, he would not simply love them but screw them till their teeth danced a wild tarantella against the roofs of their crania; instead he simply took another sip of bubble-bath and asked Scratcher if he'd seen the latest Bertolucci.

He knew there was nothing Scratcher liked to do more than talk about feature-film directors. Or was Bertolucci a firm that made jeans? He shot a quick glance at his neighbour but Scratcher launched happily into a tractate on visual dissonance in the late Italian school.

Michael crossed his legs tight as a tourniquet and fell asleep.

15

There were more set-piece battles. There were further commando-type raids and infiltrations. There were individual acts of heroism incandescently written up on the front page of Mayhem which did not always give the full story: for instance, of the female machine tool operator from Thurrock who entered the perimeter unnoticed under cover of darkness, and chained herself to a drainpipe just below the extractor fan at the back of the Leisure Complex.

She was driven off in the morning by the contrivance of Mrs Lee who cooked endless rounds of Bombay Duck in the canteen kitchens, the extractor wafting the resulting aroma straight into the face of the would-be martyr. She fainted after only half an hour, and had to be revived in one of the attendant ambulances which cost the local authority £150 a day.

And still the siege continued.

Mr Lee was implored by various outside parties to reinstate the sacked youth at the centre of it all, but he was adamant. Had he been a genuine native of Britain, he might very well have given in. But he had been brought up, far from liberal opinion, by an anglophile Chinese father who believed in the Britannic virtues of steadfastness and resolution. Mr Lee could quote 'If' at the drop of a hat, and had indeed done so in front of the television cameras. When questioned, he said the owners of the factory were out of the country, and they had placed it unreservedly in his hands, trusting him to use his judgement at all times.

The Government grew restless. It wanted its missing parts. The entire industry of conciliation was invoked. Ombudsmen spoke endlessly with anyone who cared to talk back.

The whole affair had by now caught the imagination of the country. There were almost as many journalists and interviewers as there were pickets, and enterprising operators were running a sight-seeing service from many major cities.

Rowena Tarleton-Smith, the famous broadcaster and traffic warden, hit the headlines by making an impassioned speech linking the present trouble with the public schools, and joined hands with the pickets on duty at the gate, singing songs of the industrial North West in a stentorian contralto, though the men themselves happened to come from Swindon, and didn't know the words.

The hotels, pubs, restaurants, cafes and snacketarias in the vicinity had never known such a boom, and were paying part of their profits into the strike fund in the hope of extending the dispute indefinitely.

Pundits came, expressed their views to the cameras, and went away and expressed them again in late night chat shows.

And, in the background, Bert Scrannell watched and waited, prodded a little here if things became too quiet, restrained a little there when the fierier elements looked like rushing the issue to a too hasty conclusion.

So the long summer days wore on.

'You know,' said the Chief Inspector to his driver as they enjoyed an illicit frankfurter (a stand-in for Mister Whipsee had arrived the day after the bouleversement), looking out at the hopeless prospect of meres and clifflets topped with sedge, which stretched before them, 'sometimes I think this whole bloody country is sinking into the water.'

'You're right, Rodney,' said the driver, 'and the terrible thing is, we've come to accept it, even you and me.'

They had become friendly over the duration of the siege, and used first names in private.

'If a girl's arm,' he continued, 'if a girl's arm holding a fucking great sword came out of the lake right now and waggled it at us, you know what we'd do?'

The Chief Inspector spat a segment of gristle into the dun-coloured depths. It hung there glumly, unreceived by roach, chubb or Morgan Le Fay.

'Seize it and put the country to rights?' he queried, without conviction.

'I don't think so, Rodney. I don't think that's what we'd do at all. We'd run her in for unauthorized skin-diving. Know what I mean?'

16

The hire-car jumped skittishly about over the rock-and-gravel track, leaving a long cumulus of porridge-grey dust to drench the rest of the convoy.

They were making their way across the foothills of the Sierras to Dodge City, a clapboard monument to the Wild West and the erstwhile attractive exchange rate of the peseta. There had been a spate of Westerns made in these parts in the sixties when prices were cheap and reputations high, and a dozen or so mock-towns of different flavours (American, Spanish, Indian, Mexican) spattered the hills like architectural buck-shot.

Sometimes one agglomeration would have three or four ethnic personalities within the space of half an acre.

They were, of course, mainly carpenter's façades with just a few saloon or gaol-type interiors for crucial scenes. It was the great outdoors the film-makers chiefly wanted. The stony outcrops, the ravaged water-courses, the moody peaks in the background, the shrivelled trees, the pitiless paths to nowhere in particular (with the empty Coke cans carefully kicked out of sight).

Michael and Scratcher had inspected a number of these locations, and finally selected one of the larger concourses which seemed archetypically American West circa 1880.

There was a bank, a hotel, two saloons, a sheriff's office, a general provision store, a barber's, a tailor's, even a couple of churches, and round the back where the clapboard turned to Indian adobe, there was a mouldering concourse of wagons, carriages and buggies.

It was still early, half past eight in the morning, the first day of the shoot, and Michael had his usual first-morning low. The weather, to echo his mood, was atypically overcast.

As they pulled up beside the bank (round the corner from the main street so the dust wouldn't show the pattern of their 20th century tyres) Scratcher darted out and started organizing everyone.

The cameraman cocked an eye at the cloud, shook his head (no light ever seems quite right for a lighting cameraman), and summoned the lighting crew to conference.

The chippy started nailing down one or two of the façades that had come unstuck in the last gale. And the make-up and wardrobe ladies led the four boys and girls (who had flown in the evening before) into the church and started converting them into identical-looking black-suited string-tied unisexuals.

Everyone seemed to have something to do except Michael who stood around feeling spare.

A thin, earnest, ferrety young man arrived – the client from the advertising agency. Michael said hallo. The ferrety young man did not appear to be deeply moved.

Coffee arrived. Michael had some coffee. Buns appeared. He nibbled a bun. Finally, the Unisexuals emerged from the church. In spite of himself, hardened as he was by more than a decade of film directing, Michael was impressed. The kids themselves had seemed ordinary enough in the hotel the night before, the make-up girl had converted them into something that was both (he had to admit it) erotic and outlandish.

They looked like apostate Tolkien elves; unearthly, immemorial and redolent of some Older Evil as well as underarm deodorant.

The plot of the commercial was not one of Jacobean intricacy, nor would you have included it in your Top 100 Omnibus of Stories I'll Never Forget. Indeed, it was the sort of thing that, if you left an ape with an Olivetti for ten minutes, he would have little trouble in bashing out and even improving upon.

The scenario went like this. The Badlanders ride into town, enter a rough saloon, and almost fall over at the unsavoury effluvium. They convey their feelings by general expressions of distaste. The denizens of the saloon, bad lots and loose women, (recruited from the casting agency in Almeria), not surprisingly take offence at this, and there is a certain amount of antagonistic sliding of bottles down the bar. The Badlanders respond by sliding back aerosol-cans of Badlands Deodorant. The roughs and fallen women examine them with interest, and start spraying them around, falling about with whooping pleasure (qua the bath sequence in Butch Cassidy). At which point, the unctuous Sheriff enters to see what all the fuss is about, and a rough remarks to no one in particular, 'Terrible smell around here.' More falling about. The Badlanders slip out and ride out of town, and the Sheriff stumbles into the street to gaze wistfully after them. End on crowd shot of whooping, spraying, low men and women.

Not a story to set the Thames or even a smallish effluent in Peckham Rye on fire, but Michael derived a sort of wayward pleasure from the bad taste of the Voice Over's concluding message: 'Just because you're a bad guy, you don't have to smell that way. Be bad, smell good . . . with Badlands.'

This was the civilization whose fate hung on his phallus. He did not know whether to laugh or cry.

They started shooting, and everything, for a change,

seemed to go without a hitch. They were covering the rough's confrontation with the Badlanders on the first day, and the come-uppance of the Sheriff on the second.

At around three o'clock in the afternoon, however, one of those power-failures that the Spanish do so well struck and all the lights went out. There was no generator on the location. Telephone calls were made. They would have one in an hour.

Little knots of technicians and Badlanders broke off and wandered listlessly from saddler to cantina to the little church where the padre had been so murderously gunned down in front of his congregation by El Negrito and his bully-boys in Manana Never Comes.

Michael found himself strolling, for no particular reason, towards the end of the town where the Episcopalian Church raised its clapboard neck above the surrounding shanties. It was one of the few buildings designed for interior shooting, more substantially constructed than most of its neighbours, and Michael entered, idly trying to remember what it was the parson had said to the lily-livered townsfolk in Holy Smoke, but these speculations were interrupted by a low voice from the gallery.

'Hullo, Lambert,' it said.

Good God, he remembered that voice. How could he ever forget it? But it couldn't be; it was all so long ago, and in another country, and besides . . . He jerked his head upwards like a stallion stung by a warble-fly, but there was no one to be seen. He darted round the ramshackle building and finally discovered the steps up to the gallery, but when he gingerly ventured upstairs, there was no trace of any spectator. It was just as he was gingerly coming down again, that he thought he saw the subfusc suit of a Badlander slipping out of the door.

'Hey,' he shouted. 'Hey. Come back,' and then the

name that still gave him the most peculiar sensation even twenty-five years after that extraordinary summer, 'de Blaye'.

Racing down the stairs, caution forgotten, he put his foot through a rotten plank, falling heavily on to the mock church floor in front of the mock episcopalian altar, and raising a genuine howl of pain that caused a mob of chippies, grips and roughs from Almeria to come racing in offering varying degrees of sympathy, interest and support.

They lifted Michael up, and were rather disappointed when he announced that he could walk and that his ankle was only slightly twisted.

Someone found someone else who put a bandage round the affected part, the generator arrived, the sun came out so that now they did not need the generator, the lighting cameraman went into an elaborate ritual dance with his light meter, one of the Spaniards who had got drunk refused, at first, to rehearse squirting his deodorant but, finally persuaded to do so, unleashed a jet straight into his eyes which made him cry and the Badlanders fall about with laughter, and finally they started shooting again.

Michael, all the while, was in a frenzy of mystification. Had he imagined that voice? And that Badlander uniform he thought he had seen – he had met all eight Badlanders last night and not one of them resembled the exotic de Blaye. What was going on?

Switching his directional duties on to automatic-pilot, he took a rapid stumble down memory lane.

There was de Blaye all right, looking as the young Milton must have done, 'The young lady of Christ's', a body which would have put Narcissus himself severely out of countenance, eyes that could look at you and suggest all manner of things you had not dared to think before, and a mind that was disturbing, brilliant and effortlessly corrupt.

The thing about de Blaye was that to be with him was to be alive. To be absent from him one languished in the shadows.

Michael supposed it was love he must have felt for him. It was his one and only homosexual experience, long since erased, one would have thought, by the passages of time and innumerable young ladies, but it still exercised a potent fascination. They had spent a whole summer term almost exclusively in each other's company, talking and reading and drinking (illicitly) and making love (which was beyond legislation).

De Blaye, Michael could see him now, was a veritable Ganymede. He seemed to be two sexes at once, the nearest thing you could possibly imagine to a girl without breasts, and possessed of the most soft and Michelangelo-like private areas; to coax them into life was a cross between picking fruit and playing with a sort of reverse maidenhair fern.

Although as a rule the private school he attended in Vermont was not beset by the same homosexual traditions that operated within its English counterparts, it seemed the most natural thing in the world for Michael in his seventeenth summer to surrender himself to de Blaye's irregular blandishments.

Of course, it had been too good to last. Miraculously, they had not been discovered by the school authorities, but de Blaye had gone to Greece at the beginning of the summer vacation to stay with his mother who was married at that stage to some medium-time shipping millionaire.

Michael had been desolated next semester to find that de Blaye was no longer at the school, and wondered at his friend's lack of assiduity in traversing the odd few thousand miles to join his form-mates in Vermont. But the fact was, no doubt, that de Blaye had grown tired of the affair and had found more sophisticated things to do.

At all events, Michael had to admit that, never before or since, had he known quite such pleasure. Perhaps, indeed, there was an element in his ceaseless womanizing from that time on that owed something to a determination to find an equal heterosexual (and therefore regular) fulfilment.

Suffice it to say that the appearance in the church of de Blaye's double had done more to unhinge Michael's tenuous grip on self-mastery than all the other tests he had had to endure.

The day whirred on. The sun westered, plopped into the egg-cup of the Sierras, and shooting was finally wrapped. The cortege wound slowly back among the dusty scrub. In the first car, Scratcher was in ebullient mood for the client's sake.

'Amazing. Great. Fantastic. You were ace, Michael. It's going to be a prize-winner.'

'Oh. I don't know.'

Michael hated Scratcher for his grovelling, false enthusiasm and his execrable taste. Really, the man ought to be Swiss. The only thing that made him laugh was money. The really funny things he simply resented because he didn't understand them.

'It was nothing, really,' he said. At least that was true.

When they got back to the hotel, Michael had a bath and a large drink, and went for a stroll down to the harbour before dinner.

It was just as he was skirting a large iron bollard shaped like a bull's testicle (seconds later he wondered whether this potent imagery working on his weakened susceptibilities might not have produced a doppelganger) that he saw de Blaye in earnest, leaning characteristically, one leg straight, the other slightly bent, against a breakwater, looking languidly out to sea.

'De Blaye,' he shouted, and started running. Why had he always called him by his surname? It had been an affectation of theirs, he remembered, to be intimate in person and formal in address.

'De Blaye,' he hollered again, causing an elderly Spanish couple to dive for shelter and a Guardia Civil to spring up from nowhere, rifle at the ready.

'De Blaye,' he screamed, desperately, as a generous sample of the population of Almeria suddenly manifested itself and came charging after him. But his mad sprint was unavailing. De Blaye had disappeared again. Only a cigarette end remained where Michael had seen him standing. He picked it up. It was a Black Russian, the sort they used to smoke at school. So he had been there.

The Guardia Civil shook Michael for a bit, but on finding that he was English, started telling him about his brother-in-law who worked in Ethesh.

'Where?'

'Ethesh.'

'Oh. Very nice. Muy bueno Ethesh,' said Michael humouring him.

'Si? Muy bueno Ethesh?'

And so it had gone one. Later, Michael realized he was referring to Essex, but the importance of the conversation was not so much the Guardia Civil's brother-in-law's problems with el tiempo frio in Ethesh, as that as far as Michael was concerned, it allowed de Blaye more time to become totally untrackable.

But why? For what? And anyway, it was nonsense. De

Blaye would be forty now, like himself. He would be thick in the stomach and veiny in the face, not lissom and sweet as a Pippin.

What was really amazing, he reflected as he padded back to dinner, was the realization that his homosexual inclinations were still lurking, like bacteria on Mars, waiting for a little watering to spring into life. But,then again, he did not think of his feelings for de Blaye as homosexual. They were just sexual, impure and simple. Michael was beginning to discover things about himself.

'Ah, there you are,' said Scratcher, when he returned. 'Thought you'd got lost. Can't have our director losing his sense of direction ha ha.'

God Almighty, thought Michael.

'Ho ho,' said the camera crew.

'I'm a bit worried about the product not coming over sufficiently as hero,' said the ferrety man, whose breath smelt worse than a Sheriff's under-arm. 'Is it going to be intrusive enough? Perhaps we could have a bit of a get-together over the repast.'

Two things seemed very important to Michael that night, one was to inherit his fortune as soon as possible so he would never have to smile at halitosic bores again, and the other was to get to the bottom, if that was the word, of the de Blaye affair, once and for all.

The next day dawned bright and clear. Too bright and clear, of course, for the lighting-cameraman who pulled a long face and said all the shadows would have hard edges and continuity would be a write-off, but everybody else seemed to like it.

They drove once again to the ghost town. Once more the costumes were donned. Once more the camera mounted its tripod and whirred away, playing Echo to the cicadas.

The Sheriff made his entry and was felled like an ox, suffering from a surfeit of under-arm deodorant in the left nostril. The Badlanders strutted in moody triumph, and the product as hero left nothing to be desired except, in a couple of cases, becoming affected by the heat and going off like anti-personnel mines, luckily on an isolated trestle table, though one Badlander was nearly cut off in his/her prime.

Finally, the morning work was accomplished, and they broke for lunch.

Michael had had time, during the course of the shooting, to review and condemn his rashness of the day before. Now, as he chewed his way through beans and sausalito, washed down with excellent Rioja wine, he was able to warm to the theme. The whole thing was, of course, a hoax, a stratagem of the Philosophers who had planned the whole venture, possibly using the ferrety man from the agency as their instrument, he of the mouldy exhalation. No one with breath that bad could be anything but dubious.

Michael shuddered.

'Penny for them, Michael.' Scratcher was looking at him speculatively.

'Just thinking about camera angles, Scratcher.'

'I thought you shuddered.'

'I did shudder.'

'Why did you shudder?'

'Tried the sausalito? I think it's made of horse.'

'I wish you'd mix a bit more. Mix. Jolly up the Client. Smile more. Shudder less.'

Michael wanted to leap at Scratcher and stuff a sausalito a furlong up his bottom, but he masterfully resisted the impulse, giving him instead a boyish grin.

'Thanks, Scratcher. I wish you'd give me more tips like that.'

Scratcher retired, not pleased, but seemingly baffled.

The day wore on, pungent and gritty as the sausalito itself. After a modest siesta, the roughs from Almeria were rounded grumblingly up, and certain reverse shots were taken which had not been adequately covered before. At this point, the camera developed a sort of mechanical tremens which necessitated a further interminable delay and another vehicle leaving the town and grinding up the Sierras to relieve them.

It was half past three, and hot. Some kind of scrawny bird wheeled and yelped overhead. The roughs from Almeria started drinking again. Somewhere in Hendon, a factory was turning out thousands of gallons of underarm deodorant. It all seemed, Michael thought, a very long way off. In fact, when he thought about it harder, which he found difficult, he realized that he felt distinctly peculiar – not unpleasantly so – but swimmy nonetheless. Perhaps there had been something wrong with the food.

He decided that a walk would do him good and, leaving Scratcher and the Ferrety One in close and evil-smelling conference, he headed for the Mexican Quarter, branched out through the Indian settlement and finally wended his way (his way was by now becoming increasingly wendy) to the circa 1850, Early American West, Main Street where, entering O'Riley's Hotel, he fell asleep on a sofa that had played a supporting role in A Fistful of Dollars.

When he awoke, the place was curiously quiet. He consulted his watch. I had stopped as usual. He looked up. De Blaye was regarding him with that familiar, quizzical Ganymede grin.

A projectile which, if it had been seen by the Resistance at Peenemunde would have given Churchill serious thoughts about applying for Armistice, slid slowly up the ramp of Michael's abdomen.

'Good old Lambert. Randy as usual,' said de Blaye.

'Look here, de Blaye, what on earth are you doing here?'

'I thought I'd give you a little surprise.'

'Surprise is not the word. Try flabbergast or total stupefaction. You're supposed to be forty. And why did you never send so much as a letter. I was considerably put out about that.'

'I discovered the Fountain of Youth in Arcadia. Near Mount Athos, you know. I took up with some latter-day Orpheans.'

De Blaye was given to extravagant statements backed up by recondite sounding explanations. But it wasn't de Blaye. It was a trick of the Philosophers, Michael knew it, and yet he couldn't seem to get his person to recognize the fact.

'Balls.'

'Yes, those too.'

Michael felt curiously weak except in that one area. What had they put in the sausalito? Spanish bluebottle? De Blaye seemed more than ever like a sibling of Dionysos.

'And what are you doing dressed up as a Badlander?' he rallied weakly.

'I am a Badlander.'

'No you're not. We've eight already. There are only eight parts for eight Badlanders.'

'Count us.'

De Blaye clapped his hands, and Badlanders suddenly appeared like magic mushrooms. Michael rolled his eyes. There did not seem too much else to do. It was true, count as he might, that there were only eight and yet he knew perfectly well there were nine, with de Blaye. If only they would all keep still, and not fade and dissolve like that. And why was everything so dark and suffused with a reddish glow? He had once had an overdose of hash biscuits in Chelsea which had induced the same kind of illusion, and his fuddled brain now tried to translate the confused message of his senses but with the same lapidary lack of response. He knew he should do something like drink coffee, or exercise his mind by reciting Milton, but for the life of him he could not find the strength. He knew that the Philosophers had got at him (he dimly felt that, by their own standards,using drugs was cheating) but he couldn't lift a finger to save himself.

The Badlanders now, in masque-like motion, were kissing each other with lascivious passion – whether they were boys embracing girls or boys boys or girls girls, breast to breast, tongue to tongue, did not seem to have any significance – it was an epicene pageant of pure lust.

De Blaye's right hand now strayed over his thighs while his left hand opened Michael's shirt and ran tweakingly over his chest, a thing that addled as he was, so reminded Michael of the past and inflamed the present that he sprang like a very slow Victorian wrought-iron elevator to his feet, and kissed de Blaye's carnation mouth as esuriently as if the years had castored back, and they were sitting in the woods after Preparation.

A number of things happened at this stage. Everything seemed to get darker. He and de Blaye seemed to join the masque. A jumble of images presented themselves. Girls with male organs. Hands stroking, caressing. Mouths nibbling, licking, sliding. Sensations of a myriad moth-like tendernesses. Finally de Blaye falling back, his face a satyr's, laughing, his legs spread to receive Michael's tremendous ballistic; who, when he saw that de

Blaye's posterior was, as he had often half-imagined, now that of a girl, was so overcome with surprise, lust, cannabis and sausalito, that he staggered back, involuntarily hitting a supporting strut that snapped, letting the entire side of the ramshackle building fall into the street, whereupon the flimsy roof collapsed, which in turn deranged the central façade.

The entire structure folded outwards like an orange, and when it was all over, Michael was left alone (the Badlanders and 'de Blaye' must have recovered like tigers and made off), trouserless, groggy and nursing a weapon the like of which had never been seen in the West.

The roughs from Almeria gaped and crossed themselves. The camera crew hardened individuals that they were, were visibly shaken. And the product, as hero, was incontrovertibly outranked.

Scratcher rushed up with a horse blanket and a termination of contract, and Michael boarded the next plane for London with his member contused, his mind overwhelmed with the sheer devilish determination of the opposition, but above all (he was reasonably confident), with his legacy intact.

He was realistic enough to know, however, that this was more by the good offices of Fortune rather than through the exercise of will. He could not expect to go on stumbling into timber supports for ever. There was only one thing to do, and when he got back to England he was going to do it.

17

The night was black as a Berkshire boar, and just about as smelly.

Lucy parked her car in a small dingy lane heavy with brambles and ivy-shrouded saplings on the other side of the road from the Sambrook Estate wall, where it presented a looming and minatory impassivity.

She was wearing a dark blue polo-necked jersey, black corduroy trousers, and tennis shoes, and she now extracted from her mini-Traveller a thick sack, a length of rope and a portable step-ladder.

Locking the car, she carried the step-ladder to the side of the wall, mounted, spread the sack over the glass, sat on the lenient place it provided, reached down to the step-ladder, and placed it on the other side. Dismounting, she removed the sack and the ladder, and secreted them under a holly-bush.

All trace of her intrusion now being removed, she and her rope slipped silently among the rhododendron-thickets that festooned this part of the Sambrook grounds.

It was half-past two in the morning. Even the owls seemed to have given up and gone home and, if nightingales were singing in bowers in other parts of Berkshire, they did not find inspiration here among the blissless emanations of the great house, the mass of which now presented itself to Lucy as she surmounted a knoll; a huge and brooding hulk beached on the melancholy dunes of night. No light shone from its windows. No noise came from its halls. Or perhaps light and sound did go on in there but, as from a Black Hole, it could not escape the staggering gravity, the sheer compressed density of boredom that went on inside. Whatever singularity it contained, Sambrook kept its secret.

Lucy found herself wondering once again what on earth she was doing here. She knew that if she were caught, and it came to the attention of the Law Society, she would be suspended without so much as a whisker of a wig lifted in her support. Breaking and entering, showing preferential partiality to legatee, this kind of behaviour was unpardonable, she knew it. But Lucy was in love.

She had watched the recording machine for an hour yesterday in old Tooth's office while Becket was out buying ground glass and a couple of dead jackdaws for his tea, and once (oh horrors) she could have sworn she saw the instrument quiver, but no, all was well, false alarm.

She felt very close to Michael at these times. She sensed that she was not merely looking at an electronic chip-and-printer encased in perspex, but at the very nexus of his person. She had a feeling, she knew it was silly, that she wanted to stroke it.

Of course, she had wondered with increasing urgency what she could do to help him. She did not doubt now, for one moment, that he was being pursued by the Philosophers and she would have nobbled the electronic receiver if it had been possible, but it was designed by experts, and she knew it was inviolable.

It was the last time she had spoken to Michael, when she had started by being so cross with him, that she had decided to go to Sambrook Manor and have a quick look round before he had the same idea himself. It was better that she should put herself at risk. He was so accident-prone, and there was no knowing what they might not do to him if he fell into their clutches.

It was true that she had much to lose, but half the pleasure of Love lies in making sacrifices, and when it was all over she could show him the evidence of the Philosophers' contempt of Codicil 4A, and he would inherit his fortune, and maybe take her out to dinner. The cloistered purity of her thoughts admitted no further conjecture.

So far, so good. The sky was clear but there was no moon and the night was running on starlight. She had arrived on the edge of some flower-beds which, no doubt containing a brave show of henbane and belladonna (she had as low an opinion of the Philosophers as she had of Becket), skirted the lawn, momentarily impeding her progress. She side-stepped these and, fleet as a hamadryad, sped across the grass and into the shadow of the house beside wistaria-trailing windows.

The air was warm and still. She listened intently for any noise – she had feared there might be dogs – but everything remained mercifully silent. A faint snuffling broke out, betraying a hedgehog almost under her right foot, but this was nothing she could not deal with. She wished she had some milk to give it.

She now turned her attention to the windows. They were of the mullion variety, fitted between the Jacobean stone piers, operated by a latch, and securely locked. Moving along the wall a little, however, she discovered a smaller sash window and this now yielded to her pressure. She gently slid it down, peered in, saw nothing, and decided to give it a try. Swinging her sneakered feet over the frame, she gingerly lowered herself in, knocking over, as she did so, something that sounded like the entire crockery stock of the Second T'ang.

This she could not help regarding as a setback. She

stood in the darkness, appalled and nervous, waiting for the lights and the cruel fangs; but nothing happened.

Finally, she concluded that the noise, though deafening to her, had been muffled by the wistaria and the thickness of the walls. Heartened, she shone her torch around the room, discovering that she was in a small ante-chamber, and that what she had knocked over was a large and ornate china barrel of such boisterous and outstanding ugliness that she could not understand why somebody had not done it earlier. It would have been a service to humanity.

The room, apart from these shards, appeared to contain nothing impinging on her purpose, and she made for a door in the corner which looked much more promising.

Opening it, she found herself in a large and important-seeming study, a chairman of a room, it appeared, its most obtrusive feature being a large and portentous desk which swam like a Galapagos turtle across the whole of one end.

Here, Lucy thought, this is where I shall find the documentation to get Michael off the hook; and she started scrabbling through the drawers with eager fingers. In this, however, she was disappointed. The papers she found mainly related to boring things like membership, petty disbursements, running expenses, lecturer's fees, and they contained not so much as a scintilla of iniquity.

Lucy could hardly contain her disappointment. After all this effort and risk, to look through the Philosopher's laundry bills. It was too much. Why couldn't they do their own washing? She thumped her foot in vexation. The disloyal thought began to cross her mind that she might have been deceived. The Philosophers might actually be innocent.

And then, in the bottom drawer, she found a key. It said simply 'Safe'.

Of course, she thought. They wouldn't leave incriminating evidence lying around for any burglarious solicitor who happened to come along to pick up. They would lock it away, wouldn't they? You bet your sweet life they would. She wondered where the safe might be.

She saw no sign of one as she peered about her. Classically, she thought, it would be behind a picture, and she started to examine the room's fine art.

There was a still life after (a long way after) the Impressionist School but it concealed nothing, not even the painter's lack of aptitude.

There was a landscape of the Paul Nash variety – stark with womb-shaped downs. This too proved unrevealing.

Finally, she moved on to a portrait of some Sanskrit hero, refugee from the Rig-Veda, in reds and yellows, seemingly executed in curry. And once again the prize was denied her.

Where could it be? Her eyes lit on the bookcase. If safes were not to be found behind pictures, it was possible they might lurk behind tooled leather volumes of Schopenauer.

She advanced on it, wrenching at the tomes, but all she found for her pains was an out of date Newbury Library ticket and a family of silverfish. She was growing desperate. It was now half-past three and it would be growing light in half an hour.

She gave the study a final sweep with her rubber torch and was about to call it a day and pass on to another room when she had a sudden postmonition that the safe might be in the ante-room she had just left. She went back and immediately found it lurking behind a portrait of Tolstoy. Trembling with excitement, she applied the key and the door swung open revealing a number of folders, of which one was labelled 'The Kovacs Bequest' and the other 'Operation Ironside'.

Hastily perusing the one, she discovered it lived up to all her wildest fears: there were details of surveillance fees, and disbursements to a nurse, a model, an actress, three girls, and nine dancers for Spain – What? had not Michael just flown to that country? Her heart bled for him, surrounded by all these techniques and torments. And she had called him weak! If he had not already succumbed, it was because of his fortitude and iron purpose.

She turned her attention to the other folder, and was just coming to grips with the enormity of what the Philosophers were about; the subversion of Industry, the infiltration of education, the influence on the Arts, the proliferation in the media, the erosion of morality, the propagation of apathy and do-your-own-thing, all documented and costed; when she heard sounds coming from the interior of the house – cries, heavy-booted feet and (horrors!) cerberean barking.

Quick as a gypsy, she closed the safe, stuffed the files up her jumper, swung herself back over the window and raced into the garden. But she was too late. She saw torches waving from the direction of the rhododendrons and heard the high harsh howls of the guard dogs. Mercurial with fear, she sprinted back the other way, across the far side of the house, but again she heard shouts and ululation.

There was only one way for her to go, and she went. Ahead of her there loomed a dense box hedge with a wrought-iron gate. Praying it would open, she grasped the handle, and pulled. Nothing happened. The cries were growing louder, and she could hear the scrabbling feet of the dogs as they rushed down the gravel paths.

With a last despairing heave, she wrenched the door open, slipped through and slammed it behind her smack in the vulpine snout of the leading Alsatian.

Without a backward glance, she ran down the long alley between high box hedges.

It was only after she had been running for some time that she realized that she didn't seem to be getting anywhere. There were various pathways off the main track, and the track itself seemed to keep bending. Finally, coming to a dead end, she was forced to take another path which again kept meandering, abruptly swerving, dividing, looping, and similarly confronted her at the last with a bare box wall.

She listened for pursuit, but no sound came. And then she understood. She was in a maze.

Leaning against the pungent little brussels of the box she caught her breath. What a pickle she was in! No one knew where she was. It was Saturday so she wouldn't even be missed at the office. The only appointment she had was with a consort of viols off the Bayswater Road, but they would simply think she hadn't been able to make it, and would hardly call out the police. Even if they did, they'd need a clairvoyant to find her.

The dawn was breaking, and the sky took on that lucent loveliness that elates alike the condemned man and the cockerel, but the light showed no break in the impenetrable walls. She would have to go back. She would face the dogs. She was getting cold.

But going back, when she tried, proved not so easy. The turnings in reverse seemed indistinguishable. She rapidly began to admit to herself that she was hopelessly lost, and she started to panic. She would never get out.

She would die of hunger and exposure. Were there rats in those little tunnels at the bottom of the hedge? She ran desperately from turning to turning, winding herself (although she didn't know it) further and further towards the centre.

A line from a nursery rhyme kept recurring maddeningly in her brain.

'The way into my parlour is up a winding stair.'

She tried shouting, but her voice, against the bungey citadels of the maze, sounded as if it had a sock in it.

At last, shivering, panic-stricken, and suddenly terribly tired, she stumbled into a clearing which contained a statue of Pan, a sun-dial and a small palladian temple. Here, she cast herself down upon the floor in utter desolation.

'"Here in a lonely glade, forgotten, I mark the tremendous process of the sky,"' said a voice.

Lucy looked up with mingled relief and consternation.

'What . . . who . . .' she gibbered.

'Belloc, Miss Dulcimer; hopelessly reactionary, of course, but apposite enough, and inscribed on the base of the sun-dial.'

The owner of the voice was a short-haired, whey-faced woman (the same indeed who had spoken with Michael) wearing dungarees.

'The previous owners of Sambrook,' the woman continued spiderishly, 'had a passion for neo-classicism. We will be removing the inscription in due course and replacing it with something more seemly, a text on the individual's role in society or the Inward Search for the Ultimate. Meanwhile, since we have Belloc, let us make use of him. You, like Belloc's sun-dial, lie in a lonely glade.'

Lucy sat up and tried to smooth her hair.

'You lie in a lonely glade, Miss Dulcimer.' Lucy sat up

some more at the mention of her name, 'completely in our power because you have been foolish enough to mark certain tremendous processes that are afoot. You have become caught up in matters a great deal larger than yourself, Miss Dulcimer. You have meddled, you have trespassed, you have stolen private information, and to put it in a nutshell, of which, being of macrobiotic inclination, you will find we have a great many, you are going to have to take the consequences. But please do not think that we are displeased with you. Far from it. We have plotted your every move. We have read you like a book. Not a very profound or very well-written book, but literature nonetheless. You have been surveyed since you left your flat in London. You have been observed at work. You have been monitored at home. And now you have played into our hands exactly as we knew you would. You see, you, Miss Dulcimer, are going to have the honour to be our ultimate weapon.'

Lucy had recovered something of her spirit during this sinister harangue – anything was better than the oppressive desolation she had felt in the long green catacombs of the maze.

'I see what you are now,' she said heatedly, a pretty flush suffusing her cheeks or it might have been the reflection from a covey of small rubescent clouds that had come up for the day from Wales and were drifting vaguely round overhead. 'You're simply cheats and bullies. You're just after the money and you'll stop at nothing to get it. Call yourself Philosophers? If you're a philosoper, Genghis Khan was a universally-loved family provision merchant and fruiterer in South Mimms.'

'You are wrong, Miss Dulcimer. We are lovers of wisdom. And our wisdom leads us, in order to further our philosophy, to examine one of the great untapped tensions in mankind. Not a political division, Miss Dulcimer. That is superficial stuff. Politics has been the great red-herring of the past two centuries. But there is a temperamental, an emotional, a spiritual division. You know at the moment we have East versus West, Left versus Right. The tension I'm talking about is North v South, Up versus Down. What do you think of that?'

'I . . .'

'Exactly. Now. Our natural home is Down, Miss Dulcimer. Do you understand the beauties of Downness? The serious, the earnest, the slow, the grave, the minor (I speak of keys), the dun, the subfusc. There is too much Up in the world, Miss Dulcimer. It pains us. It interferes with us. We cannot approve of it. And so our Plan is this. Without declaring our Aim, which would be foolish (people would think we were just another political party), we will exploit the existing tensions to our own advantage. For instance, at the moment, the West is much more Up than the East. So we encourage the Trotskyites, the Maoists, the Liberation Fronts. They are our tools. But if they become frivolous or in any way not properly intense, we drop them. We do not approve of laughing Communism, or indeed laughing anything. The committed, the drab, the dull, the bitter, the boring . . . these are our natural bedfellows, Miss Dulcimer. What pleasure one gets from saying those words! What an army of potential recruits! You see, for us, Miss Dulcimer, to paraphrase the psalmist, "Joy may endure for a night, but Heaviness cometh in the morning". That is our watch-cry. Heaviness! I see you are moved. You are privileged to be the first outsider to hear it. I feel perhaps that you, having more than a touch of Up in your make-up, may need a little persuasion before you completely come round to our point of view, but we shall work on it, Miss Dulcimer, we shall work on it, and I am sure you will see things our way.'

Lucy, at the end of this bizarre homily, tried on several expressions, but none of them seemed to fit.

'You're deranged,' she said weakly, 'I've never heard of anything so preposterous. Or are you pulling my leg?'

'We do not pull legs, Miss Dulcimer. The ambulatory limb we regard as purely for locomotion.'

'I shall expose you, then.'

'Fortunately for us, Miss Dulcimer, you will not be in a position to confide in anyone. In cooking your goose, if you will forgive the excess of metaphor, you have burned your boats. And now, Miss Dulcimer, if you will permit me . . .' She took the files that were slipping out from under Lucy's blue jumper . . . 'I think we had better show you to your quarters.'

She took Lucy by the arm, quite hard, and escorted her back through the labyrinth to the wrought iron gate.

'You'll never get away with this,' said Lucy hopelessly. 'There's too much good in the world.'

'People often say that to us, Miss Dulcimer. It's funny how desperation evokes cliché. I'm afraid you'll have to resign yourself to the fact that, if you take a good look at the state of the West, everything's going our way. The only thing that can thwart us now is lack of immediate funds. And that's where you come in.'

'Oh Michael,' thought Lucy, 'if you could see me now, I'm sure you'd ask me out to dinner.'

18

Michael arrived back in London still considerably bemused by the contents of the irregular Spanish charcuterie and, although the English sun was clearly out to show the returning native it could knock spots off its bully-boy counterpart in Andalucia, he drew the curtains on the day and went to bed.

The next morning, however, he woke clear of eye and chipper of limb and went down to see Tom whom he found in optimistic mood exercising a bull-worker to the limits of its tensility and sipping yeast bouillon.

'They found it,' said Tom, 'throbbing monster. Parked on West Byfleet Station. So I got it back after all. Not too happy about the sound of the differentials. Think they may have thrown a cog. No sign of the bleeper, needless to say.'

Throbbing Monster returned, Tom was once more able to go into training for the Miss Wonderful round the corner. Michael was happy for him, but he declined the offer of grape-nuts. He had sterner things to do.

'They tried to get me again, Tom. In a ghost town. They spiked my sausalito.'

It was Tom's habit to become increasingly serious and practical, the more bizarre and far-fetched the anecdote you were relating. At the same time, he had a knack of latching on to the least important aspect of your tale.

If you said to him 'There's a yeti in the bathroom eating cream-cheese out of my shaving mug', he would frown in a helpful concentrating sort of way and say:

'Yeti, right. Cream-cheese. Think I've got it. Shaving mug. What sort of cream-cheese? Any chives?'

And so it was now.

'You mean the long thin sausalitos that taste like dog's weewee or the thicker ones with the consistency of pipe-dottle?'

'It really doesn't matter, Tom. The point is, I only escaped because the whole building collapsed. Damn lucky not to get hurt. It's gone far enough, Tom. That's what I came to say. I've got nothing to lose now.'

'Eight million pounds?'

'I've as good as lost it. Unless, in some way, I can catch them on the hop. I have to take the fight to them. I'm going in there.'

He knew the Solicitor girl would be annoyed with him, but there it was. It wasn't her fortune. Or her parson. Besides, she looked rather sweet when she was cross.

'I've got to find evidence that they're tampering with the terms of the will, and God knows what else besides. Terrible things are afoot, Tom, besides which a Venusian tyrranosaurus in the High Street with mandibles the size of the R101 would be worth only a back-page mention in the local gazette,' he continued strongly.

'Was that the ill-fated dirigible that caught fire coming in to land at New York, or the one that ended in a holocaust near Beauvais?'

'Never mind, Tom. I'm going. Now.'

'Tell you what. I'll come with you this time. Keep an eye on you. Take you in the Throbbing Monster.'

'I wouldn't dream of it. It could be dangerous.'

'Safe as houses, old boy. Just a dropped cog or two. Don't you like driving in her? Why don't you like driving in her?'

Michael did not feel the exigencies of the situation

permitted too many recapitulations of his drift, so he let the matter drop, agreeing to let Tom take him in the long-suffering Porsche, but insisting on his maintaining a watching brief outside the walls rather than accompanying him into the interior.

Apart from a disinclination to jeopardize his friend in the unimaginable awfulness that lurked among the dungarees, he had reservations about Tom's usefulness in a tight corner. To be with Tom in a tight corner, he had found in the past, was to be in two tight corners. Tom tended to panic, thrash wildly about, and trip over things.

They agreed to go that evening, and Michael spent the rest of the day mustering what he considered to be the necessary equipment (much on the same lines, as it turned out, as Lucy's but including a liberal supply of dog-chocolate and aniseed essence). He told Tom that he might need to be inside Sambrook for at least twenty-four hours, and urged him to bring whatever sustaining crunch or brittle he felt was suitable to sustain his vigil without the walls.

The day sped by in a welter of Kendal cake, hemp rope, collapsible ladders, brandy and mental fortification, perfumed by strange odours from below as Tom cooked roughage crackers.

The Sabbath sun sank in a burst of flamboyance, converting the sooty tenements of Barons Court to Moghul palaces of rose and gold. The homing drivers poured back along the motorway, eager to return to yet another repeat of 'Seven Brides for Seven Brothers' on TV, with a sense of a weekend well-spent if ignobly earned. Underwear, freshly washed for the week ahead, semaphored waggishly from a thousand bed-sitting room windows. Everything was as usual. It was Sunday evening again in Kensington. All over London, candidates for the mouse race, riders for the slow-motion Wall of Death, nerved themselves variously for the coming week, oblivious of the battle between Negative and Positive, Up and Down, North and South, that was about to rage across the battlefield of Michael's pudenda.

'"The day thou gave us, Lord, is ended,"' carolled Michael. Now that action was upon him, he was suddenly in buoyant mood. No more skulking, no more waiting for an irresistible force to meet his only too moveable object, but a commando raid right into the heart of enemy territory. He felt he could hold his head up again.

As they packed the impedimenta into the Porsche, the world was, he sensed, a finer, cleaner place. He smelt Freedom and Nobility, he told Tom; but Tom demurred.

'It's the new leatheraroma interior car disinfectant spray I've been using for her,' he explained. 'I gave her a squirt when I got her back from the station. Didn't know who'd been sitting in you, did I?' he crooned to his iron charger.

Just after eleven, they were off.

When they reached Sambrook, it was after midnight. (Tom stopped several times to listen to what he insisted were suspicious tinkles from the engine.) The night was as dark as it had been for Lucy's escapade, and just as redolent of piggy middens.

As it turned out, the spot where she had elected to park was vacant. The Mini-Traveller had been removed. Ignorant of Lucy's fate, Michael and Tom selected it just as she had done, for the convenient shelter it afforded.

Michael took the ladder and the rope and the rest of his tackle, and moving up to the wall, proceeded to scale it. Tom appeared to be in an ecstasy of concern.

'I don't like it,' he kept repeating. 'I don't like it.'

'Just stay here, Tom, if you don't mind, and I'll pop

over again, probably about the same time tomorrow night. If I haven't come out again by the morning after that, ring Lucy Dulcimer.'

'I don't like it.'

'Goodbye, Tom.'

'I don't . . .'

But Michael could delay no longer. He lifted over the ladder, placed it on the other side, leapt down into the spinney, hiding the ladder under the same hollybush Lucy had used, and made his way through the trees towards the rhododendron grove.

At one point, he made a considerable detour, dropping a little aniseed in case of guard dogs, and then struck off again for the house, hitting it slightly further up the flank than Lucy had done, which simply meant he had more locked mullions to try before he found the sash window which gave access.

Sliding it noiselessly up, he scrambled in and, in his turn, tipped something over with his foot in the process which exploded with the concussive exuberance of a supernova.

He made to scramble out of the window again. Thought better of it. Froze. And when still nothing happened – no cry, no dog, no bootfall, he shone his torch cautiously across the damage. A repulsive faced ceramic Buddha on a cedarwood pedestal had departed this life and was no doubt even now queuing up to reincarnate as a toby jug, a staffordshire spaniel, or a chamber-pot.

He ventured into the next room, found the desk, discovered the key and, going through a similar deductive process to Lucy's, at length located the safe, and extracted the vital documents.

Huddling in a corner, to hide the light, he was able to give the file marked Operation Ironside a rather more informed attention than his predecessor. The details within smacked incontrovertibly of the illicit. He discovered payments of, for instance, £5,000 to Weasel in the Home Office, £3,000 to Black Rat in the Atomic Energy Commission, and £7,000 to Vole in the BBC (thus confirming Michael's suspicions that people in the media were overpaid). But there was no indication as to how the operation was run or from whence it drew its power source.

Michael reasoned that what he was looking at was simply the records of one section of the grand design. He understood, however, why the Philosophers needed the money. Their outgoings seemed to be colossal. But to thwart them, rather than simply to preserve his legacy (and he now felt thwarting was the order of the day) he realized he needed to get his hands on the whole specification of the project. Details of disbursements were not enough. He had to have The Plan.

At this point, he suddenly saw lights among the trees, and heard deep-throated baying away in the woods where he had planted his aniseed all-sorts.

Cautiously closing the window, he tiptoed back into the study, inched open another door, and issued into a corridor of great length which offered a generous choice of possible escape routes.

He shone his torch furtively to see whether the door nearest him had any kind of title upon it. It contained the legend 'Lecture Room'. The next door had one of those clothes-peg men on it, indicating that even Higher Thought had Lower Functions.

The one after that said 'Restricted; Authorized Personnel Only'. This was more promising. Michael pushed the door (it had no handle) expecting to find it shut fast but, to his surprise, it yielded to his pressure, and he went in.

It was only when the door clicked behind him that he realized that an exit the same way was impossible. The wood was smooth, and there was some kind of catch on it which stopped the door swinging open.

'Very well,' thought Michael, not yet seriously disconcerted. 'Then it cuts out the debate as to what I do next. I go forward.'

But the heady wine of action was beginning to lose a little of its fizz. Had he been wise in trying to tackle this machiavellian organization with all its seeming subtlety and power entirely on his ownio?

There was another door ahead which, similarly, swung open easily and closed immutably behind him. He now thought he could hear, somewhere below him, the steady hum of machinery. Ahead, the way was lit by dim lights, and there appeared to be, at the end of a short passage, what looked like a staircase going down; but, just at that moment, he heard heavy steps coming up towards him. There was no time to think. He darted at a door on his right marked 'Top Security', slipped through and pressed it shut just as the lobster of his previous visit came into view. Michael heard him pass, return, and stop by the door. He heard his heart pounding like a caged goblin. And then he heard a telephone sound, somewhere back in the darkness, and the lobster hurrying off to attend to it.

Michael breathed a gale of relief and looked around him.

He was, it seemed, in some kind of control room, dimly illuminated by lights that shone from knob-sprinkled panels under a beefy bank of closed-circuit television monitors. On each screen was a picture of what he supposed was some room of the house or quarter of the grounds. He observed with some misgiving that the whole route he had taken, including the sash window appeared to have been under surveillance. There was indeed one screen which even showed Tom reading Health and Efficiency and eating a sesame biscuit.

The notion that he could have been overlooked at every stage of his infiltration gave him a nasty turn. Though, when he came to think about it, it wasn't exactly surprising. It was simply the latest in a long line of eaves-dropping on his activities. This time, though, perhaps he had been in luck. The room appeared to be empty. He may indeed have been seen by the cameras but who had been watching the monitors. Quis custodet ipsos custodes?

He looked more closely at the bank of panels. A group of them caught his particular interest. They showed aspects of what looked like a vast subterranean workshop-cum-laboratory built round a huge central shiny black pudding. He read some of the notices surrounding the black pudding, hoping for enlightenment. Words like 'Accelerator', 'Vortex spin', 'Neutron press' loomed out at him. What could this mean? They were perfectly familiar to him, of course, from his science-fiction studies, but he had hardly thought to have come across them in the course of an ordinary working day, not that this day was exactly ordinary working, but he knew what he meant.

Casting about in his mind for explanation, he turned his attention to another bank of monitors. These showed kitchens, a refectory, a laundry, dormitories; nothing strange here. Other chambers seemed to be reserved for theatrical or perhaps philosophic-religious activities, sets and draperies were in evidence; there was also a work-shop. These might or might not be sinister, but they looked more whimsical than menacing.

Moving now to the extreme corner of the bank, he noticed one monitor which chose, for whatever prurient reason, to focus on a girl asleep in bed. There was something, even at a distance, that suggested to Michael that he knew her. What could this mean? He waited, in a fever of curiosity, until at last she moved in her sleep allowing him to see a little more of her face.

'Miss Dulcimer,' he gasped involuntarily.

She sat up and rubbed her eyes.

He could hardly believe the evidence of his senses. He said it again.

'Miss Dulcimer.'

Incredibly she could hear. She cupped a hand to her ear. She looked about her. Seeing a knob just below the monitor that said 'Speaker volume', he twizzled it.

'MISS DULCIMER,' he boomed.

'Michael . . . Mr Lambert.'

'PLEASE. MICHAEL WILL DO.'

'Perhaps you would like to call me Lucy?'

'Lucy.'

'Do you think you could turn the volume down a little?'

He twizzled obligingly.

'Better?'

'Wonderful.'

'You're not . . . working for them?' he asked tentatively.

'Of course not. I came to find evidence. They caught me and now they're keeping me here.'

'That was terribly decent of you.'

'No . . . really. I couldn't just stand by and let them get away with it.'

'Where are you? Which room?'

'I don't know.'

'This is terrible.'

'You must take care. They'll catch you too.'

'Do you know what they're up to?'

'North and South, Up and Down. Does that make sense?'

'Not exactly.'

'The Nasties against the Nice. They don't put it like that, but I think that's what it boils down to.'

'I've got to find you.'

'Don't worry about me. It's you they want. They need the money desperately. It's for something they've got to have before they're able to put their plan into action. That's all I've gathered. Fly while you can.'

Lucy was sitting up in bed, cheeks flushed, hair tousled, the light of love in her eyes and the language of Charlotte M. Yonge on her lips. She looked young and very defenceless.

'I can't possibly do that,' protested Michael.

But at that moment, the whole screen went dead, the lights came one at full wattage, and a voice coming from the ceiling remarked:

'And there, for once, Mike, you've hit the nail in the nuts.' It was the voice of Treacle.

19

To say that Michael was flabbergasted would be to employ too milk-and-watery a word. His jaw hit the floor, his cortical hemispheres whirled like catherine wheels, and his seat of reason turned to junket. If smoke did not come out of his ears, it was only the fault of the plumbing. He could not remember ever having been so shaken.

'You?' he exclaimed. 'You? Treacle?'

'Yes,' she replied, after the manner of Tarzan and Jane. 'Me. Treacle.'

'What the hell are you doing here?'

'I didn't reckon on the way you threw me out, so I went over to them, didn't I? 'Smatter of fact, they put me on to you in the first place. I was a Philosopher too. Once.'

Michael suddenly felt trapped. He sensed that if he now tried the door through which he had entered the control room, he would find it locked. He did, and it was.

'So what are you proposing to do with me, Treacle?'

'We've got a nice little surprise in store for you, mate.'

He tried to be reasonable.

'Now look, Treacle, you're not a bad girl. You don't want to be mixed up with people like this. They're like dry rot. They'll take all the life out of you and leave you wandering round for ever like an Oxford Street shopper.'

It had started to happen already. The dottiness and life he had once sensed in her seemed shadows of their former selves.

'Who's in charge here, Treacle? I demand to talk to the Master or whoever he is.'

But her voice was fading.

'Master,' she whispered, and was gone.

At this juncture, a particularly jumbo-sized screen in the centre of the console suddenly activated itself. A pair of piercingly dull eyes looked out at Michael from a face that (horror of horrors) appeared to be so much the essence of negativeness that it was in fact, as in photography, negative. The face itself was dark. Only the thin lips and the eyes were light.

'Fool,' a voice of chilling sibilance remarked. 'Fool. Fool.'

'No thanks, I'd rather have the mousse.'

Michael was trying to feel brave but secretly admitted to himself that causes for optimism had stopped coming off the production line.

'I could crush you,' continued the apparition. 'Like an ant. I could snuff you out like a moth in a candle.'

Michael noted an absence of subtlety in his choice of similes, but felt that now might not be the moment to contest the issue.

'I could expunge you like a broken fly on a windowpane.'

There was a pause. Michael realized he was expected to make some kind of counter comment.

'Hold on,' he said, 'I wouldn't do that.'

'I would,' said the apparition, 'I would, all that and more. I would flay you alive, cover you with honey and leave you tethered to a termite's nest. I would pull out every hair on your body and with a pipette drop the most exquisite venom down the resultant orifices. I would fill your wretched belly with accelerated freeze-dried peas and make you drink Diet Pepsi till you burst open like a ripe gourd. I would . . .'

'Please,' said Michael, 'you're making me thirsty.'

'But,' said the Voice, 'I cannot do that. First, thanks to the madcap jade Kovacs and the indisseverable web of electronics she has spun round her legacy and your genitals, we have to get you to bed. I assure you, Mr Lambert, it will go the better with you if you oblige me. But just in case you still will not do it, even now, at this late stage, of your own volition, we have prepared one or two little, how shall I say, divertissements to encourage you. Entertainments, I may say, worthy of a sultan. We have been preparing for you, you see; and you are a lucky man indeed, Mr Lambert, to have so much care, imagination and sheer technology devoted to the satisfaction of your lust. Let me rest your mind on one matter, however. I understand in Spain a certain substance was inserted into your food in order to encourage a sense of . . . confusion. This will not happen again. Our strength is in the mind, Mr Lambert. We do not need crass chemicals. There will be no force. And no drugging. We will break you, I assure you, without them. And now, Mr Lambert, on with the motley. I almost envy you. Gentlemen in London, now abed, would pay a small fortune to participate in some of the frolics which we have laid on for you – absolutely free. Let us hope you will be a worthy recipient of our hospitality.'

'No,' said Michael stoutly. 'No, I won't, never, not on your life. You can lead a horse to water but you can't make it drink.'

'Come now, Mr Lambert. Let us not shilly-shally. Enjoy yourself while you can. You're only middle-aged once.'

The negative face faded from the screen leaving Michael in a mingled state of indignation and despair.

What had they got in store for him? Was there no escape? What hold had they got over Treacle? More important, what were they going to do with Lucy? He had to find her.

He bounded to the door and rattled it fiercely, but it was not the sort of door to be intimidated by threats.

Then, suddenly, behind him he heard music, and turning to face the screens, he saw, on the jumbo size, a very pretty girl of around twenty who looked in some way (so much of this whole affair seemed to have been built on dream-like echoes from his former life) curiously familiar.

The girl was driving an old MG with the radio on playing Beethoven at full throttle. She turned in at a driveway, parked the car outside a small Georgian house which again he dimly recognized, and went in through the front door.

The camera followed her inside, and showed her taking off her coat in the hall, and going upstairs to her bedroom. She was wearing a black dress in the style of the very early sixties, and this, with a sort of teasing self-pleasure she proceeded to take off, revealing a slip of charmingly adhesive and slippery texture. Silk again. When as in silk my Julia goes.

'Oh come now,' he said, 'you'll have to try harder than that.'

He was not a callow youth to be unhinged by celluloid stripteasery, and (judging by the clothes) a couple of decades old celluloid stripteasing at that. Then something happened that considerably shook him.

He had, of course, seen pornographic films, on and off, not because he particularly enjoyed them but at stag parties, seminars, and witty little gatherings in Putney, where they were de rigueur. He thought he knew all about blue movies, but he had to admit he had never seen one where the girl actually stopped what she was doing and spoke to him.

'The art of love, Michael,' she said intelligently, 'like any other kind of art, consists in never having to try too hard.'

And, with that, a door he had not previously noticed, opened. This caused Michael momentarily to cringe (fearing the crustacean janitor and Baskerville hound) but, on investigation, it revealed a room within, identical to the one on the screen, with (what was more) the identical girl in the identical posture sitting on the identical bed in the identical slip crossing legs of identical lissomeness and looking as if identical butter would not melt in her identical mouth, and smelling of stephanotis which was different but something of a bonus. The fragrance stirred in his memory.

Michael went back to look at the monitor. Then he returned to the door. Then he reverted to the monitor, wondering, professionally, at what point they had cut from filmed material to live-action.

And then he went back, through the door, to the live-action, before he properly realized what he was doing.

The door swung shut behind him.

The girl smiled at him cordially, running her hands down hips that made his own fingers wander instinctively towards them like the fronds of the trailing arbutus.

'Like a drink?' she said.

'Tha . . . um . . .' said Michael, remembering himself and scuttling back to the door. He must remain sober, retaining all his faculties. 'No thanks. Sorry. Er, sorry.' As if they were in a country hotel and he had mistaken his bedroom.

He noticed that there was a television set in the corner of the room which, in its turn, also seemed to be a monitor. At the moment it was focussing on the girl's thighs.

He began to get perversely excited. He knew it was mad. He knew he was letting the side down. He understood, or thought he understood, the enormity of the evil he was up against. But the idea of making love on camera curiously aroused him. It had been one of his frequently declared whimsies, and was something of a standing joke among his colleagues. And now, wonderfully, here it was, absolutely on a plate.

'I say,' he couldn't help blurting, pointing to the television, 'good film. Wonderful supporting cast.'

'I'm glad you like it. I was just wondering whether the plot couldn't do with a little livening up.'

No, no. This wouldn't do. He strode masterfully to the door, but it had no handle.

'I wonder if you could show me the way out?'

'There is no way out.'

'Yes. Well. About that drink.'

She went over to a cupboard that turned out to be a well-stocked bar and poured him a bumper of brandy. He eyed her nervously as he gulped. She really was the most amazingly pretty girl; oval face, green eyes, dark hair with a hint of the autumnal, a mouth that seemed both vulnerable and succulent; the sort of face you couldn't imagine doing anything dirty with until you saw her body. She had the figure of a courtesan and the face of an angel. And now he remembered who she was and when he had met her. She was an Oxford girl.

'Now do you remember me?' she said.

With a grave and perhaps enigmatic smile, she folded one of her superb pins across the other, and regarded him across the top of her glass. She was pondering, her face seemed to say, considerations of timeless profundity; serene, perspicuous, universal. Lowering his head just a fraction from the serene and lofty gaze, he could see she was wearing (oh joy, oh misadventure) stockings rather than the hated tights, topped with a tantalizing glimpse of black silk drawers.

'Do you remember?' she said. 'He who hath deeper digg'd Love's mine than I say where his centrique happiness doth lie . . .'

As he watched her hand slipped down and, still with the grave timeless expression on her face she started idly tweaking her knicker elastic.

'Don't,' he implored.

'What?' she said, dreamily. 'One never gets tired of Donne does one?'

He shifted his gaze to the television set; it did not help. She was running her fingers, in close up, across elysian fields.

'Would you mind not doing that?' he blurted.

'Mind you,' she continued patting her pussy, 'I think there's more of the purely lyrical in Marvell. "An hundred years should go to praise thine eyes and on thy forehead gaze, two hundred to adore each breast and thirty thousand to the rest." All that green imagery, too. I always think Marvell is the poet of green, don't you? "Stumbling on melons as I pass, ensnared with flowers I fall on grass". So fecund, don't you think. So thrustingly fertile.'

'Oh yes, anything,' he mumbled rapturously, 'anything you say.'

He remembered her now: Hermione Mount-Hesketh. That house he had watched her drive up to was her father's. He had kissed her in that very bedroom. She had been up at Somerville, a Zuleika-like legend in her year with an inexhaustible retinue of admirers, and Michael himself, for one glorious month, had headed her swain list.

They had gone to garden parties, picnics, Eights Week dances but more poignantly and memorably, they had explored the Matthew Arnold country round Oxford: Godstow, Wytham, the ferry at Bablockhythe, Cumnor Hurst, Wychwood bowers, and the fritillary-spotted meadows by Fair Rosamond's Nunnery.

They had quoted extravagantly to each other, drunk Entre Deux Mers and made passionate foreplay (she would never actually sleep with anyone) among the long grass.

'Do you remember?' she said, '"Where black-wing'd swallows haunt the glittering Thames"? What fun it used to be. How sweet you were.'

Of course, it had had to end. She met a lordling who owned an Aston Martin and took her to the Four Hundred, and the harebell happiness she and Michael had enjoyed in the field was replaced by the callow razzmatazz of the turbo-prop set. (That was what Michael had thought anyway.)

Michael would never forget the way she wore her subfusc so demurely while her legs went secretly soaring up like Late Gothic pillars to the clerestory of her stocking-tops. Or the way her knees were smokey black like Venetian glass, smooth as paperweights under the nylons, as she lay, drinking sherry and quoting Keats, in front of his Garden Quad gas fire after she had been up before the Proctors.

The only thing that troubled him, in the midst of his recollection and delight, was the realization that Hermione Mount-Hesketh must now be in her late thirties and no doubt a wife and mother, if not a redoubtable old bag, while the creature in front of him, so similar, nay identical to the literate enchantress of his youth, could be no more than twenty two.

It made him gasp anew at the ingenuity and inexhaustible research that had gone into the planning of his undoing. First de Blaye, and now Hermione. What other seminal (if that was the word) liaisons of his past were they going to pull out of the hat?

Meanwhile he had somehow to survive this one. He shuddered with mingled disgust and bafflement.

'Hermione,' he said, 'I know you're not Hermione but let's call you Hermione. Who are they? What do they want? What are they doing? It's something big, isn't it? Huge, cosmic, vile, that sort of thing?'

Michael had a lively sense of the dramatic, a tendency often exploited by the women in his life. If you wanted him to believe a tall story, whereas with most people you would play it down and make it appear likely, with Michael you had to go the other way. He would only believe you if you piled Pelion on Ossa. It explained why he was now, in a curious way, in his element. All his life he had been waiting for something Big.

'What's going on?' he reverted to his theme, 'who is the Negative Man? Is he a Philosopher? Is he trying to harness some kind of power? Is it some sort of Force they're after?'

Unfortunately for Michael, and perhaps for physics, his grip on the empirical processes of science was tenuous in the extreme. He would have been hard put to it to tell you what actually happened in Archimedes's bath. He might have had some natural aptitude, but his Physics Master had terrorized him when he was thirteen, throwing chalk and opprobria, and keeping the whole class in until he had done his formulae correctly.

In accordance with his theory of Batsmen and Bowlers, however, it was quite natural that he should wish to be strong in this area of weakness. He knew he could never master the facts so he had taken up the fiction. Hence his regular assimilation of quasi-astronomical tractates, treatises on hyper-space and postulant romances on the Origin of Matter.

He now began to see some connection between the Philosophers' Negative-Positive tension and the Negative man's quest for power. It was all inextricably bound up.

Again, he got the feeling that he had been here before; and then it came to him. It reminded him of his own unfinished film-script. There had even been a character called Dr Zero modelled on his Physics Master. How searingly prophetic he had been! How his Physics Master would squirm!

'It's Anti-Matter,' he said to Hermione Mount-Hesketh's doppelganger, 'they're harnessing the power of the Negative Proton?'

She nodded enigmatically. So that was what it was. He felt a sense of awe but not of fear. He had stumbled across a nexus of intrigue and subterfuge and dirty-dealing that posed the biggest threat to mankind since sliced atoms.

Hermione nodded again and took off her slip. Her brassière was almost completely transparent and slightly glossy, making her breasts shine like crystallized plums.

'They're building a Black Hole,' she said. 'First of all he'll threaten to gobble up Berkshire, and then when the government gives in, they'll take charge. Such fun.'

'Ohmygod,' said Michael, remembering an article he had read in Science Tomorrow which hypothesized that tiny black holes could be constructed and used as energy sources. 'This is terrible. And why does he look negative like that?'

'There was an accident.'

Had he slipped through the Hole and been rolled-up in another dimension? Had he just got pulled inside out by a narrow brush with a singularity? You couldn't expect a girl with a pair of Victorias like that to understand the niceties (or even the nastinesses) of astro physics.

'I've got to stop him.'

'Don't be silly. You can't stop anything. You can't stop yourself. Anyway, life's going to be so much simpler. I mean, everything's confused at the moment, like oil and water, bubbles of Up and Down. "Tis not what once it was, the world; but a rude heap together hurled". With Negative in charge, you'll know where you are. You've no idea how satisfying Nothing can be. "Apples of ashes, oh how bright, waters of bitterness, how sweet, Oh banquet of a foul delight, Thou has prepared, Dark Paraclete." Get it?'

It was true that Michael did wonder for an instant whether she was making a fool of him, though he felt disinclined to believe that such a thing could be possible. He also noticed that she was taking his trousers off. Was he dreaming? Even he realized that she was talking something that teetered ominously on the verge of balderdash but somehow there was a bizarre credibility about the whole farrago.

Completing her labours, she lay back on the bed watching him as he kicked off his shoes, divested himself of socks. A quirk of his, this. He would never, whatever the exigencies of the moment, however close the world might be to succumbing to the powers of blackness, make love in his socks. But what was he thinking of? Making love? Never. But why did he feel so weak? Was the

Negative Man getting at him already, tugging at his will like a sea anchor?

He could see the little white omicrons of her knees shining through the dark stockings, and he started kissing them delicately. She pulled him to her, and his hands flattened like bats around her bra-hook.

'Oh Hermione,' he breathed.

'"Nothing,"' she said, '"Thou elder brother ev'n to Shade, thou had'st a being e'er the world was made, and well fixt art of ending, not afraid."'

Her bra, unfixed, sprang from her breast with the exuberance of a breached dam, and like the hart desiring the waterbrooks, his mouth drank thirstily from her twin bibbles.

Even so, he might yet have drawn back, had not his eyes lifting for a moment, caught sight of the television screen. The monitor happened to be pointing straight up her legs to an unequivocal manifestation of pleasure.

'"Are not Abana and Pharpar,"' he quoted, since quoting seemed to be the game, '"rivers of Damascus, better than all the waters of Israel?"'

'Stop fucking talking,' she said, 'and start talking fucking.'

And this was the girl or the clone of the girl he had so loved and who had so teased him, never allowing him (or anyone else for all he knew) the searing pleasures of penetration.

It was too much. With a hoarse cry, he tore down the deliquescent silk. A thousand spiders, with chilli powder on their feet, seemed to be scuttling up and down his member. He could see himself now, poised above her like a rutting demi-god, as she writhed and moaned and quoted beneath him.

It was at this moment that something happened he did not normally associate with coition.

The floor gave way.

As he slid down goodness knew what nameless abyss, he called out to her.

'Yum,' he shouted, trying to combine in one syllable both admiration and despair.

She appeared to understand.

'It was Nothing,' she said.

And he fell into a gulf of blackness. As he dropped (his brain dimly registered that he seemed to be in a sort of chute), he wondered fleetingly why they had let him off the hook. An instant later he realized that this time they were merely playing with him. They were proving their mental superiority. Hermione had been put up to be what she had always been, a tease.

Now they had him in their power, they were going to make sure of his moral as well as his physical disintegration. Total surrender seemed to be the name of their game. They wanted to leave him Nothing.

Somewhere, beyond the blackness, he thought he could hear anti-laughter.

20

It was not so much a sheer drop as a steep incline, but it was as black as a hole can possibly be without finding itself in trouble with the Astronomer Royal, and Michael was not at all sanguine about its outcome.

Was this the well of nothingness he had read about, from which no traveller returned, and no light could emanate? Was he going to be stretched to the thinness of a scream as he whirled through the Schwarzkild Radius, past the Event Horizon and into the singularity at the centre?

He thought, on the whole, probably not. Black Holes, he felt, would not smell of canvas nor be quite so scratchy. But where was he going to end up? Dim memories of Alice in Wonderland, evoked perhaps by Hermione's literary ramblings and distant memories of water-meadows by the Isis, assailed him. What was it the White Rabbit had said? 'Oh my ears and whiskers.'

'Oh my ears and whiskers,' he repeated aloud, hoping the distant laughers would think this irritatingly cool and poised.

The truth was that he wasn't feeling irritatingly cool and poised. For a man who had been even toying with the idea that he might be sucked into a Cosmic Cloaca, he was feeling very randy indeed. Indeed, as he fell, he was host to a number of emotions which, as so often during the past weeks, were of an extraordinary miscellaneous and conflicting quality. You could easily reconcile fear, horror, surprise and affront; but add lust, nostalgia and frustration and you had a peculiar-flavoured mixture more suited to the smorgasbord table than the seat of the senses.

But even as he was savouring these feelings, earing and whiskering as he went, he was aware that his rate of descent was lessening, and before he could say Charles Ludwidge Dodgson he was precipitated through swing doors and on to a floor which smelled of polished linoleum.

Picking himself up from the cold surface (he was naked except for his shirt and he didn't even have any socks on, dash it) he stared about him incredulously. He was becoming inured to surprises, but this one was medulla-bending.

He was in a perfect replica of his old nursery. The blue paint, the Peter Pan wall-paper, the rocking horse, the toy cupboards; everything was immaculately in place. Even the ancient gramophone with the horn was there by the window, and he knew that the records lying beside it would be the ones he had played till their grooves wore out.

He walked, clutching a teddybear to cover his conspicuous parts over to the window and examined them. Yes, there they were: 'Barnacle Bill the Sailor', 'I wonder where my baby is tonight', and 'If I give up the saxophone, will you come back to me?' He picked up one at random, put it on the machine, wound it up and applied the needle. How it all came back.

But he didn't stand long in idle reverie. It was one thing to be impressed with the Philosophers' once-more unerring homework, but it was a task of a great deal more urgency to get the hell out of the place. Past experience suggested that they weren't in the business of giving him a magical history tour just for the pleasure of making his mind boggle. They were after something, and it was only their own arrogance that had stopped them taking it already.

He darted about trying the doors and windows, but none of them proved responsive. The only exit was up the chute which had deposited him through one of the toy-cupboards. He tried its one-in-three slope but there was no purchase, and he slid back. He lay down on the little rug beside the railway train, and tried to think of a ruse.

'Get up at once, Master Michael. You should be ashamed of yourself lying there like a lummox, a fine thing for a young gentleman.'

It was unmistakably the voice of Nanny Berryman.

Nanny Berryman had been a West Country girl, from Devonshire if he remembered rightly, known to Michael's English grandmother who had sent her over to New England to help look after him. He had loved Nanny Berryman. In an austere New England household, she had had the warmth and sweetness which his stepmother and father so significantly lacked. She had also been extremely fond of him, a little too fond, Michael's stepmother decided, after finding her soaping Michael beyond the dictates of hygiene one traumatic bath-time.

Nurse Berryman had been sent home on the next boat. And now here she was again. Michael marvelled anew at the devilish ingenuity of the planning. Who had the Philosophers consulted? Where had they mustered their material? Nurse Berryman, indeed. No one could have been better summoned-up to promote his parson's standing in the world. Why, it was she who had first christened it, he seemed to remember.

He couldn't help being excited.

'I see the Parson's at his sermons again,' said the voice.

There she was standing at the door to the bathroom which was now just ajar. She looked more wonderful than ever.

'Lor, luv you, Master Michael,' she said, coming into the nursery, 'but what a fine big boy you are now.'

'Look,' Michael expostulated, remembering his predicament in the midst of his pleasure, 'this is ridiculous. I can't possibly . . .'

'Ridicklus? Ridicklus? What sort of talk is that? Ridicklus? You ought to have your mouth washed out with soap. Can't? Did I hear can't? Can't's a word we don't use in the nursery. Come over here at once. It's past your bath-time. You look half-asleep. A nice hot bath'll put you to rights.'

It was true. He did feel, after all the excitement, dreadfully tired. A nice hot bath was just what he needed – with a nice hot cup of cocoa to follow, but still he found the energy to resist.

'No,' he said, and he found himself stamping his foot. 'No, Nanny. No, no, no.'

'Oh,' said Nanny Berryman, smiling and limbering. 'Oho. We're in a pet, are we? We're having a temper tantrum. Temper, temper. What a little turk. You better come right now or it'll be smacks on your bottomley.'

And she advanced on him with her sleeves rolled up, and her mouth pouting like a pincushion in playful indignation. What a sight she made! Her fair curly hair (a wisp escaping from her cap) her upturned nose, her skin fizzing with health, her big young bosom jutting out under a wonderful piste of starch. She would have made any farmer a wife in a million and (thought Michael) now she probably did. Meanwhile here was her alter ego.

How quick she was. How nimble on her pumps. Help! Nanny, don't!

'No. Look. Wait,' he put the rocking horse between them. 'Where's the Black Hole?'

He had to find out if Hermione had been telling him any part of the truth.

'Black 'Ole? Black 'Ole? Don't know of no Black 'Ole. You been playing down the cellar again? I'll skin you, I will. I told you, didn't I, but you don't take no notice of Nanny Berryman. We'll have to soap you extra special if you been down there. I 'spect you got potatoes behind your ears and all.' And she came out at him, seemingly from both sides of the rocking-horse at once, and grabbed him warmly by the bottom.

'Whooo. Ooooooo. Nanny.'

'What a lot of fuss. Never met such a fusser. Come along now, duffer.'

She led him towards the door and pushed him gently into the bathroom. Fragrant it was, as it had always been, smelling of pink geraniums, muggy with steam. His duck and his torpedo boat were waiting for him in the water.

'Off with your shirt and get straight in.' She felt the water. 'I'll just get your Cousin Libby, what a little slowcoach and then we'll begin. Won't be a jiffy.'

Cousin Libby? Horrors. He remembered Cousin Libby. She was a pretty little minx who had taken him into the garden shed one day and compared notes with him as to how exactly they both did a pee. Yes, it was true. Sometimes they had bathed together. How soothing the water was.

Michael felt the tensions, frustrations and anxieties peel off him like balsa-wood cement.

But this would not do. He must not be lulled by Nanny Berryman and her soft soap. He looked round, soggily galvanic. The window! It was unlocked.

Even as he drew the catch, however, manically furtive,

he heard Nanny's sensible shoes on the linoleum again, accompanied this time by the shuffle of slippers. The door opened and Nanny ushered in Cousin Libby.

Cousin Libby was dressed in a Flopsy Bunny dressing gown and had a ribbon in her hair. She did indeed resemble the real Cousin Libby in almost every detail, except that she was somewhat fuller in the chest. Somehow Cousin Libby, who should have been thirty-eight by now, was only eighteen. But Michael was not complaining. The idea of having a bath with Cousin Libby under the soapy auspices of Nanny Berryman was giving him disturbing intimations of delight.

Cousin Libby took off her ribbon, shook out a profusion of golden ringlets, removed her Flopsy Bunny dressing gown and stepped into the bath (which had taps set in the wall half way down one side and was big enough for three). Whoever designed her had indeed given her breasts but had omitted to etch in the pubic hair.

It made for a powerfully erotic effect, and Michael couldn't keep his eyes off her.

'Come along, slowcoach. Quick's the word and sharp's the action. Let's get those potatoes out.'

First Nanny turned her attention to Cousin Libby, however, wiping her face with a flannel and then busily soaping her chest. What a sight they made. Nanny like some goddess of the fields, a veritable Ceres with her wheat-gold locks and her cornucopic bosom, tending and plucking the young nymph's apples.

Cousin Libby's foot inserted itself under Michael's posterior, and wagged impishly about. This was too much for Michael.

His member rose like a deep-sea diver, and bobbed

about on the surface waiting to have its headpiece unscrewed.

'Oooooo,' lisped Cousin Libby, as she sent the torpedo boat skimming across the surface towards it.

'Ouch,' shrieked Michael as the plastic prow caught him sharply in the buoys.

'Drat,' said Nanny as the soap slipped out of her active hands and flew like a bird under the bath.

She scrabbled around for a bit but eventually gave up.

'That was your fault, Miss Libby,' said Nanny, not in the least put out, 'that's what comes of playing the giddy goat. Now I'll have to go an fetch another bar of Coal Tar from my cupboard. You be good, mind.'

And she padded out to her room, closing the door behind her.

'Would you like to thee my bottom?' enquired Cousin Libby, sweetly.

'Now look here,' said Michael, the pain caused by the torpedo boat had temporarily cleared his brain of desire, 'don't come that with me. You're not Cousin Libby. You're an impostor, just another bit-part in this appalling charade. See your bottom? You ought to be ashamed of yourself. Out of the question. I never heard of such a thing. Well. All right. Just a peep.'

Cousin Libby, smiling impishly, got up. Her body, sketchily festooned in Baby Bubbles Bath Foam, was awesome in its perfection, and its lack of secondary characteristics around the pubis gave it a delinquent appeal that may have been shameful but was infinitely hard to combat.

'Ready?'

Cousin Libby turned round so she had her back to him, looked wantonly over her shoulder and shook the golden profiteroles of her hair.

'I bet you've never theen anything like thith before,' she said.

And she bent over.

Averting his gaze as if from the Gorgon's head, although by God he could feel the pull of those taut hamstrings, blindly, desperately mustering every apothecary's scruple of self discipline he possessed, Michael leapt at the small window whose catch he had previously unleashed, and clutching a face-towel to his tumescent member, he cocked a leg over the sill just as Cousin Libby became aware, possibly for the first time in her life, that her bottom was not the centre of the Universe. Michael's apostasy from what had hitherto been an irrefutable axiom, struck her in very much the same way as Galileo's impinged on Urban the Eighth.

She did not exactly have him arrested, imprisoned and threatened with excommunication, but she hurled a spontex loofah with considerable force at his retreating right buttock and yelled:

'You rat.'

And it is quite conceivable that, in similar circumstances Urban the Eighth would have done the same.

'Get him,' shouted Nanny Berryman, coming back at that moment with a monster slab of yellow soap, her rage making Michael shiver with delight and alarm. 'Don't let him get away. I'll give him what-for, you see if I don't.'

For a time, there seemed a chance that they might actually pull him back. He was stuck, half in, half out of the window in a posture that caused his already assaulted parson a considerable further degree of discomfort. His legs were free, either side of the sill but his head and shoulders were stuck under the window frame.

'You little brute,' cried Nanny Berryman, cruelly

belabouring him with half a kilo of coal tar, 'what you need's a good hiding and I'll give it you directly.'

'Thquirt him with the hot tap,' suggested Cousin Libby helpfully. 'Make him beg for merthy.'

But just in the nick of time, by squashing his globes to a flatness that Mercator himself would have commended, he was able to gain an extra millimetre or two which allowed him to remove his head, swing his other leg over the sill (The Baby Bubbles making it difficult for the two myrmidons to hold on to the captive limb) and, sending up a prayer to whichever saint it is that looks after bachelors and celibates, he launched himself, with a strong sense of fires and frying pans, into whatever it was that lay beyond.

As he fell (and this gave him more cause for concern than any imprecation, parting fusillade of bathroom accessories or sound of pursuit) he heard the bathroom window slide down with a finality, he felt, that indicated he had merely been through yet another stage of his amatory assault-course, and that there could be more and worse to come, with no possibility of evasion.

It is always disconcerting to fall when one cannot see the ground, but it is bleak to know that when one lands one is not going to be any the wiser.

Michael fell with a heavy heart, and was not much comforted by the thought that this did not necessarily accelerate his rate of descent.

21

The siege of Babylon, as it came to be called, was not yet the longest on record, but it was conducted with notable vigour, both by the Unions and those encamped around, and by the defenders, Mr and Mrs Lee.

There was an attempted take-over of the premises – not, of course, by the workforce but a taskforce representing them, comprising the cream of the municipal workers. It had been driven off by a combination of mounted police and a fortuitous thunderstorm, this last especially disconcerting the lavatory attendants who regarded sudden floods with almost superstitious horror.

It was subsequent to this that the Mister Whipsee van had been overturned. The Cypriot driver had thought to vary his musical offering – perhaps in deference to the thunderclaps – with something more martial, and had switched to The British Grenadiers. This (with its implications of the troops being sent in and, who knows?, race memories of Peterloo) incensed the thwarted crowds, and over it went – soft ice cream, Whipsee specials with chocksticks, Koolafrutes, frankfurters, onion rings, paper doilyettes and all – in spite of the pleas of the proprietor.

'I will play only Blueballs of Scotland,' he reiterated, but the Clydesiders were deaf to all blandishments.

The mess was appalling, though popular with the local dogs.

Later, there was a night attack with a couple of firebombs hurled out of the darkness, but they exploded harmlessly on the back of the urinals which were constructed of asbestos board and remained as impervious to flame as they were to the wilder sprinklings of the staff. The perpetrators had not been caught though the police made a terrific effort, chasing flying shadows along the sallow-fringed isthmuses of the hinterland, but in the end only succeeding in arresting each other.

22

As it happened, Michael did not have far to fall.

In the manner of one treading on a phantom step at the bottom of a flight of stairs, he landed sooner than he had expected with the sensation that his feet had been impacted half way up his shins like Jose Ferrer playing Toulouse Lautrec.

Picking himself up, and clutching his towel to his long-suffering parts, he became aware that he had been mistaken in thinking that Nanny could be put off so easily. Clearly she and Cousin Libby had thought better of it, and even now were showering him with soap, lavatory cleaners and cocoa beakers.

It even seemed to him that Nanny had hitched up her skirts and was starting to clamber out after him.

'Thtring him up by the tethticleth,' he heard Libby inconsiderately recommending.

Realizing he had been wrong to rate pursuit so lightly, he turned and ran. His eyes, becoming accustomed to the darkness, informed him that he was in an external basement-level passage-way, constructed to allow light to penetrate the lower windows of the house and grilled to prevent access to intruders. Or extruders, he thought despondently.

He had now run the entire length of the house without finding access, and was beginning, in his exhaustion and despair, to get extremely testy. Here he was, a man of forty, charging about with an inadequate towel round his waist like a callow fourth-former escaping from a beating by the Upper Dormitory. What was he doing here? Where was the Black Hole? Did it exist even? If it did, his science fiction told him, they would have to make it rotate extremely fast to get any power out of it, power being presumably what they wanted. How were they making it spin? How do you get hold of a Black Hole in the first place? Was his reason tottering? Was he the victim of the most subtly planned deception, or was he the one man who could save the world from a hell plot? Why did his sexual organs have to be tied up in all this?

Tired and frustrated, he was beginning to think that he would simply yield to the next tasty ordeal they had prepared for him, go home and sleep for a week, and let the world fend for itself; but he knew that was just what they wanted. How they would crow. They were deliberately wearing him down, and he was damned if he was going to give up like that. It wasn't just a matter of civilization, it was a matter of self-respect. Lucy would never look at him again as she had done so recently on the monitor; the light would go out of her eyes. She would consider him a worm.

But what was all this about Lucy? Why was he having these feelings? Was it because she was the only woman who had ever seriously put herself out for him? Was it because he had suddenly felt a surge of something quite extraordinary when he had talked to her for those brief televisual minutes? Where was she anyway?

He shivered, resting in the shelter of a moss-covered buttress. A dawn wind smelling of honeysuckles and grass-cuttings reached chilly fingers down to him through the bars.

It seemed to Michael that, as he stood there, swaying with fatigue under the grill, with the starlight hissing and spitting overhead, he had spent his whole life searching for something he desperately wanted, but with his head in his trousers and his balls in the air.

What was it that he was looking for? The dong with the luminous nose, the burning pestle, where had it led him? It was all a waste, a desolation. Let the rocks groan with continual surges.

He had often said to his friends that he was waiting for a knock on the door, someone (not some dreary moral re-armer or woolly do-gooder) but someone who said: 'You're needed now in Tierra del Fuego.' He would go like a shot. A mission, he used to say jocularly, rather than emission.

Now for the first time, he felt that in some bizarre sort of way he really meant it, that he was trembling on the verge of a discovery that made it all make sense.

If he hadn't been so tired, he would have felt almost exuberant in spite of his position. This was the Quest he had expected for so long, a Quest he could undertake with his head in the air and his balls where they belonged.

The next thing was sleep. Whether he should first try to look for Lucy, throttle the Negative Man, put the Black Hole out of action, or thermidor the Lobster was entirely academic at this point. He needed shut-eye.

Finding a little door leading into a store-room under the drive, he stole in and crept under some sacking. It was not the most luxurious pit he had ever slept in, but it did the trick wonderfully. He might have been more at home in the bed Nanny had made up for him in the robin redbreasty bedroom next door to hers, but he could not have dropped faster into the land of Nod.

He could not tell afterwards how long he slept, but he knew that a confusion of images had jostled about among his Alpha Rhythms: faces, familiar scenes, peculiar circumstances; but when he woke it was with a clear head in a warm dark place, and it was not the same place that he had gone to sleep in. So much for no drugs. Someone must have given him a shot. But not perhaps to molest his person directly. Just to prepare him for further molestation. Where was he?

Not on a bed, certainly. There was no spring in the arrangement. Possibly on a sort of sheet on the floor. His shirt had gone but . . . what was this . . . he was naked except for . . . my god . . . nappies. This was monstrous. He had committed himself to a Quest. Were they trying to make him crawl? Did they not realize he was tantamount to Sir Perceval? Who ever heard of a knight in a nappy?

He was distracted from these speculations by the lights coming on. What he saw made him gasp and pinch himself like a harpy with a severe self-disgust problem.

He lay on a little mat, on a sheet, in a clearing as it were, under a colossal pair of recumbent thighs which, as he watched, appeared to be slowly advancing as if to envelop him.

It was, at the same time, astonishing and loathsomely enticing.

The huge thighs inched forwards implacably, making his little clearing smaller and smaller. He put a hand out to feel it. The thigh bounced a little. He was going to be smothered by a vast tide of flesh-coloured latex.

How fitting an end, he thought. But how sad that he had only just acquired a sense of purpose. At all events, he wasn't simply going to lie down and let them walk all over him. He had to get out of here. He struggled to his feet, hobbled by the towelling, suddenly realizing why babies were always so bow-legged, and looked frantically about him. The other end of the small chamber was smooth and impenetrable except where the legs went out (and that was impenetrable to all save the legs). He looked up at the looming hams. There was only one thing for it.

Up above him there lay a dark aperture, a huge latex crevice, which was the only visible point of egress in the place. Was this the Black Hole? It was towards this that he was being irresistibly coerced.

Had he been somehow shrunk like Alice, and was now being run over by a life-size Rubber Companion? Or was he normal and the Thing brobdingnagian? While he wrestled with these questions, the thought uppermost in his mind was still his role as a quester. If he went through these fell portals, could he maintain credibility when the tale came to be told? Consulting his memories of Celtic Romance, he reassured himself that the Quest could lead to some very humiliating passes indeed (what about the Knight who had to sleep with the Loathly Lady?) and that if the End was sound, the Knight could undergo all manner of vile and perilous tests – even, he told himself, a Chastity Test as Sir Gawain had done and come out with more or less flying colours, give or take the odd smirch.

A Chastity Test! It suddenly put the whole thing in perspective.

But the Knight could not go about his business in diapers. Rapidly divesting himself of these encumbrances (but retaining the safety pin in case he met a Beast) he started to climb up the vast, billowy, surging thighs into what would have been in real life the very portals of pleasure, and soon he was deep within soft folds of wonderfully simulated plastic labia, and thrusting himself ever upwards into he knew not what.

The experience, though alarming at first, began to be amazingly soothing. Phrases like 'The haven where I would be' crossed his mind. The only thing that made him nervous was his little electronic monitor. He had no idea how much contact would set it off, though he had been assured that only actual congress would trigger it. Even this concern, though, was ceasing to matter to him. As he wriggled up the wonderful burrow of the uterus, he felt he had never been more at ease.

Arriving in the dark satiny cavern of the womb, he made himself at home. Adopting the required position (one does not stand or sit cross-legged in the womb, just as one does not keep one's hat on in the hall), he looked foetally around him.

The place was not entirely dark but was lit by a subdued red glow all round. How nice, he thought. How entirely fitting. I could spend a lot of time here. It did cross his mind that maybe he should get on with his search, but Lucy seemed a long way away, and he was sure she wouldn't mind waiting. Meanwhile, in spite of his recent sleep, he felt he needed rest.

He huddled himself into a delicious placental languor and emptied his mind of conjecture.

He was aroused some time later (how much later he could not tell as time seemed to have no meaning here) by a faint movement from the other side of the chamber where his drowsy eyes discerned an exact replica of himself, lying in the same position, sucking its thumb and kicking softly at the wall.

A few minutes (hours?) later, and they had rolled together, and he was able to discern that his twin was a female. He was not annoyed to be sharing his quarters. Quite the reverse. He felt gratified and warm towards his second self. Could it be possible that, in that other life, he had originally had a twin? He seemed to remember hearing something about it. At any rate, he felt now an instinctive bond, a deep-seated emotion of delight to make her reacquaintance. They clutched each other without feeling called upon to comment on the situation.

A mild trembling of the frame, however, did not considerably divert his languorous attention. Something else seemed to be coming with rather more disturbance than he had caused, up the genial passage. What could it be? His eyes rolled, his twin wriggled.

Then suddenly there popped into view something which the ancient fertility dancers of Thrace, the Bog People of Tollund, the duck-billed warriors of the rain-forest and indeed the Cl housewife of Staines, would have taken as the Sign they had all been waiting for. A monstrous male organ advanced like the serpent in the Magic Flute, or a very old doorman, puffing and creeping and red in the face, and stood apoplectically in the vestibule of their chamber.

It was so big and jolly and well-simulated that Michael, in his curiously lulled condition could only gape in awe, while his own suddenly sympathetic little phallus beat a morse code of admiration against his stomach wall which in turn persuaded his twin to grasp it for all the world as if she were pulling a pint.

In this posture, they awaited further developments. They were not long to come.

The rosy monster drew back – and then suddenly lunged forwards towards them like a playful puppy – a sequence it repeated with increasing rapidity and gusto a considerable number of times . . .

A bead of moisture the size of a football issued from the vertical mouth. The walls of the cave trembled and pulsated. Vast rumbles and diapason gasps suffused the fabric of the chamber as if the Flying Scot were ravishing the Caerphilly Castle.

The activity had a curiously arousing effect on Michael. He could feel his twin beginning to roll on top of him . . .

Then, quite suddenly, as in the emptiest corner of remotest Space a madly flying neutrino particle can hurtle through, so, at that moment, a flicker of an image of Lucy crossed his mind. The respectable office, the demure blouse, the candid eyes, the softness of the nape, the kindness and bravery of what she had done for him.

He was damned if he was going to be manipulated, quite literally it seemed, into making her sacrifice null and void.

'No,' he shouted at the rubber penis.

'No,' he yelled at the irresponsible foetus beside him.

'No,' he hollered just in case anyone else had failed to get the point, and he jabbed his nappy pin into the taut inflated integument of the floor.

There was a blast like the combined brass section of cherubim and seraphim at the Last Great Battle. There was a rushing mighty wind. There was an indignant squawk from the foetus who kneed him smartly in the groin. Someone said 'Fuckinghell' in a voice he couldn't help thinking he recognized but couldn't place. And suddenly the air was full of flying latex.

The ceiling came down like a Big Top. The giant penis went hissing and whipping round and round the womb like a mad thing, and finally collapsed in a little shrivelled heap at Michael's feet. And the foetus, most limberly, turned and ran.

Michael, under the whelming tide of tattered gonads, hacked his way out with his trusty nappy-pin. He found himself in a bare barn of a room with various lighting and electrical equipment, relics of his recent ordeal, still strewn around the premises. Formerly hidden by the outsize thighs, there was a door at the far end and, over the door, a television screen. While he looked at this, as if for some kind of explanation, the face of the Negative Man appeared.

'You unspeakable hound,' said Michael, weakly.

'So, Mr Lambert. You enjoyed our little game? It gives back-to-the-womb a new meaning, does it not?'

'Why don't you climb into your Black Hole and bugger off into hyperspace?' replied Michael, combining impoliteness with astrophysical inaccuracy, and wishing he didn't feel quite so naked.

'Come, come, Mr Lambert. Have a care. Do not think that just because I am impervious to insults that I tolerate them. I can become unpleasant to the point where hardened men fall on the floor and eat fluff. So far we have just been playing with you, but now we have a harder test. You will be this time between the devil and the deep blue sea. The devil will be . . . well, you will find out. The deep blue sea is down there.'

The scene shifted, though the voice went on talking. Michael saw a long room which reminded him of his early days as a proof-reader in a direct-mail warehouse. Rank upon rank of listless women sat behind their Olivettis typing out items whose boringness came across as strongly as the smell of rancid haddock.

'That is the Pool, Mr Lambert. Down there are thirty typists who have been denied television for six weeks. Watch.'

All at once a trap door opened in the low ceiling. The girls rose as one, slavering in anticipation.

Michael turned away, appalled.

'They can strip a man in thirty seconds,' said the Negative Man. 'I say again, have a care, Mr Lambert. If you fail to be moved by my next little set-piece, that is where you could end up.'

'But,' Michael stammered, 'but look here. You told me it's all going to be in the mind. Those typists don't look very philosophical to me.'

'In the long run, Mr Lambert, Philosophy is one thing. £8 million is another. We have tried to play this thing by the book, and there are certain er colleagues of mine who would wish to continue to do so, but time is running out, Mr Lambert. Have a care. Rely on Nothing.'

'But . . . look here . . .' said Michael.

The screen was already blank.

23

In the study to which Michael had been shown when he first came to Sambrook, a dungareed man and woman were going through the bills with their chargé d'affaires, a person dressed in blazer and grey flannels.

'This is indeed serious,' the dungareed man was saying, 'the bank has already voiced concern. Do we really need the extra material?'

'If you wished to do the thing by force, we could have the money tomorrow,' said the chargé d'affaires.

The couple paused. They did a great deal of pausing. It was part of their philosophy.

'I can't see . . .' started the chargé d'affaires, but the couple motioned him to silence.

'When you first came to us with this scheme,' said the dungareed woman, and stopped.

'We agreed no physical coercion,' the dungareed man completed her sentiment.

'Of what use is the money,' said the dungareed woman.

'If we violate our sacred beliefs?' confided her companion.

'Your sacred beliefs aren't going to get the Bank Manager off your back,' said the chargé d'affaires. 'Sacred beliefs do not butter the parsnips. But as it happens, I agree with you. I do not advocate coercion.'

Pause.

'Your plan has been very costly,' announced the dungareed man.

'In business,' countered the chargé d'affaires, 'an

investment of £800,000 is considered minimal for an £8 million return.'

They looked at each other without relish.

'We could probably make a fortune from that chastity gizmo, you know,' suggested the chargé d'affaires.

'It is required in situ as of the moment,' said the man. 'Do not let us cloud the issue. And I do not like that "we". It is our monitor.'

'We must keep our eyes on the ball just now,' said the woman. 'Later we will clap monitors on everyone.'

The man thought of something else.

'What about the Black Hole?' he demanded.

'Is it necessary?' asked the woman.

'Necessary? It's the very nub of the Plan. It's the threat in the background. The cosmic dimension.'

'It is very dear,' said the woman.

'You can't have a revolution for nothing,' said the chargé d'affaires.

There was a very long pause indeed during which the chargé d'affaires got up and walked out.

24

Michael, as he addressed himself to the door in front of him, tried not to think too hard about his predicament. The first step was to frame insouciance in words. Words, he had found, are the stepping stones to emotion.

'Danger is the Tabasco of the man of action,' he tried, though even as he said it, he doubted whether the devil-fish in the Pool below would be much deterred by such a consideration.

Finding no succour in syllables, or in anything else for that matter, he turned the handle and went in. The Quest must go on.

He found himself in a small curtained room, a boudoir, a miniature Bower of Bliss. For some reason which he could not immediately identify but which was to become painfully clear in a few moments, the decor of the place was redolent of the 1930s. He recognized the style, of course, instantly. Had he not pastiched it in a dozen commercials? He almost expected to see Mae West lying on a sofa having her grapes peeled, but instead there was a girl of such piquante and individual beauty, it seemed to go straight to his vitals.

At Scripture, in school, he had sometimes stumbled across the phrase 'His bowels yearned'. That was exactly how he felt now. His bowels, he sensed, had never featured in the yearning stakes before, but this time they went to the head of the field. Indeed yearned hardly did justice to his sensations. It would have been more accurate to say that his bowels leapt, writhed and knotted themselves about his back-bone in a manner only emulated by the Serpent Nidhogg round Yggdrasil the Tree of Life.

The girl smiled at him with great love.

'Come on, Mouse,' she said, extending her hand.

'Merciful heavens,' he thought, caught between more warring emotions than Queen Phaedra.

Only one person had ever called him 'Mouse', deriving it from his Christian name and the Hollywood rodent. It was his stepmother. The wickedness and subtlety of the Negative Man's choice was as cruel as it was well-judged.

To many people, the sight of their stepmothers in early youth would not be in the least bit troubling. Some stepmothers are, of course, simply appalling. Others are comfy but dim. Others are perfectly splendid but do not induce sensations of vertigo. Michael's stepmother was different.

She was his father's second English wife (the first, Michael's real mother, having died when he was two). This one had been the belle of Buckinghamshire when she had been a girl, and there was many an ageing lordling who remembered her, even now, with tears compounded of grief and frustration, and who had, the year she came out, pursued her up and down London from Chelsea Barracks to the Tower, and to more country seats than you could conveniently employ.

She had been glorious. Of a little above medium height, she was lissom, yet well-rounded with charming legs and a wonderful bosom, but her chief glory, apart from features that seemed to combine tenderness, intelligence and sensuality, was her complexion in which pinkness and whiteness, like aggressive strawberries versus militant cream, strove with each other for supremacy, only producing an endlessly delectable palest pink syllabub.

Her golden hair was bright and abundant and freshly-disclosed-looking. Her green eyes were bright and full of important mischief. If you looked at her mouth for long, you were in danger of hurling yourself into it, such a dizzying lust could it induce.

Michael, from his very first awareness, like all the other men around, had fallen in love with her.

But she had not been a good stepmother. She believed that a child's place was in the nursery while her place was in someone else's bed. Not that she had ever been unkind to him; simply absent; hence his love of Nanny Berryman, and his undying adoration of herself.

Finally, she had become bored of the puritan ethic and the New England mahogany (she had only married Michael's father because he was wealthy, good-looking and different from the voluptuary lordlings, but, in her inexperience, she had mistaken different for better), and ran off with a jolly New York banker (for whom business was not so much a way of life as a lay of wife, usually somebody else's). With him she had lived happily for at least three years before she fell in love with a polo-playing Argentinian. And after that Michael rather lost count.

Her life had been a succession of raffish escapades conducted with such seeming innocence that you simply couldn't blame her; but finally Nemesis had overtaken her in the shape of a cattle-truck on the Corniche, and she had perished gloriously, and rather fittingly, with her Italian prince and her Rolls Royce, plunging into the drink from a very great height.

Michael advanced towards the sofa where she reclined (it stood towards the back of a room with one end against draped curtains). He felt as won-over as a dowager at a seance.

'Hello, Steppie,' he said, simply. It had always been his name for her.

She patted the sofa, indicating that she wished him to sit down, and then she kissed him most tenderly. He realized, as she did so, that she provided yet another, possibly the deepest, most emotional reason for his obsession with women. He had always been looking for her replica, the only mother he had ever known. And here it was.

He returned her kiss with more than affection. She opened her arms and he fell into them like a drop of water returning to the Sea. She smelt as she had always done, a scent that had haunted him at odd times all his life. He would break off from friends in the street to follow that nostalgic fragrance carried by heaven knew who, sweet yet light, troubling yet pure as a dewpond.

He sank into her bosom homingly while she cuddled him and made the soft noises at his head that she had so signally failed to do when she came up to his bedroom to say goodnight.

He lifted his head and saw her looking down at him, her mouth slightly open, and he felt, stirring in his head, that vertiginous sensation which made one want to lose oneself in its depths.

'I'm so sorry, Mouse,' she said, equivocally, and she opened her mouth to meet him.

Her kiss was softer than the underfeathers of a pochard, and tasted of roses and Chambolle Musigny, and he clung to her as a nymph to the surface of a rain-butt, bobbing and stirring to the swell of her body which he could feel trembling and welcoming him under the sheath of her dress.

He could feel her legs parting, and he knew that he

was lost, totally and irrevocably, but he could find in himself no censure.

Part of his brain questioned, it is true, the probity of sleeping with his own stepmother but (leaving aside the precedents of the Pharaohs to say nothing of Hippolytus), the other half told him that this could not possibly be her. One half in tremolo or was it Vox Angeli recalled Lucy and the legacy, the other half in Tromba with pedals extolled the glories of the matter, one might even say the mutter (he could still joke) in hand.

'Steppie,' he said. 'Oh, Steppie.'

Somehow she was out of her dress and lying in front of him in that delicious pink lingerie she got from Paris. He clung to her legs as he had wanted to do so often as a child, and buried his head in the soft cushion of her thighs.

As she stirred and trembled beneath him, half pulling him on her, half pushing him away, he looked up at her, wanting one more glimpse of her face.

What he saw made his blood run cold, the scales fall from his eyes and a thousand horror-struck clichés run babbling to and fro, jamming the switchboards of his reason.

Tom, his Tom, neighbour Tom, he of the exercise bicycle and the bullworker, Tom of the nut-cutlet and the Throbbing Monster was peeping out of the corner of the curtains with an expression of lively interest tinged with envy on his face, and rush-matting dungarees on his well-developed corporation.

Without bothering to demand what his business was, how he had managed to get in, what he had done with the Monster, how he had been suborned by the Philosophers, Michael leapt to his feet and rushed at him – more, it was true, for explanation than for retribution –

but Tom, misreading the intention skipped to one side and rushed back behind the sofa.

Michael, having reached the curtains, peeped out himself. What he saw, now he was alert and the adrenalin was coursing freely through his corporation, appalled but did not surprise him.

The sofa was on tracks that ran as far as, and a little way beyond, the curtains. The tracks ended in front of miniature buffers and a sort of slide – cunningly devised, as he reasoned, to tip the sofa up precipitating its occupants into what he now saw was the Pool below.

Even as he watched, a heavy dark-haired typist, horribly nubile, became aware of his gaze and stared back at him, signalling her fellows, her eyes glazed with lust, dribbling a little. They even started to try and climb up the chute, piling up chairs and desks in their attempt to get at them.

He turned back to Tom who, for all his biceps, cringed behind the rounded arches of the sofa.

'No,' Tom implored, 'I didn't mean to. Really. They came and got me. Said they'd been watching. Gave me a nut-burger, actually. Tasty. Can't be bad. I thought, maybe you're wrong. Said I was one of them, did I but know it. You know. Diet, exercise, mental poise. It's me isn't it? Said they'd give me a Lamborghini. Said I could have a look in if I kept quiet. Covered by monitor anyway, so it's no worse. Didn't mean to pry, old lad. Wondered what your secret was, that's all. Like my dungarees? How do I look? I look younger, don't I?'

Michael left the curtains and came back towards him, almost (though vexed at Tom's inconstancy, not surprised by it) with a mind to thank him for having broken the hideously mesmerizing spell of his mock-mother, and generally to forgive him; but Tom, misreading his intentions, leapt round the sofa again, tripped on the carpet, fell on the mock-mother who shouted (how unlike Steppie) 'Gerroff', and set the whole equipage in motion, rolling it judderingly back towards the curtains.

Michael watched, in powerless consternation, as the sofa gathered momentum, shot through the drapery with its cargo of over-developed muscle and syllabub limbs, and deposited the freight into the chamber below which was now packed tight with typists, their pink cardigans and flouncy petticoats horrifyingly accentuating the relentless gleam of their swept-away glasses.

As the two bodies hit the serried ranks, the surface seemed to seethe and erupt as the typists scrabbled implacably at their victims, indiscriminate of gender.

'Aaaaaaaah.'

'Oooooooooooh.'

Michael heard the two shrill despairing cries, but which one emanated from Tom and which from his mock-mother he could not tell. He caught a flash of syllabub leg and something that could have been Tom's torso, solarium-brown, thrown up for an instant in the pullulating welter, and then they disappeared under a frenzy of threshing.

Stripped in thirty seconds, the Negative Man had said. Michael thought it had looked more like fifteen.

25

Once in the relative freedom of the passage (peeping Tom must have left the door unlocked), Michael was able to collect his wits – wits which over the last hour or two, had become curiously fragmented.

He knew now that the forces ranged against him were unspeakably evil, and that, even before he rescued Lucy, he must destroy whatever ghastliness it was that they were so loathsomely perpetrating.

He had been relying on Tom to summon help. But the help Tom would have summoned was Lucy. It was clear there was now no help to be had. Michael knew that the ball was not only in his court, but it was an incredibly heavy ball to boot. If there were balls on the planet Jupiter, this was the sort of ball they would have.

He thought he understood what had to be done.

Finding his way to a back staircase, he glanced out of a window and was surprised to find it was already dusk. (All his ordeals had been, if expertly, artificially lit and his sense of time was thrown.) The evening star had already taken up its position, like a granny with train-fever, for the night, in a sky of muted turquoise and cochineal. In the park, the fallow deer were drifting towards the wood, while the dungarees padded studiously back to their herbal tea.

He had been in the house, though it seemed like an eternity, less than twenty-four hours. He looked enviously at the quiet fields and the trees, vulnerable against the grey declining light, cannon fodder for the Black Hole.

What a promising grey it was, luminous and tender, as different from the virulent non-colour of the Philosophers as cheese from chalk.

Did they really mean to swallow Berkshire? Just like that? Would it go all at once? Or in bits? Reading (burp.) Newbury (hic). Windsor (I beg your pardon).

Stealing down the stairs, he continued to the very bottom where, from the lukewarm smell of sour cooking, he judged the kitchen to be. In spite of the unappetizing odours, he suddenly realized he was intensely hungry. He peered in. There was an Aga, cupboards, a Welsh dresser and a great scrubbed table with (thank heaven) a loaf of bread and some tomatoes standing beside it. Seeing no one, he darted in, helped himself to a couple of slices and a tomato or two, and skipped back just in time to escape an oafish dungareed scullion who came through, rattling a pan.

When he had wolfed the last pip, and the coast was clear again, he cut across the kitchen and followed a dimly-lit passage towards the interior of the house, hoping that he would come across something that would direct him to his goal.

He was in luck. A double-door with a red sign on it saying 'No Admittance' hinted that he was on his way. A further heavy safety door convinced him.

He pushed it open (not stopping to wonder why it wasn't locked) and found himself in a long, low, nefarious-looking corridor full of the imperceptible but pervasive sound of machinery.

Doors gave off the passage with red letters inscribed on them 'Main Drive', 'Vortex', 'Accelerator', and 'Control' – the very words he had seen on the black pudding earlier.

Michael's slippery grasp of physics was not such as to

allow easy familiarity with the problems of the manufacture, or capture, or maintenance of a Black Hole, or even a nodding acquaintance with these cosmic unfathomables but he had already recalled from 'Black Holes Can Be Friends', that if you wanted a Black Hole to be of any use to you, you had to keep it in rapid circulation.

Beyond this, he reasoned that if you wanted to control or indeed destroy something, the best place to start would be at a door marked 'Control', a conclusion, he felt, that even the Physics Master couldn't refute.

If he could get his hands on the drive operation, and stop the spin he could send the Negative Man's source plummeting to the Earth's nadir where, if it was a small handleable Black Hole which this presumably would be, though it might slowly ingest the molten core, it would be unlikely to do much harm for the foreseeable future; its effect being not unlike trying to suck the Atlantic dry with a drinking-straw (see 'Whither Anti-Matter'?).

He approached the door marked 'Control' and, taking his courage in both hands, still found he had one to spare for the handle.

26

Although he was now used to scenes of outlandish curiosity and his suspension of disbelief stretched by one bizarre experience after another, now made the Sydney Bridge look like a game of cat's cradle, what Michael saw now caused him to reel back, gaga with astonishment.

He had expected Science but he seemed to have stumbled on Myth. He had read that at the frontiers of physics, both magic and fantasy can take over but he had never foreseen anything like this.

Somewhere an Aeolian lute played.

The chamber he had entered was dimly lit, and gave the impression of some kind of classical temple. In the centre of a small court was a sunken circular recess which seemed to glow with a fitful incandescent light, and which emitted a sound unlike anything he had heard before, a cross between a gargle and a big end going.

Presumably in its depths lay the Black Hole itself, the power source at the centre of all this web of intrigue, hungry for Berkshire and anything else it could lay its hands on.

At the rear of the chamber was a small domed portico supported by pillars in which stood a statue of what looked like Aphrodite surrounded by little gambolling loves and cupids.

The whole thing, the statue, the eerie music, the subterranean groaning, the low wall round the central well, the subdued lighting, gave the impression of a place of human sacrifice converted for use as a wine bar.

At this point, to his utter bemusement, the statue and its little attendant group started to move, and suddenly the whole lot of them were coming towards him.

The door clicked shut behind him, and he braced himself for the latest and quite possibly the greatest of his trials. This time it was Love herself who had come for him.

Aphrodite was, as one would expect, divinely Lovely. She moved with a light step and an airy grace, her long golden hair flowing about her as wantonly as her gossamer-thin peplos which parted as she walked, revealing legs more classically superb than anything Praxiteles ever put chisel to and scarcely concealing breasts as round as pedimental windows and pointed as finials.

Michael could feel the deity emanating from her (or else it was being sprayed by unseen nozzles), and his retinas clouded involuntarily with desire like protein on soft contact lenses. He squirted thoughts of Lucy energetically round each eye ball but it didn't seem totally to shift it.

As she approached, he became dimly aware that her gambolling retinue were not, as they had seemed at a distance, cherubs, toddlers and little eyasses, but a squad of dwarfs rendered singularly evil-looking by the polystyrene wings that were loosely affixed to their busily-wagging shoulders.

Keeping his back to the wall, he sidled round the chamber as the group moved forward.

This can't be happening, he thought, they've broken their word, they've come for me at last. But with this realization came the knowledge that the Negative Power of which Hermione had babbled, was not inevitably victorious. If they had to use force, it meant they weren't totally confident. The knowledge lent him strength; a strength it became apparent he was going to have to call upon imminently.

The dwarves were the first to attack. Bobbing and surging, they clutched at his knees, tripped him up, and before he could recover himself, they had hauled him over to the portico where they ripped off his white coat, humped him onto a plinth and started to tie him down tighter than Gulliver. He struggled mightily but they were amazingly powerful.

The plinth, he noticed, had started to vibrate in a trembly, insidious manner like a water-bed mounted on an invalid carriage.

At last they had him pegged out, and Aphrodite, who had been watching the proceedings from a distance, advanced and stood beside him. The dwarves backed away, mumbling in awe. Slowly, slowly, she mounted the podium. Slowly, she peeled off the peplos revealing a body that made Botticelli's vision of Venus look like a corn dolly. Slowly, she knelt over him, her ringlets touching his face, her breasts hanging like Chinese lanterns, luminous, lambent. Slowly, she brought her thighs up close to his face, and he lay there, powerless, looking at a spectacle that would have induced rampant priapism in a garden hose.

For a moment, induced by the wobbling bed and the beckoning bosoms, his diapason swelled, seemingly about to burst into its usual voluntary. But, just as suddenly, it subsided. For the first time in his life, Michael could feel no response. It had all been too much. Parson refused to climb pulpit.

The dwarves shrieked and gibbered with frustration. Aphrodite scowled and bit her lip. And Michael examined his feelings. He was part appalled by his unprecedented mechanical failure, part relieved at being so unexpectedly let off the hook. An idea came to him.

'I'm not into bondage,' he said. 'I think maybe if you undid the straps . . .'

The suggestion seemed to make sense to them, and they untied him with a will, expecting, at any moment, life to surge back into the recalcitrant member; but, just as the last strap was unleashed, he bounded up (knocking one of the dwarves flying) and raced for the door at the far end of the chamber.

The dwarf sped like a golf ball across the floor and disappeared with a shrill squeal down the central hole.

Michael waited breathlessly for the incredibly attenuated sounds that would indicate that the dwarf, stretched now to ten miles long had crossed the point of no return and was entering the Singularity perhaps to be spewed up again in the searing holocaust of a white hole halfway across the Universe.

'Oh fuck,' said Aphrodite, 'that's gone and done it.'

And they all rushed to the brink and craned over.

Michael, who had stopped in mid-career, now joined them at the edge, appalled in spite of his own predicament, at the fate he had inflicted on a fellow-creature.

'Quick,' said a particularly malevolent-looking gnome at Michael's side, 'fetch a ladder, arse-hole.'

'I'm afraid that won't be any good,' said Michael, ignoring the gratuitous opprobrium, 'he'll be stretched like spaghetti now. He's passed the Schwarzkild Radius.'

'Radius my left tit,' replied the dwarf, 'that's an old well down there. Get a rope someone. Rupert can't swim.'

Finally an extending ladder was produced from somewhere, looking, Michael thought, strangely like the one he had left so many experiences ago under the holly tree, and Rupert was hauled up, spluttering and vicious-tempered.

'I don't understand,' said Michael to Aphrodite, 'this is the nerve-centre, isn't it? This is the Room of Power. Why isn't that the Hole? And if it isn't, where is it? It said Control on the door.'

'That was advice, dear,' said Aphrodite, 'not description. That was what you needed. Control. Or didn't as it turned out.'

A terrible fear that he had been taken for some kind of monumental ride at last began to penetrate Michael's blinkered brain. But a ride how far? And where? There might be no Black Hole. It was conceivable that the Negative-Positive nexus was codswallop. But the electronic bug was still on his parson, and someone had spent a great deal of time and money trying to nobble it. And there was Lucy still upstairs waiting to be rescued.

'Out of my way,' he screeched, pushing the loveliest of all the goddesses brusquely aside, and charging through the end door like a triceratops at a tupperware-party.

And then he stopped dead, amazed, gratified and horrified at what he saw.

Coils of metal, bowels of zinc and nickel, festoons of plastic capillaries, flourished and gleamed and twinkled in the light of banked computers.

So it was not a hoax. He rushed back, seized his ladder from a dumbfounded midget, raced back to the computer room and started laying about him as if the future of Berkshire and lord knew what else depended on it.

Casings collapsed, the viscera gaped, faint fizzings emanated from shattered fuse-boxes, and suddenly a further door opened and a wizened figure in white overalls appeared.

'Spot of bother?' it said. 'Thought we weren't going to

activate this part.' And then, when he had taken in the destruction. 'Fucking Hell.'

It was the engineer to whom Michael had gone for his tailing device. Michael's heart missed a beat. All the strands seemed to be coming ominously together. Treacle, Tom and now Wally. What was going on? Who was behind all this?

He noticed that, behind the façades of the computers, there was nothing – no circuitry, no crystals, no core – and that the shattered entrails had led nowhere. It was all a typical film-company mock-up job.

Wally evinced considerable surprise at seeing Michael and a degree of furtiveness he would never have suspected in him (though Wally's chip-witholding wife would).

'Good grief,' cried Wally, ducking and scuttling.

Michael was too quick for him, leaping prodigiously and arresting his progress with a hand on his collar.

'What are you doing here, Wally?'

'It's a long story,' said Wally, hang-doggedly.

'I'm sure it is. But I've all night at my disposal.'

What, he wondered, was Wally's role here? Though an able enough technician, he certainly wasn't a qualified astro-physicist or force-field engineer, so that finally put the kibosh on the Black Hole. And then there was the question of coincidence. Why was Wally, who worked in films and lived in Battersea, here at all? And why was Wally so keen to evade him? It all pointed to a deliberate and sustained plot to pull the wool over his eyes. It made him – when he thought of the endless obstacle-race he had had to go through, and the trouble, and the time, and the humiliation, and the money, and Lucy – all at once furiously angry.

'I thought you were a mate,' he shouted, shaking Wally like a rat. 'What a bloody fool I've been.'

'Don't be too hard on me,' Wally muttered, 'I was short of money.'

Money, thought Michael. Was there no limit to the depths people would go to, grovelling before the Golden Calf? But he realized he was in no position to pontificate, gadgeted as he was about the pubes, and prepared to endure a condition in a will that a high-minded man would have turned down with a contemptuous 'tush'. No, he wasn't exactly a pattern of probity.

A familiar voice broke in on his thoughts. 'So you have uncovered our little deception?'

Michael whirled like a dervish.

The Negative Man was leering at him from a monitor high up on the wall.

'You are to be congratulated, Mr Lambert, on being as credulous as you are lecherous. (We will draw a veil, for the sake of your reputation, over your flaccidity in the last episode.) I would have thought a backward five-year-old would have seen through the flimsy veneer of likelihood we have daubed across some of our stratagems. But you are so full of yourself, you are so besotted with the trees, you cannot see the wood.'

'But I damn well can now, and I'm going straight to the police. Black Hole my backside.'

'You forget, Mr Lambert, you are still in our hands.'

This was very true.

'And so is Miss Dulcimer, in case you had forgotten.'

'If you harm her, I'll . . .' And he would, by God.

'There is no question of our harming her, Mr Lambert. We might have to tell the Law Society of her breaking in here, her attempts to remove our property – false documents, Mr Lambert, carefully designed to play on your absurd obsessions and prejudices – her . . .'

'You can't do that. You'd ruin her. She lives for her work,' Michael blurted.

'We're not suggesting that we harm her, Mr Lambert. Far from it. We're suggesting that you do it for us. Well . . . harm isn't exactly the right word. Ravish. Enjoy. Get the leg across. You must take her, Mr Lambert. Use her. Make the beast with two backs.'

Michael now allowed the full tide of realization to flood over him. Everything was made clear. He was trapped. Somehow, the Philosophers were still at the bottom of it all. They had made him the victim of a gross deception that was all the more galling because he had swallowed it so completely. He doubted whether a Black Hole itself, the real anti-thing, the genuine anti-article, could swallow Berkshire or indeed Betelgeuse more effortlessly than he had gulped down their offerings. His little knowledge, his callow romanticism had led him up the garden path and across the nebulae . . . in pursuit of what? Money? Of course. Lust? It went without saying. Certainly, he wasn't the only one. They were admittedly the twin obsessions of the age, but that didn't excuse him, it exacerbated his opinion of his own weakness. He had willingly undertaken the mockery of his six-month term. He deserved all the subsequent humiliation. How piffling had been his aspirations, how worm-eaten his goal posts. His potential millions now seemed worth less to him than a quiet mind, and he knew, like Mark Antony, he would give up all his future conquests for true love.

Conjectures of chalets at Courchevel, visions of gaping-crotched international houris failed to compensate one iota for his sense of complete despair and futility.

> 'Then Old Age and Experience, hand in hand
> Lead him to Death and make him understand
> After a Search so weary and so long
> That all his life he has been in the wrong.'

Lucy was the only person he wanted to see. And yet this unspeakable hound was suggesting something that would make their meeting impossible. Lucy was to be the innocent victim of his weakness and selfishness. He addressed himself once more to his tormentor.

'You loathsome toad,' he said, feeling that he was doing the batrachian species a grave disservice, 'you never escaped from a Black Hole, you're not a manifestation of Anti-Matter. You're just a dirty voyeur too frightened to show your face.'

'You're wrong there, Michael,' said the Negative Man, but this time in tones that were curiously familiar, taking a small metal object like a jew's harp from his mouth, and proceeding to remove a great deal of shady make-up with a wisp of Kleenex.

Slowly, a dab here, a wipe there, the mirthlessly smiling features of Scratcher emerged.

'Scratcher,' Michael gasped, 'for God's sake. Why?'

'Bread, for one thing. When the Philosophers first looked me up and told me about your little windfall. Well . . . I naturally wanted in on it, didn't I? And when they explained how they felt I could help 'em, the whole thing just seemed to flesh-out. Nurse Lundquist had been *their* idea. Just shows you, doesn't it. Amateurs' night. Well, *my* first thought was that pricey but limited little scenario with Coucou. But that was still Elstree stuff. I soon saw you were going to need a rather more er barocco approach. Even you weren't going to part with £8 million just like that. So . . . I got to thinking . . . drew up a plan, got together a presentation . . . charts, figures, video, all the business . . . and sold them on this big production number. Take it or leave it, I said, no skin off my nose, I don't need the money. Besides, I said, there are techniques here of computer editing and hologram opticals that could well stand you in good stead in the areas of persuasion and surveillance when your precious revolution gets under way. Funny, isn't it, how people outside the industry are so curiously impressed with the technical side?'

'But . . . my past . . . all the details . . . how did you . . .'

'That's what finally sold 'em. Me knowing you the way I do.'

'But you don't.'

'They didn't know that. Besides, what I didn't know I could always find out. A word or two with some of your ex-girlfriends. A bung or two to your cleaner. Remember the diaries you lost – the books, the letters, the old photos, the film script – make a lousy movie, incidentally . . . That was me. And then of course there was my knowledge of the film world – all my contacts – researchers, technicians, designers, wardrobe, props. It was too big an opportunity for the Philosophers to let go. They never had such facilities. And me? I'd always wanted to do a big production. Never been able to get a feature together. You didn't know that, did you? They won't be laughing at me now. Enjoy the Typing Pool touch, did you? Cubby would like that. Put it in specially even though it is a gnat's outside the brief. The girls are small-town drama students who think they're doing a Living Art weekend . . .'

Scratcher paused, breathless with self-interest.

'But . . . the Black Hole . . . the negative dimension . . .'

'Just to confuse you, to wear you down with your own hobbyhorses. It was true that they wouldn't allow any force to be used. I came very near to it once or twice, believe me. But it wouldn't have done. No, no. The very point of the whole thing was to get you through the, shall we call it, the carnal assault course, and then drop you in it right at the end – at your moment of psychological weakness. Mission, or shall we say, emission complete.'

Michael swallowed.

'Good work. I have to say that. I mean . . . the organization must've been incredible,' he said.

He was clutching at straws, but he knew that Scratcher had always been susceptible to flattery.

'Took a bit of getting-together I can tell you,' said Scratcher almost chattily, and Michael's spirits momentarily lifted. 'Added years to my life. But now I can go to Hollywood.'

Scratcher's face took on a dreamy yearning expression that was almost more repugnant than his former malice.

'That's one of the reasons I've got it all on tape,' he continued, 'so I can show it to Cubby and he'll see I can really make it in the big-time.'

In spite of his predicament, Michael suddenly gave in to an uncontrollable desire to laugh. It was ill-advised. Scratcher instantly reverted to his poison vein.

'The other reason, of course,' he said acidly, 'was that I wanted to make you look ridiculous.'

Michael had to admit that Scratcher had succeeded triumphantly in all his aims. He had never felt such a pratt.

'Why? I still don't understand.'

'Because I dislike you intensely. Good reason, isn't it? But don't get the idea that your humiliation was devised entirely for my benefit. The Philosophers would never have bought that. I made sure it had a practical purpose for them, of course. Like, I mean, in case you want to cut up awkward afterwards, you wouldn't want your friends in the advertising or indeed any other world to see those tapes now, would you?'

'You Kong-size turd.'

'I didn't expect you exactly to fawn on me, Lambert. I've known you a long time and, frankly, you nauseate me. Your arrogant air, your approach to women . . .'

Of course, thought Michael, that's what's underneath it. Scratcher, unattractive, clammy and domineering, had been secretly hating him ever since they had met. He thought Scratcher was mad but, he had to admit, the man had displayed genius.

'Do what you like,' he said, 'but at least leave Lucy out of it.'

'That is precisely what we won't do. She is to be the instrument of your forfeiting the legacy. Indeed, unless she is, we will ensure that she never practises as a solicitor again.'

'I'll disembowel you when I get out.'

'I don't think so. Remember, I have the video tapes.'

Michael thought of another useful consideration; at least a possible wriggle out of the impasse.

'I'm impotent. I can't do anything if I'm impotent. I've lost my powers.'

'You'll have to find them again, won't you?'

'Let me speak to her.'

'Oh, never fear, Lambert. You will. You will.'

Scratcher's smirking features faded like a Cheshire Cat from the screen, the door opened and two very large lobsters in white coats came in. Michael threw an amateurish right hook at the first one while the other secured his arm and thrust a hypodermic needle into it with all the fastidious imprecision of an Austin Rover spot-welder.

27

After so long a confrontation, the end came with extraordinary suddenness.

When Mr Lee received the official letter telling him that Her Majesty's Government was no longer prepared to wait for the parts in question but had made arrangements with alternative sources (no doubt the dreaded Japanese), he finally knew where his duty lay.

He marched out onto the forecourt, a slightly ludicrous figure in his agitation, and waved the communique at the duty picket officer, addressing him before he could show even superficial outrage or summon the disapprobation of so much as a babe for peace in the crowd.

'You idle man,' declared Mr Lee.

His father had served for some years with the Hong Kong police force and had instilled in his son a due sense of the mystery of the parade ground.

'You idle man,' he repeated, the military adjective of rebuke sounding sweet in his ears, 'now look what you have done. You have cut off your noses to spite your faces.'

The pickets who had been somewhat starved of event recently, and had been taking their time over breakfast, stared at the little Chinaman, momentarily impressed with his vehemence. Sid Brewfitt was located indulging his passion for forcemeat fritters at the Fast Buck Snack Bar in Ebenezer Street, and summoned to the scene.

'Well,brothers,' he mused, wiping a crispy morsel from his moustache, as he listened to the pickets' resumé, 'I do

not wish at this stage to react prematurely, but it would appear to me to be a clear case of management shortsightedness and industrial blackmail.'

Suddenly, it seemed, the whole street had woken up. There were cameramen and police everywhere, sensing tension.

'I would advise you,' said the Chief Inspector to Mr Lee who was clearly in a state of great agitation, 'I would advise you to say nothing that might be construed as an incitement to violence.'

'Fuck that for a rark,' said Mr Lee. 'I am up to here.'

It wasn't very high, but neither was Mr Lee. Sid Brewfitt took advantage of the fact.

'You're up to here,' he jested ponderously, 'well, let me tell you, we're up to here.'

And he held his hand at his own head height above Mr Lee's shiny black bonce.

'That does it,' said Mr Lee, 'you can send your pickets home.'

'Home?' said Sid Brewfitt, as Bert Scrannell edged up behind him. 'Home? You can't do that. This is an industrial confrontation. We stay here. This is a public place. Nobody tells us to go home.'

'You can stay here forever if you like,' said Mr Lee. 'But I am closing the factory.'

'You can't do that,' reiterated Sid – then, switching to another favourite leit-motiv, 'this is people's lives you're playing with.'

But Mr Lee was adamant.

When the crowd was informed of the management's decision, there was a great deal of hissing and booing but, in spite of Sid's appeals for solidarity, the tension had gone, and almost immediately people started to drift away, disappearing down the streets of Babylon like nymphs down a water butt.

With almost incredible rapidity, considering all the brouhaha, the area reverted to its habitual isolation.

'The days of man are but as grass,' said the Chief Inspector, 'for he flourisheth as a flower of the field. For as the wind goeth over it, it is gone: and the place thereof shall know it no more.'

His driver would have liked to have made a suitable reply, but there's not much you can say to a psalm. Besides, after so long a spell of enforced inactivity, he was experiencing a little wind of his own.

Sid Brewfitt suddenly realized that he was out of a job.

Bert Scrannell looked on, pleased with the outcome. It almost looked as though he might be smiling, but he was, in fact, simply breathing through his mouth. (Satisfaction merely served to pinch his already dangerously tight nostrils.)

Finally, assured the whole business was over, he walked to a telephone box at some distance from the scene, and dialled a London number.

'Babylon falls,' he said, 'stop. One two zero, I repeat one two zero jobs lost, stop. Marionette management in callous closure situation, stop. Whitehall shops overseas for arms while British workers starve. No, no. Delete starve. It'll offend our friends at social worker level . . .'

He paused, more for breath than anything else, his gaze traversing the Light Industrial Area littered with the debris of ten thousand snacks and mealettes.

'While British workers go hungry, stop,' he concluded. 'No one could possibly object to that. Meanwhile, the Army's new laser sights will be duly delayed and, even when provided, will be vulnerable to our Japanese associates.'

28

When Michael came to, he found himself sprawled in a big wing-back chair that, as he struggled into consciousness, he dimly recognized as part of the furniture of the room in which he had encountered his mock-mother. He struggled into consciousness a little more.

Memories now of his recent conversation with Scratcher came stumbling on parade, bugling to his sleepy senses to take up their stance round the perimeters of his frontal lobes with more than usual devotion to duty.

Without moving, he noted that the chaise-longue of his earlier encounter had been removed and a large double-bed with a brass headpiece substituted.

At the same time, he became aware that someone was applying a damp cloth to his temple and murmuring endearments in his ear on a scale which suggested considerable attachment.

His drugged eyes, rolling about in their sockets like drums in a hurricane, were able to ascertain, by dint of much swivelling, that the kind person was none other than Lucy.

'Wake up, darling love,' said the pride of Kent University's School of Jurisprudence.

Michael's mouth felt like a charred string vest, but he attempted to convey the fact that he was sensible of her presence.

'Awawa,' he began.

'Oh. Mr Lambert. Michael . . .' she exclaimed, blushing prettily, wondering whether he had heard her.

She was wearing a light blue dress, obtained from the wardrobe-lady, Michael imagined, which accorded sweetly with her eyes. Her enforced durance did not in any way seem to have impaired her complexion.

'Awawa, I mean, when did they get you?'

'I've been here three days now.'

'I'm terribly sorry. Are you all right? I mean . . . they haven't done anything to you?'

'Nothing. Nothing unpleasant, that is. Apart from keeping me here, they've treated me marvellously. Scented baths. Amazing clothes. Champagne. Rather a lot of fish. I don't mind if I never see another oyster again in my life.'

'"Fish dinners will make a lass spring like a flea",' said Michael, glumly.

'What was that?'

Michael felt he couldn't keep it from her.

'They want you to sleep with me.'

'What?'

Michael gave her a run-down on his recent experiences. Lucy listened wide-eyed, not knowing whether to laugh or cry.

'If we don't make love,' he concluded, 'they'll see you never practise again.'

'But that's terrible. I couldn't possibly agree to it. You'd lose your legacy. Eight million pounds.'

Lucy, was it possible, appeared to have no worries about the act, or the affront to her person; she was only thinking of him.

'It's very sweet of you to put it like that,' he said, 'but I don't mind about the money any more. All this has made me see things in a rather different light. Life, I mean, and that sort of thing. It's all been sex up till now, you were right when you said that to me, and a desperate scrabble for money, and it's ended up in my being made a fool of, and you being dragged in, and it's time I stopped that's all. I'm forty-one next month. It's time I started enjoying myself. Yes, I know it sounds soupy, it's time I started living. You're only middle-aged once.'

Michael gave a small rueful grimace, but Lucy was listening with eyes shining like halogen headlamps.

'That's the most wonderful thing I ever heard,' she said. 'I think I ought to tell you, Michael, that my interest in your case has not been entirely altruistic. In fact,' dropping the legalese altogether, 'I'm crazy about you, and I think you're a darling.'

'That's terrific,' said Michael with relief. 'Because I was just going on to say that what with my idols' feet all turning to clay – money, sex, science fiction – you're the only thing I feel strongly about, and I thought I'd lost my powers, but suddenly I want to make love to you very much indeed but in a good way, you understand, not *at* you but *with* you.'

And they kissed each other rapturously while a camera in the ceiling twinkled joyless approval.

Michael, his powers miraculously restored, allowed his mouth to nibble the meadowsweet softness of Lucy's cheek and neck and ears, while his hand adored her breasts.

Their breathing grew more rapid. Gasps were uttered. In the next room, Scratcher watched the proceedings with more than financial interest.

Suddenly, urgently, Michael drew back.

'No,' he said, 'when we make love, I want it to be at home, not . . . forced like this. I won't take advantage of you this way. They're watching us. It's humiliating.'

'I don't mind. I want you.'

And so they kissed again. His hands now strayed to

her legs, lying, wonderfully welcoming and secret under the sky-blue dress, while she did things to him she had never thought to do to anyone.

Then it was her turn. She sat up, mustering every ounce of resolution.

'No,' she said, 'I won't let you. You'll lose everything. You'll have to go back to detergent commercials and the Philosophers will get the money and keep spreading their horribleness and Scratcher will get his satisfaction, and I just won't let it happen. I don't mind giving up my job.'

'Do you really mean that?' said Michael.

The thought of the commercials, the endless pursuit of pifflingness, gave him a nasty twinge.

And so they drew apart and sat there for a minute or two, thinking their thoughts while Scratcher gnawed his lip. Then Michael took her hand.

'Your work matters much more,' he said, 'I don't mind commercials. I've done them for eighteen years. A few more won't hurt. I could always get another job.'

'I'm sorry. I won't let you do it.'

'I insist.'

He reached over and started to kiss her again. She kissed him back and pushed him off, both at the same time.

'Take your hands off me.'

They were struggling now, and Lucy was crying a little. In the next room, Scratcher was getting impatient.

'Come on, come on,' he muttered, his finger toying with a switch as his other hand strayed over the misshapen bulge that betrayed the appalling boa constrictor in his trousers.

'Stop,' cried Michael, 'we can't fight about it.'

Lucy dried her eyes and sniffed.

'Of course I want to do it,' she said, 'it's just that . . .'

'I know,' said Michael, 'but we have no alternative. If we don't, we'll get thrown into the Pool.'

And he told her how they were in the room which had been so indelibly printed on his memory.

'I know it'd be a moral victory for us not to make love now,' he said, 'and moral defeat's intolerable to Scratcher and the Philosophers, but victory would not be sweet. Tom's scream will haunt me for the rest of my days. I'm not letting you be catapulted down there. So on the whole,' he said, taking her in his arms, 'I think we had better push ahead with our original plan.'

The scene that now took place caused Scratcher actually to steam up the glass of the monitor screen.

Michael forgot his erstwhile temporary inability as totally as Lucy forgot her shyness.

Like a bead of dew on a trellis of gossamer, like Peer Gynt on Troll King's Orders, like a tassel on a tit, Michael was suffused with a sort of incandescent tremble. All the frustrations of the past weeks seemed concentrated in his reactor whose needle rose and rose, far beyond critical stage.

Lucy smelt of fresh hay, claret and honeysuckle, and her body was full of undiscovered treasures. He took her in his arms, and for an interval, rational thought was erased.

When they resurfaced, they found Scratcher gloating at them through the monitor.

'I expect you feel better now,' he said vilely, 'that must be a great weight off your . . .'

But a sudden eruption from the door stopped him short.

A posse of amazonian croupiers charged into view with a striking redhead at their tail.

'Ohmygod,' said Michael. 'The Foxy Lady.'

'I told you I'd be watching you,' she said.

'All right,' said Michael. 'I'll take what's coming to me. I failed. I deserve it.'

'Do it to him, do it to him,' mumbled Scratcher thickly.

But the Foxy Lady was staring at Lucy, open-mouthed.

Michael moved protectively as if to shield her from any vile advance, but she motioned him aside.

'My oath,' said the Foxy Lady, 'but it's Kubla. Khan,' she added as if in explanation to Michael, 'as in the damsel with a dulcimer.'

Michael nodded, understanding nothing and certainly not Lucy's reply.

'Copperknob,' she said.

For some reason the Foxy Lady didn't strike her dead but continued to smile repulsively.

'We were at school together,' Lucy explained, getting up and tucking the sheet around her. 'I was a new bug when she was Head of House. Don't get batey with Lambert, Copperknob. He's not a bad egg really.'

Scratcher cursed, and the door clicked shut. One of the amazons tried the handle but it was locked.

'Haven't you forgotten something?' hissed Scratcher's voice, now coming from behind the door. 'There's only one way out.'

They all gazed at the chamber below where the typists, scenting prey, had once more gathered in anticipation, led by a particularly ferocious-looking specimen in polka dots.

'Funnily enough,' said the Foxy Lady, 'we did have a contingency plan. At Foxy Lady Casinos, we leave nothing to chance.'

She extracted a small two-way radio from her bag, pressed the switch, and said, 'NOW.' There was a scuffling noise outside, and the protesting Scratcher was pushed inside by a second group of black-frocked myrmidons. Before they could stop him, however, he seized the key, turned it again in the lock, and cast it with a cry of triumph into the depths below. It was received with an ominous swirl of expectancy.

The Foxy Lady pointed to the bed which Michael had by now also vacated, and Scratcher was thrust unceremoniously upon it.

'Now look . . . wait a minute . . . there's been a mistake,' he gabbled. 'I let you in on this so you could . . . No. Wait . . .'

But the croupiers were already trundling the bed forward towards the curtain where, smartly upending it deposited the odious creature upon the jostling bevy beneath.

'NO,' shrieked Scratcher to the Drama Project. 'No, you fools . . . it's MEEEEeeeeeee . . .'

There was a threshing of a myriad petticoats, a horrible flurry of angora jumpers, a high-pitched squeal, and silence.

'Poor old Scratcher,' said Michael at length, drawing on sketchy memories of Bond, 'he was always wanting to scoop the pool.'

29

As it turned out, the Philosophers, so intent were they on the acquisition of the legacy (they had their henchman Becket lined up to inform them as soon as the little recorder showed its tell-tale fibrillations), had made one vital mistake.

Their right hand had not been fully conversant with their left. The Activist wing had not shared its secrets with its Thinkers. And vice versa.

What the Activist in the street (led by Bert Scrannell) had been doing for the last six months was, of course, picketing the very electronics factory which, with all its disruptive possibilities as well as its financial assets, the Thinkers had been plotting to inherit.

The factory, lacking the instinct for compromise and flexibility, which an owner might have instilled, simply had not had the will to survive.

The result was that, when the Philosophers (who of course had had the Infinite on their mind as well as Michael's seduction, and electricians and carpenters all over the house into the bargain) came to collect, they found the whole place in the hands of the Liquidator.

Michael and Lucy, who did not care about the money for themselves, had been concerned that the Philosophers would indeed use their acquisition for grey, disruptive ends. (Scratcher and his actors, like all good liars, had built on fact.) So they were now understandably cheered.

'To think they went through all that effort,' said Michael when Lucy came to the Hospital to collect him after the removal of his monitor. 'They must be totally cleaned out by now. Which reminds me. I've got a Final Order on my rent. And a rather bleak appointment with the Bank Manager. And then there's the telephone bill, and the garage, and of course Copperknob, school chum or no school chum . . . And I don't think the only job I've got on offer – a rather moody little documentary on the Decline of the Village Pond for a local Water Authority – which I'd actually quite like to do – is going to net me that kind of money . . .'

'Oh,' said Lucy, pointing at the parcel she had collected from the nurse, 'I was meaning to tell you. The one thing we can salvage from the factory is the monitor itself. Technically, at the moment of liquidation it was a personal fixture or fitting bequeathed to you under the terms of a Will, which gives you an inalienable claim. Apparently, it could be worth rather a lot. We've already had a substantial offer from an American surveillance organization specializing in divorce, and another from a consortium that manages top sporting personalities. In fact, Copperknob herself has seen in-casino applications . . .'

'Happy endings worry me,' said Michael. 'Life isn't like that.'

'There's no law against it,' said Lucy, who knew about these things. 'Besides I should've thought the last thing you want's a sting in the tail.'